Crossing Double

A Heartbreaker Novel

Tamra Baumann

Published by Tamra Baumann
Cover Art by Coverinked www.coverinked.com
Printed in the United States of America
Crossing Double
ISBN   978-1-947591-04-2

This book is dedicated to my critique group. Sherri, Louise, and Robin, I appreciate you all so much!

Contents

Chapter One

S ara Chapman slapped the button to silence her radio as she drove on the 5 to a charity event. She couldn't take another moment of her fiancé's voice—well, now her ex-fiancé as of two minutes ago. Who broke up with someone at a press conference? And then to drive the stake even deeper into her chest, Scott announced he'd be marrying her best friend? When had all that falling in love happened? And why was she the last to know?

It was hard to see through her tears as she negotiated the busy California highway. Drawing in enough breath between sobs so she wouldn't pass out was becoming increasingly difficult. And she might possibly throw up. The last thing she wanted to do was face the press she'd invited to the shelter. Embarrassed and humiliated, all she wanted was to go home and crawl under the sheets for a week.

But, she honored her commitments, unlike her now ex-fiancé, so she wiped the mascara streaks from under her eyes, threw her shoulders back, and pulled herself together, probably the last to arrive at her own event.

She parked her car in her usual spot at the rear of the shelter and got out. Plastering on a fake smile, she made her way past the barriers that held back the paparazzi stacked five deep. It'd be nice if the press would focus their cameras on the real celebrities who were there raising money for the LA homeless shelter. Not on a person who was famous only because her parents were. Except now she'd probably found her own fame—for the most embarrassing breakup in the history of the entire world.

The thought made her want to cry all over again. She bit her bottom lip and focused on her anger instead.

Unfortunately, after what Scott had just done, the day wasn't going to be about a good cause anymore. The press smelled blood in the water, and they'd want their bite out of her, so she needed to make sure to keep the shelter front and foremost if she could. Scott had surely timed his announcement that way on purpose. He hated that she regularly volunteered to help "those people."

Sara stepped onto the raised temporary podium erected in the shelter's parking lot and smiled at the aging movie stars, the local radio celebrities, and the soap stars she'd recruited. All of them whispering their condolences for her newly failed engagement as she hugged them in honest gratitude. It was as if they'd all gotten a push notification to their phones about her humiliation the way cell phones in the vicinity of bad weather approaching sounded an alarm.

One of her mother's good friends, Chantel Goodwin, once a Hollywood legend and now a host on the Southern Eats Channel whispered with her Alabama twang, "Wait until Annalisa hears about this, darlin.' She'll make sure that little spoiled pissant never works in Hollywood again."

Sara kissed Chantel's cheek. "Mom's too busy to worry about the likes of Scott. Thanks for coming. I appreciate it."

Sara made her way up to the mic. She'd had a nice speech ready, but quickly did some editing in her mind. She wanted to get out as fast as she could. "Hi, everyone. Thanks for coming today to support this amazing cause. Home for All thanks you." She held out a hand toward all the wonderful stars who'd shown up at her request. "All these amazing celebrities thank you, and I thank you. I know the press has a ton of questions you'd like to ask me about Scott's announcement a few minutes ago. I promise we'll get to that, but first, we're here today to help people who truly need our support. Let's keep our eye on the meter over there and see how close we are to saving this amazing nonprofit shelter after I add this check for one hundred thousand dollars!"

A cheer went up as the meter, which looked like a giant thermometer, rose slowly toward the goal. As it moved, the director of the shelter, Timmy Sanchez, whispered in her ear, "You've been amazing, but we're still going to be short."

Sara whipped her head toward him. "I thought with my donation, we knew we'd have enough?" She'd invited the press to a victory party. Not another personal defeat. Two in one day was more than she could bear.

Timmy shook his head as the meter moved excruciatingly slowly. "We had pledges, but only half made good on them."

Crap!

Sweat dripped down Sara's back as she stood in the warm LA winter sun. She had to save the privately funded shelter. The amazing things they did every day were a needed service the city couldn't provide.

3

She scanned the crowd for any possible late donors and noticed the press wasn't even looking at the meter, they were just waiting for it all to be over so they could ask her about her failed engagement.

What was she going to do? Maybe she'd call her mom and ask her for the money. She hated to ask, though, because she'd been trying to stand on her own two feet lately. "How short will we be?"

"About two hundred thousand."

Roughly one hundred and ninety-nine thousand less than she had in her savings account. "Okay. Tell them to slow that thing down even more. I need to make a few calls." She grabbed her phone to call some of her pals just as it dinged with a text. It was from the traitor, Scott.

Hey. Do me a favor? Return the ring to my mom. I'm going to repurpose the diamond for Brandi.

Sara's vision blurred as she reread the text. What a piece of...lying...no good... Who did he think he was? He hadn't even had the balls to text her first before he'd simply announced to the world that he was dumping her.

Timmy whispered, "It's as high as it's going to go. What are we going to do?"

She glanced at the diamond gleaming on her finger. Hell would freeze over before she'd give Scott the ring back to give to someone else.

She whispered, "Did Scott make good on his pledge? He'd promised to send fifty K."

"He didn't." Timmy cringed. "I wasn't going to say anything after..."

"No worries." Surely her rich former fiancé had just forgotten to send in his pledge money because he was so busy falling in love with another woman. He'd definitely want to increase his donation as an apology.

She turned to the mic again. "It looks like we're a bit short. But as most of you probably already know, Scott, my former fiancé, has plans to marry Brandi Walters now, and I wish them both well. But that leaves the question of what to do with this." She yanked off her engagement ring and held it up high. The bright sun sparkled off the mammoth rock worth half a million dollars. She beamed a triumphant smile he would surely see later online.

I won't allow you, or any man, to humiliate me ever again.

She handed her ring to Timmy. "Scott has always wholeheartedly supported this shelter, so he'd be happy for me to give this to you to cover our deficit. I'm sure someone out there would love to get a screaming deal on this gorgeous ring. So, crank that meter up guys, and let's party!"

The press all reached for their phones, no doubt searching their archives for the value of the ring that had been posted to every gossip site Scott could blab to after he'd given it to her. Cameras whirred as the celebrities led the way to the free champagne and food she'd arranged to be donated from some of LA's finest chefs.

In the rush for the food tents, she quietly slipped away to avoid any more questions. Everyone who'd seen the story knew Scott had blindsided her. He'd said as much in his announcement. What they didn't know was that he'd done it to pay her back for changing from her party girl ways into a responsible person. She'd grown up, while he hadn't. She'd known deep down they'd never work anymore in the long run. She'd just been too hardheaded, or maybe too softhearted, to accept they were over.

She wouldn't allow the tears that wanted to escape as she slipped out the back of the party and jogged toward her Porsche.

Even though she'd changed, she'd thought she and Scott had truly been friends and that he would never do what he'd just done to her. Scott had been the only guy she'd given her full trust to. Watching her father dump one woman for the next had made her leery of men. Her mother never marrying hadn't helped. Maybe all guys were like her dad.

Men could go suck it as far as she was concerned. She'd just focus on finishing her degree. She didn't need a man to be happy.

When she leaned down to open her car door, a stab of guilt hit her. Was she any better than Scott for what she'd just done out of hurt and anger?

Maybe she shouldn't have donated the ring. But then, she was actually doing Brandi a favor. No woman wanted her former best friend's engagement ring.

∞ ∞ ∞

Undercover FBI forensic accountant, Brent Keiser, AKA Brent Jackson for his current assignment, tossed the strap of his leather courier bag—one that held conflicting financial data—over his shoulder and then beeped the locks closed on his electric car. Drawing in the warm, salty ocean breeze into his lungs in mid-December and appreciating his relocation to Malibu even more, he walked to his office in Holden Chapman's house.

His buddy Rick, a former classmate at the academy, never let an opportunity pass to poke fun at Brent's cushy assignment investigating a rich movie star. What he wouldn't give to have just one exciting story from the field like his coworkers did on their Friday beer nights, though. Ledgers and stock trades dulled in comparison to the stories that included zinging bullets and high-speed chases.

A red Porsche with music blaring from the open windows zoomed up the drive and skidded to a stop in front of the mansion. It was a Tuscan design with arched stone windows and tiled roofs, a home the size of a hotel.

He started walking again before the occupant opened the door to get out. The long, tan legs owned by the daughter who lived there were a temptation he didn't need. Sara Chapman was beautiful, and everything he'd *never* wanted in a woman. Not that he really knew her. Being a former homeless kid, he just didn't care for what spoiled rich women like her represented.

Sara called out, "Brent?"

He stopped in his tracks. She knew his name? They'd only spoken once when she'd asked him to write her a check for a charity few days ago. He turned and forced his eyes to stay far above her pretty legs. "Yes?"

Her dazzling smile shone as bright as her sunny yellow dress. She flipped her curly light brown hair over her shoulder and said, "Can I talk to you for a minute? I think I might have screwed up yesterday."

He'd seen what she'd done on the news. Everything Sara did was newsworthy because she was the daughter of two of the most famous stars in Hollywood. Well, her mother was still at the top of her game, but her father had been struggling for parts and up to some criminal financial dealings, according to their intel. Hence the undercover assignment. "What can I help you with?"

"My ring." She transferred her behemoth purse to the other arm and lifted her left hand that sported a white circle on her finger. Once, a huge engagement ring that could've supported a family of four for years had occupied that finger. She said, "Scott is threatening to sic his lawyers on me. I might need some more money from the investment account. I've only got a grand or so in my personal account."

Brent started walking again, trying his best to ignore how nice Sara smelled when the light breeze tossed her pretty scent his way. Like purple flowers and fresh linens. "He didn't care for your donation on his behalf to the homeless shelter?" The same homeless shelter she'd had to perform community service at two years ago after a night of partying with her spoiled friends had gone bad. He wasn't sure yet if she donated because she cared or to repair her reputation. Or perhaps to legitimize dirty money as a tax write-off.

Sara caught up with his long strides and walked beside him under the portico that led to his office. She only came up to his shoulder because she'd opted for flat sandals rather than her usual skyscraper heels. It was his job to notice those things, or so he told himself every time he started to appreciate her beauty.

She sighed loudly. "I'd just read a text from Scott asking me to return the ring because he planned to repurpose it. When the director of the shelter said they were still hundreds of thousands short, I just sort of lost it."

He slipped the key into his office door lock and tried his best to hide his grin. As much as he didn't care for Sara's lifestyle, no one deserved to be dumped on national television like she had been. He couldn't blame her for slipping off the rock and making a show of donating the engagement ring to the shelter in front of the press. Served the guy right. "You could've chucked it into the ocean. At least you gave the ring to a good cause." He'd spent his share of nights in shelters growing up. Not that he'd ever tell anyone that.

"Right?" Sara flopped into one of the guest chairs in front of his desk and crossed tanned legs. "He's just mad because the public is on my side."

Brent slipped his bag's strap off and sat behind his desk. "This sounds more like a legal problem than an accounting one."

"That's where I just came from. The lawyer. She said an engagement ring is a conditional gift, and it matters who breaks up with who. Everyone with a pulse saw him break up with me real time on TV. So that's on my side." She stood and paced. "Scott is claiming something about emotional abandonment, though, because I hadn't been to the set to visit him in four months. We'd been drifting apart."

Four months? That *was* a long time not to see a fiancé. "I'm not qualified to..."

"He wouldn't listen." She stopped pacing and laid her hands on his desk. "I'm writing my thesis. I have just one more semester to go. I can't jet off at the drop of a hat anymore. I have responsibilities now I didn't have before." She closed her eyes. "Everyone has dropped me, if you want to know the truth. None of my girlfriends even bother to ask me to go out with them anymore. They say I've become *boring*." She flopped into the chair and blinked away tears.

He needed to get her back on track before he'd feel the need to wrap her in a hug and console her.

Besides, she could be a criminal. He hadn't proved all the players' involvement yet, but something was going on with her account. "Where do I come in here?"

"Sorry. Stressful week." She wiped her cheeks. "I wanted to know if I have five hundred thousand dollars to give to Scott. If the press gets wind of his abandonment allegations, it'll become even more embarrassing. I just want to focus on finishing my counseling degree and getting a job."

Who didn't know how much money they had in the bank? He'd been acutely aware of every cent growing up. Was it a clever ploy because she and her father were onto the investigation? Had his cover been blown? "Let's check and see."

He tapped keys on his computer but could have told her to the penny how much was in her account. He'd lived and breathed all of her father's complicated accounting mess for the past six weeks. That and because, unbeknownst to him until college, he was apparently a genius, especially with numbers, according to the FBI. That's why they couldn't "waste" his talents with typical fieldwork.

Sara glanced around his office as she waited. "Why didn't Justin decorate for Christmas in here? The rest of the house looks like Toyland on steroids."

"I told him not to bother." He continued to tap keys. "I don't believe in celebrating holidays."

"None?" She leaned forward and tilted her head. "Not even a picnic on the Fourth?"

"Nope." Not since his mother had died. What was the point? He had no one he cared about enough to celebrate with. "How much do you *think* you should have in your account?"

Sara's bewildered frown still lingered. "I have no idea."

Maybe she could act as well as her parents? "Not even a guess?"

Her palms lifted. "I don't get control of that money for four more years. When I'm thirty. My father controls the account. He still resents that my mother made him start that investment account before he got married the first time. She'd correctly predicted his numerous marriages and the mountain of alimony bills he pays each month. She'd been looking out for me."

Brent leaned back in his chair. Her mother was stinking rich too, so Sara probably didn't have to worry about money from her father. "They never married, right? Your parents?"

"He asked, but my mother said no. Can't wait for dear old Dad's wedding number five this weekend. To Veeeroonica." She turned away and stared out the window. "You probably think I'm stupid for not paying attention to that account. But the few times I looked, it was pretty much empty."

It took all his control to stop his brows from lifting. That made zero sense. "Did you actually see the statements?"

"Mr. Barker only showed me when I pressed him." A sad sigh escaped before she said, "I still really miss him. He was like a grandfather to me."

Barker's death created the job opportunity the FBI had pounced on to place Brent inside to take over as Holden's business and estate manager. They thought they'd hired a person who'd had a string of bartending jobs since graduating with a business degree from a local community college, not a highly trained agent.

Ignoring the tug at his heart for her obvious loss of a loved one that he knew well, he asked, "Maybe he showed you the wrong account? I've found a few mistakes since taking over."

"Doubt it." Sara shook her head and pulled her attention away from the window and back to his desk. She picked up the Rubik's cube he often used when he was thinking. As she twisted, she said, "My father is that type who's there for me when things are fine, not so much when things get tough—or he's about to remarry again. He loves me. I try to focus on that. But I don't depend on him. My mom promised to help me as long as I'm in school. After I graduate, I'll be on my own and happy for it."

"And yet you asked me for a hundred-thousand-dollar donation the other day as if you expected the money to be there." Maybe he'd catch her in a lie. It made his heart rate pick up.

She nodded. "When I called and asked my father for a fifty-thousand-dollar donation to help save the shelter last week, he said I could use my own money for a change. Evidently, he'd sold some real estate for me I never knew I'd owned. I thought I'd better grab it before it was all gone again, so I doubled the donation. When you didn't blink at the amount, I figured I'd gotten lucky and the money was still there. I'd rather give it to a good cause than one of his many ex-wives."

Or maybe her father needed a tax write-off. Laundering money through real estate and donations was a common way to clean up tainted cash.

What kind of father would use his only child's account to do that? Or was she involved too? Because her account was certainly involved.

He didn't want to give her the five hundred thousand to pay her scumbag spoiled ex back, though. It was money he might be able to return to injured parties. "Maybe you should let the lawyers work things out. If they say you have to pay, then we'll give him the money back. I'd hate to see Scott win."

"Thank you." She smiled weakly and set the cube back in its place. All the colors perfectly matched.

He picked the cube up and turned it around in his hands, checking to see if all the sides were correct. "Wow. You did that really fast."

"Yeah. Old party trick. So, how much is in my account?"

Party trick? He'd never met anyone who could solve the puzzle faster than he could. It was a little annoying. "There's just over two hundred million now." He turned his screen filled with transfers into her account.

She blinked in stunned surprise as she studied the screen closely, as if she couldn't believe her own eyes.

Her reaction *seemed* genuine.

She finally whispered, "Holy crap. I guess we'll be fine, then, if I have to pay Scott back." She stood to go. "If you're not busy on Christmas Eve, we always have a dinner for everyone who's still in town. You're welcome to join us, of course."

He ignored the invitation. "You don't go to your mother's house?"

"My mom's plane always picks me up at nine to take me to Albuquerque right after. You should join us for dinner. Zoila will be offended if you don't come and eat her food." Sara pointed to the illustrated mug on the desk. "Caffeine. Funny. See you around."

After the door closed behind her, he picked up his coffee cup. He'd totally forgotten which one he'd chosen to use, but she'd been right. It had a picture of the molecular structure of caffeine on it, but no label to identify it.

Seemed the spoiled little princess was smarter than she let on. Perfectly capable of orchestrating the elaborate money laundering scheme he'd yet to fully crack. But something inside him still didn't want to believe Sara was involved. Confusing as it was, he couldn't screw up his first solo undercover assignment.

He needed to separate his attraction to her from the job. Besides it being a handbook violation to date suspects, Sara was waaaaay out of his league. No way he'd screw up his plans for any woman, no matter how beautiful. He'd joined the FBI for their stability and amazing retirement plan, and one day, he'd own that house on the water he had his eye on. Free and clear, so no one could ever take it away from him. Solving the mystery of Sara and her father would get him a promotion and one step closer to fulfilling his dreams. Nothing was going to get in the way of that.

Especially not beautiful, smart, spoiled Sara.

Chapter Two

After her meeting with Brent, Sara headed toward the kitchen to find some empty carbs to drown her sorrows about losing Scott as a friend. But not as a fiancé. They would've never worked, and it was almost a relief now that she'd thought things through. Brandi, on the other hand, violated girl-code big-time, and that still stung.

On top of that, she was still reeling from the news about how much money was in her account. But it'd never be there in four years. Her dad would divorce Veronica long before then, and she'd end up with it all. Why the man never insisted on a prenup was an unsolved mystery.

How her dad had come up with that much money when he'd been complaining nonstop about the cost of his upcoming wedding was the bigger mystery, though.

"Hi, my love." Zoila, short, dark haired, plump, and like a second mother to Sara, dropped a spoonful of dough onto a cookie sheet. She looked up from the batch of chocolate chip cookies she was making. "How are you today?" She'd been trying to only speak

English since Veronica banned Spanish from the house because she couldn't understand it. Veronica was a pain in everyone's butt.

"I'm hanging in. Barely." She reached out for a cookie and got a hand slap. "What?"

"These are for Mr. Brent. They are his favorite."

"Oh. I thought you were making them for me. To cheer me up after what Scott did."

Zoila shook her head. "I told you Mr. Scott is never going to be the one for you. That he lack character. But me? I'm no gloater, so I make your favorite chocolate mousse anyway. In the fridge."

"You're the best. Thank you." Sara kissed Zoila's cheek and crossed the kitchen and pulled out a little cup of goodness from the commercial-sized stainless fridge. She grabbed a spoon and planted herself at the kitchen island.

A can of whipped cream suddenly appeared beside her too. Since she'd been a kid, it had become a tradition that Zoila snuck Sara a can of whipped cream all for herself whenever she was sad about something. It was a silly tradition, but she loved Zoila for it.

While spraying on as much fluffy goodness as the cup could hold, she said, "I invited Brent to have Christmas Eve dinner with all of us. Doubt he'll come, though."

"I invite him too. He say he busy. But Mr. Brent? Now he a man with character. Nice, likes my cooking, only two years older than you, and very, very handsome too."

Sara nodded as she stuffed her mouth full of chocolate decadence. "If you're into the Superman/Clark Kent look." He also had pretty blue eyes that contrasted with his dark hair, and he spent lots of time in the gym, not that she'd stopped and gawked or anything. She'd just noticed. But he never smiled. It was odd.

Sara scraped her bowl clean, then leaned her head back and sprayed whipped cream straight into her mouth. She mumbled around the fluff, "But who wears a suit every day to work in a home office? Mr. Barker wore jeans and polo shirts."

Justin, their house manager, flopped onto the stool beside Sara. "I'm into the Clark Kent look, but I think Brent is more interested in you, Sunshine." He took the can and sprayed whipped cream into his mouth too.

Zoila said, "Hey! That only for Miss Sara! Not pushy men who make themselves too much at home in my kitchen." She grabbed the can away from Justin and threw it in the trash mumbling in Spanish about being a piggy.

Sara hid a grin. "Brent thinks I'm an airhead. It's written all over his face."

Zoila turned to put another tray of cookies into the oven, so Justin snatched two that were cooling and handed her one. "That's not what his face was saying the other day. I was trying to have a scintillating conversation with him, and then you walked by wearing that killer blue dress. You know, the one you wore with the Versace pump platforms? His head turned so fast, it's a miracle he didn't give himself whiplash. Which reminds me. Your mom's monthly clothing shipment arrived an hour ago."

"Great. Thanks."

"Try not to get too excited there, Debbie Downer." Justin's shoulder bumped hers. "To quote your mom, 'One must always look camera ready. Especially because you are a Botelli.' Good words to live by, if you ask me."

Those words had been drilled into Sara's head by her mom since she'd been old enough to walk. Sara and her sister, Dani, had high standards to live up to when out in public. Her mom's reputation meant the world to her, while her father seemed totally indifferent to his.

"But maybe just once, on a lazy Saturday afternoon, I'd like to look like a Chapman."

"Why would you ever want that?" Justin shook his head and leaned closer. "Tell your mom when she's tired of you, I'm available for adoption. You're an ingrate."

Zoila called out, "What you don't know, Mr. Smart Mouth, is that Miss Sara donate all those clothes. Many single mom and poor high school girl have nice things to wear for proms and job interviews because of Miss Sara."

"You do?" Justin frowned at her. "How do I not know this?"

Sara opened her mouth, but Zoila interrupted, "Because she not all braggy like you, so stop poking at her. She need a break. She sad about losing her friends. Even if they both have no character. Not that I ever say so."

Justin grinned and rolled his eyes at Zoila's gloating. "Brandi's always been about as loyal as an alligator, and screw Scott. Especially when *you* could have Superman with a snap of the fingers. Unfortunately for me, Brent's just not into blond men who look like pop stars."

Justin did look a little like a pop star. Tall, thin, and often dressed in tight leather. Always much more blinged out than her. Her tastes ran toward the simple.

Zoila turned back to her cookies and gave them both the stink eye for stealing Brent's treats. "Well, Mr. Brent. He a good man. He not give me a hard time about the food budget like cranky Mr. Barker did."

Justin grabbed another cookie, just barely avoiding Zoila's swat. "I've called your beloved Mr. Brent over here because we're all having a fitting. Veronica and Holden just finished theirs a few minutes ago. The new M-R-S wants all the *staff* to look presentable at the wedding on Saturday. It's my job to dress you hooligans. Luckily, Trina brought tons of choices." After Justin finished off his second cookie, he said, "And you, Sunshine, have to look amazing. Scott called and asked if he could bring Brandi as his guest. Veronica said yes, of course, because having both of you will be good for publicity."

Sara's stomach dropped. "Nope. Not happening. I'll talk to my dad. He'll uninvite Scott."

Justin grabbed her hand and gave it a quick squeeze. "Your father loved the idea. He wants the press there too."

Utter betrayal filled her for the second time in as many days. She stood and rinsed off her bowl and then put it into the dishwasher. "Dad really needs another big part. I guess he could use all the publicity he can get right now." At her expense. What else was new?

When she looked up, Brent was standing next to Zoila. How long had he been there? The guy moved as quietly as a ghost.

She circled the island to settle onto her stool again with Brent's cool gaze, like ice cubes on the back of her neck, sending a tingle down her spine. The guy really didn't like her.

Justin, with pity etched on his face, said, "We'll make Scott sorry he ever let you go. Can you find a date?"

A date? She'd been engaged. It wasn't like she kept a harem of men waiting in the wings. "The wedding is day after tomorrow. There's no time for me to find a date on such short notice."

She met Brent's steady, steely blue-eyed gaze. Betrayal moved aside to be replaced by absolute mortification. She was already a loser in his eyes, and now she was one who couldn't even find a date for a wedding. She quickly looked away and said, "Maybe I'll just go to my mom's early for Christmas break. Skip the wedding. My dad won't even miss me."

Zoila shook her head. "*We* will miss you. Especially on Christmas Eve. This house is only happy because you make it for us, sweetheart."

Brent cleared his throat. "Why am I here?"

Justin's grin turned mischievous. "Because Sara needs a date for her father's wedding. And tag, you're it."

When a frown crossed Brent's face, Sara dropped her forehead onto the cool granite countertop. One more rejection to top off her week.

Can things get any worse?

∞ ∞ ∞

Brent glanced at Zoila to see if Justin had been kidding. Her head bobbed up and down with excitement, and she said, "You make a good date for Miss Sara."

Apparently, it wasn't a prank.

The last thing Brent wanted to do was accompany Sara to her father's wedding. He'd planned to use the wedding as an opportunity to check out some of the people whose names he kept seeing on various real estate contracts. The guest list had shown most of the people involved in Holden's business dealings would be in attendance.

Sara, her forehead still on the countertop, whispered, "Give Brent a break guys. He clearly doesn't want to take me." The defeat in her voice warred with his conscience.

Even though his mother hadn't been the most reliable, or made the best decisions in her life, she'd insisted on one thing: that her son never treat women the way she'd been treated by men who never saw past her bimbo exterior. "I'd be honored to be your date, Sara."

Sara's head whipped up from the island, and she blinked at him. "You would? I thought you couldn't sta—"

"Perfect!" Justin grabbed Brent's arm and tugged. "I'll start with you. I have just the suit in mind. Trina can tailor it for you if need be. Sara, you come too, please."

Tailor? Crap. How would he explain his gun?

He stopped walking, and Justin, who couldn't weigh more than a buck thirty-five to Brent's two-ten, almost pulled his own arm out of the socket. "Why are we stopping?"

Brent glanced at Sara, who was still looking at him like she expected him to take his invitation back. "I'll email you guys my measurements. I have something pressing."

Justin shook his head and tugged again, but Brent stood his ground.

On a long sigh, Justin said, "You work for Holden Chapman, therefore, there is nothing more pressing than making sure his wedding is perfect. Am I right, Sara?"

She nodded. "It won't take long. Trina's fast."

If they busted him for the gun, he'd make up something about living in a sketchy neighborhood. From what they were "paying" him, that'd make sense. "Fine. After you, then." He held a hand out for Sara to go first.

"Thank you." Sara led the way toward the rear of the home, past a large, plant-filled solarium that looked out over the ocean. He'd never been past the kitchen before, so he took mental notes of the layout. Sara continued down a series of wide hallways past what must be a theater based on the little lobby area with a ticket booth, candy counter, and a popcorn maker like in a real theater. She finally stepped into a large room filled with rolling racks of clothes.

"I'll be right back, guys." Justin hurried inside and started rifling through the racks.

Sara stood quietly beside him as he checked out the rest of the room. To the right was a beauty salon set-up his cosmetologist mother would have loved to work in, complete with sinks, dryers, and shelves of hair dyes to choose from. On the opposite wall, big padded chairs stood in front of huge lighted mirrors. There were counters filled with a selection of makeup like he'd never seen before. Even more little plastic boxes and brushes than when his mother had worked at the department store doing eye shadow demos.

Holden and Veronica, the future bride and groom, were sitting in the chairs getting their hair and makeup done, looking like blond gods. In the mirror's reflection, Holden's eyes locked with his, and Sara's father lifted his chin slightly in greeting. When Holden's gaze connected with Sara's, he quickly looked away. Probably feeling guilty for inviting Sara's ex to the wedding. Who'd do that to their kid?

Veronica winked at him as she droned on about something into her cell phone. Her knowing smile was the same she'd worn the last time she'd rubbed up against him when they ran into each other in the kitchen a few days ago. She'd made it clear she'd like to get to know him better in the biblical sense.

Sara must've seen him cringe as a woman put lipstick on her father, because she whispered, "Don't worry, we won't make you wear any lip gloss today." She smiled as her gaze lowered to his mouth.

It sent a zap of heat straight to his gut. "Appreciate that."

A woman with spiked red hair, a top that barely held her assets in place, and pants so tight she might as well have not bothered wearing any at all, joined them. "Hey, gang. Who's this, Sara?" Her blue eyes zeroed in on his.

Sara held out a hand his way. "Trina, this is our new business manager, Brent. Justin guilted the poor guy into volunteering to accompany me to the wedding."

Her eyes did a quick up-and-down inspection of his body. "Nice to meet you." Trina frowned as she tapped a finger on her full bottom lip. "I'm thinking of dressing Sara in pink. You're okay with wearing a pale pink shirt, aren't you, Brad? I want you two to coordinate."

Pink? Hell no! He'd never worn a pink shirt in his life.

"It's Brent. And I'd rather not." The guys at happy hour would never let him live it down if they saw him with Sara in the tabloids the day after the wedding wearing a pink shirt.

Veronica called out. "No pink at my wedding!"

Trina's brow arched. "Then I guess we'll go with Justin's choice."

Seemed not many in the house were fans of Veronica's.

Justin returned with a dark suit and a blue dress. "Here, you two. Try these on. Wasn't sure on your fit, Brent, but you can adjust the tux pants at the waist."

Not sure if he was expected to strip right there, or worse, if Sara was going to, because that might be too much for any man to bear, he locked gazes with Trina. "Shirt?"

"Your date doesn't waste words, does he, Sara?" Trina turned and grabbed a white fancy shirt and a dark blue tie that matched Sara's dress off a nearby rack. Then she grabbed some shoes. "Hmmm. Big feet. What are you, a thirteen? No, I bet fourteen." She looked up and hitched her brows.

He nodded. "Fourteen."

"Lucky Sara." She handed him the shoes.

Sara rolled her eyes. "Give the guy a break, Trina." She looked up at him. "Ignore them. They all live to tease around here."

He followed behind Sara's tan legs, while trying his best to not look at them. But then his gaze found her butt, and that was nice too.

He needed to find the missing money before Sara drove him nuts.

When she stopped abruptly, he nearly ran her over, stopping just in the nick of time.

She pointed to her right. "You can take that one." Then she circled behind a matching silk privacy screen of her own.

His shoulders and head stuck up over the folding screen, so he had to crouch down a little when slipping out of his gun holster. Just the top of Sara's head was visible over her trifold screen as her yellow dress landed over the partition and then a black bra joined it.

The thought of Sara topless just a few feet away was a pleasant one he needed to shake off. He quickly slipped his holster onto a hook and then added his sport coat over it. After he'd slid out of his slacks, he folded them neatly and was about to lay them on a chair when he spotted a legal-size envelope lying on the seat. The return address was Golden Bear Real Estate Group. Holden's fake holding company.

Was it a test? Did they suspect he was investigating them?

Screw it. No way he'd pass up a chance to possibly find evidence to crack the case.

He glanced around one more time to check that everyone was still occupied, and then he reached for the papers inside. It was an offer to buy another piece of real estate for cash. His heart pounded in anticipation.

He grabbed his phone from his suit pocket to shoot pictures of the pages inside. He'd study them later, but the contract might be just what he needed to bust them all.

Keeping his breathing steady and his heartbeat in check, he shot the last of the pages.

Just as he started to return the pages back to their envelope, Holden called out, "Hey, new guy?"

Dammit. That's me.

He stood up and looked over the screen. Both Veronica and Holden were staring at him. Fixing a bland expression on his face, he said, "Yes?"

Holden frowned. "Did I leave an envelope in there?"

"Let me look." Brent quickly slid the papers all the way back inside and folded the flap tight. "Is this it?" He held up the envelope.

"Yeah." Holden nodded. "Bring it here will you?"

"Sure." Brent was in his socks and boxers, so he quickly pulled on the new suit pants, but they didn't fit. There were some adjustable things on the sides he couldn't figure out.

Fingers snapping, Holden called out, "Need those papers, buddy."

"Yep. Coming." He slipped the white shirt over his shoulders, forgoing the tiny black buttons. "Be right there."

Giving up on the side things on his pants, he snatched up the envelope, held on to his pants and jogged across the room to hand it over. "Here you go."

Sara's father, tall, golden-haired, Botox injected, teeth bleached, and skin unnaturally tanned, took the envelope from him. "Thanks, pal."

Veronica, a blonde bombshell, and an equally fake counterpart to Holden but only six years older than Sara said, "His name is Brent, babe." She smiled at him while her gaze ran across his bare chest. "Will you save me a dance or two on Saturday?"

"I'm not much of a dancer."

"Pity." Her lips formed a pout that'd make a two-year-old proud.

He was about to leave when she added, "When I get back from my honeymoon, we'll have that meeting. Okay?" She smiled like a cat about to dive into a bowl of cream as her gaze did a full up and down over his body again.

The woman had no shame. She was setting up a sex date right in front of Holden.

Sara moved beside him and said, "Let's finish getting you dressed so you can get back to work, Brent." Sara's hand slipped around his arm, and she yanked him toward his dressing area.

He glanced down at Sara and nearly swallowed his tongue. Her shimmery dark blue dress fit like it was made just for her, highlighting all the parts that made her so perfectly a woman. The soft curve of her breasts and those hips. God. Her tall shoes made her legs go on for miles.

Once they were behind his partition, she frowned. "Figured you might need some help back there."

What he needed help with from Sara was off-limits. "Thanks. Do you know how these things work on the sides of my pants?"

Sara nodded and got to work on his waistband. "You have a small waist for such a big guy. All those crunches we see you do in the gym every morning, no doubt." She tightened up the sides of his pants with a violent tug, and then lifted his hand and buttoned up his cuff. "I'm sure it's part of what Veronica wants to 'meet' with you about." Sara yanked up his cuff on the other side, none too gently.

He'd been using Holden's gym because it was top-notch. Maybe he should start using the crappy one in his apartment building from now on? But then, it sometimes gave him the opportunity to talk to Holden, so he'd stick with his routine. "I would never cross any lines with your future stepmother."

"Veronica will never be any kind of *mother* to me." She shook her head as she jerked his shirt together and started working the tiny black buttons. "Zoila told me Veronica has been hitting on you, so I think it's best we keep you fully clothed. Your abs alone could tempt a nun."

He looked down. Sara had just buttoned up his shirt like he was a little kid. And because she'd seemed so upset by Veronica's flirting, he'd let her. Maybe he'd better handle tucking in his shirt on his own, though. She was being a little violent, and there were parts he'd rather she not shove around.

When her hand reached out to grab his suit coat from the hook, his shot out and covered hers. Couldn't let her see the gun underneath. He'd just ignore that soft skin under his. "Other one."

She huffed out a breath. "Sorry. I'm a little distracted."

By his abs? That shouldn't make him want to smile, but it did.

"This wedding is such a joke," she said.

Oh. So not him. The wedding.

She grabbed the other suit coat from the hook along with his tie and wrapped them both around his shoulders. She whispered, "I hate that my dad keeps marrying the same kind of woman. They only want to be with him because of his fame, but then they figure out he's not nearly as loaded as they think he is, and they leave him. But only after they've slept with the pool guy and the gardeners, just to make things worse. No offense."

Was he supposed to take offense? "Like I said, I'm not interested in Veronica."

"Yes. But you're a man. And most cave to women like her eventually. Scott did."

So, this was about Scott? Or her father? Hell, maybe it was all about Veronica. It was hard to keep up. "Scott slept with Veronica?"

"No. Brandi. Same thing." She started in on his tie. He should probably stop her, but she seemed determined to continue dressing him, and it wasn't a hardship, so he'd let her do her thing.

When she was done, he glanced in the mirror. She'd made his tie look really nice. He should have paid attention to how she'd done that. "May I point out that your father does have money now. Even if it's in your account, he's got control of two hundred million. That's no drop in the bucket where I come from. So maybe Veronica will be the one who stays?" Was that helping? Maybe not.

She pushed on his shoulder. "Sit." After he complied, she slipped on one of the shiny shoes. "That money won't last six months. You'll see."

So he'd done it before? Laundered money through real estate. But then where did it all go?

She laced up his other shoe then stood up and studied him like a bug under a microscope. "Just need to fix this." She leaned closer, so close her subtle sweet perfume filled his senses, and then she ran her fingers through his hair, straightening it. It sent a nice shiver up his spine.

She whispered, "How could my father not see that Veronica wanted to lick you like an ice cream cone back there? Is he blind or just totally oblivious?"

He wasn't sure if he was actually supposed to answer that, so he stood up and looked at himself in the mirror. He'd never worn clothes so nice.

Justin appeared. "Look at you two. Like the top of a wedding cake."

Ignoring Justin, Sara said, "I wish my father would just quit marrying them. Save himself the grief of getting yet another divorce and just live with them until it sizzles out."

Brent glanced at Justin and held up his hands, palms up. In a what-the-heck-do-I-say gesture.

Justin nodded in understanding. Then he walked over to Sara and took her hands in his. "Hey. Can you please stop long enough to see what I've created?" He turned her around to face their reflection in the mirror. "You guys look amazing."

Sara blinked at their reflection as if finally seeing them clearly for the first time. "Wow. We really do." Her gaze raised up to meet his. "You clean up nice, Brent. Thanks again for being my date." Her eyes filled with tears as she left.

He turned to Justin. "What did I do?"

"Nothing." Justin smiled. "When our sweet Sara gets upset, she doesn't scream and yell. She cleans, straightens, or fixes things. Consider yourself fixed." Justin turned and disappeared.

Fixed? He'd been broken for so long, he doubted anyone could ever fix him.

Chapter Three

The thought of seeing Scott and Brandi together at her father's wedding haunted Sara all night. So much so, she rose early on Friday morning to beat the crap out of a punching bag in her dad's gym. Not that little one that looked like a volleyball. Nope. She was going for the fat, round one that hung in front of her looking all intimidating.

She poked it with a finger, and it barely moved. The bag was really heavy and almost as big as she was. She'd never hit a person in her entire life, and she didn't want to start by clocking Scott and Brandi at the wedding if she lost it, so the plan was to get her aggressions all out before she saw them again.

After she slid her hand inside a boxing glove, she lifted it up. Now what? How was she supposed to tie the thing with only one hand? Use her teeth? That might work. She pulled the lace tight and placed it between her teeth to hold it. But that still just left one hand to tie it tight. And then only her teeth when she put the other glove on. Oh, forget it. She didn't want to hit that heavy thing anyway. She'd probably break her wrist and then Scott and Brandi would win. Again.

She threw down the glove and glanced at the new stationary bike that had shown up a few days before. It had a built-in screen and speakers. A spin class might do the trick.

She rummaged around in her father's locker area until she found some padded bike shorts and a brand-new pair of riding cleats she'd never seen before. Must go with the new bike.

After changing, she walked to the bike, figured out how to turn it on, and then clipped her shoes into the pedals with a solid click. Like a ski boot clicking into a binding. The shoes fit nice and tight on the pedals.

The screen showed twenty options for different classes. It even had scenic rides. Maybe she'd take a ride through Tuscany first to warm up. Or maybe Paris. Yeah, Paris sounded fun, so she poked the icon, put her earbuds in, and got lost peddling down a cobblestone street. Much better than being violent. So relaxing, she could almost smell the buttery pastries in the windows of the little shops as she peddled by. And the flowers, they were all colors of spring and so very pretty. She should probably stop meandering through the countryside and take a real spin class, the kind that made her sweat and huff, but she was having so much fun, she decided to do the trek across Australia next.

A movement to her right pulled her attention from her ride past the Sydney Opera House. Brent had joined her and was doing his ab crunches again. He must've been there for a while because he'd worked up a sweat that made his shirt stick to the outline of his six-pack abs.

Why did men look great when they worked out and were all sweaty, and women just looked gross? She hated to think what she must look like with her hair in a ponytail and her bangs plastered to her damp forehead. But then, why should she care? The new plan was to stay away from all men until after she finished school. Then maybe she'd get lucky and find a trustworthy guy to marry and have kids with. If that kind of man even existed. If not, she'd be like her mom and have kids on her own.

She glanced Brent's way again and caught him looking at her legs. Probably because her form was wrong or something. She went back to her ride but lost interest. Maybe she'd switch to the elliptical for a while.

She shut down the program and yanked her earbuds out. After pointing her toes, she jerked her foot to the right, but her shoe wouldn't release from the pedal. She tried her left foot, but that one wouldn't give either.

Great. Her feet were stuck on the stupid bike.

She reached down to release the top strap on her right shoe, ratcheted like a ski boot, but apparently, she'd adjusted it too tight, because it wouldn't budge either. It was new and stiff and probably required two hands. She let go of the handlebar and leaned down with both hands but stopped. If she fell off while attempting to escape her new shoes, she could break an ankle. Or her neck.

A deep voice behind her said, "Need a hand?"

Of course, he'd be right there to witness her humiliation once again. But she'd look like a bigger idiot if she sat there and waited for him to leave so she could call Zoila to come save her. "Yes, please."

He reached down, grabbed her shoe's heel, and then gave a quick twist. Sure enough, her right shoe came free. That his bicep had flexed nicely wasn't enough to make her forget her embarrassment, but it'd come close. He had a mighty impressive body.

She closed her eyes to block out any more bulging muscles and let him do the other foot before she opened them again.

"Thank you." It'd just sound like an excuse if she explained everything was new and adjusted wrong, so she climbed off the bike and sat on the floor to remove her shoes. To her surprise, he flopped next to her and unlatched the mechanisms for her. He smelled like a combo of sweaty male and woodsy deodorant. It was actually...nice. She could only hope her sweaty socks weren't stinky.

He gently pulled the shoes off her feet. "I tried this bike out yesterday too. Someone had adjusted the men's shoes all wrong. They should be at a lower setting so you can clip out easily. Want me to fix those for you?" He pointed to her shoes.

Wasn't he going to tease her about getting stuck on the bike? Everyone teased her about everything. No one in her house ever took her seriously. Especially when it came to her studies. They all assumed she'd been taking her time finishing school so her mom would keep the checks coming, but that wasn't true. She was going to shock them all when she graduated top of her class come next May. Well, except for Zoila. She knew the truth. "I can fix them. I should have checked before I got on. But thanks."

"Okay." He hopped up and held out a hand to help her up.

She slowly took his hand, surprised at how callused it felt for an accounting guy, and stood. "Thanks for saving my life. I could've been stuck on there for days, and no one would have noticed with all the wedding prep going on." She smiled at him, not that she expected one back.

"I would've noticed. You're my date tomorrow." Without a smile, he gave her hand a quick squeeze. "What time should I be here?"

Yeah. That. "Depends. Do you want to ride in one of the limos with the wedding party early or take my car?" She didn't want to make him drive on top of everything else.

"Right." He dropped her hand. "My electric car would embarrass you."

Crap. She hadn't thought that. It probably made her sound like a snob. "Not at all. I'm all for preserving the environment too."

His right brow cocked in disbelief. "That's why you bought a Porsche?"

"No. That was a gift from my mother. If I were buying the car, I couldn't afford one as nice as yours." She wasn't going to tell him that her mom had given her the car for staying on the Dean's list at school. She'd taken a long time to figure out what her major would be and was a little old to be waving her report card around like a kid.

"Okay. Then what time would you like me to pick you up?"

"How about three o'clock? But after we make an entrance for the press, you don't have to hang with me. I plan to leave as soon as I can anyway. I'll grab my own ride home."

"I'll take you home whenever you're ready." He shrugged a shoulder. "I hate weddings."

Her curiosity was piqued. "You don't celebrate holidays, and you hate weddings. What makes you happy, Brent?"

He crossed his muscled arms. "Not everyone grew up believing in the tooth fairy and unicorns like you." He grabbed a towel and walked toward the locker room.

She called out to his back, "Since we don't get to choose how we grow up, maybe it's pigheaded to judge people for it?"

Brent stopped walking and glanced over his broad shoulder. "I meant it metaphorically." He turned and disappeared through the locker room door. No doubt to put on one of the suits he wore every day.

Metaphorically?

Now he'd gone and intrigued her. Her studies for her counselor degree made her want to know what made a guy like Brent tick. Specifically, what it'd take to make him smile.

Her phone rang on the bike where she'd left it. When she saw who it was, she grinned despite her mood being tainted by grumpy Brent. She hadn't seen her mother for months, and she missed her. "Hi, Mom. How are you?"

"I'm wondering the same about you, sweetheart. Seeing Scott and attending another of your father's weddings tomorrow can't be a fun prospect."

That was the understatement of the year. "I'll live. I always do."

"And the new guy? Brent, is it? How are you two getting along?"

Why would her mom ask about him? Unless she'd had another of her prophetic dreams. Sara was the only Botelli woman who didn't have any "woo-woo powers," and that was fine by her. "I'm certain I've never mentioned Brent to you. What's up?" She jogged to the locker room and tucked her phone under her chin as she changed in one of the stalls.

"I'm not sure, entirely." Her mother drew in a deep breath. "My dreams have been unusually vague. I think your father and some new business partners might be in trouble. Financially."

Nothing new there. Her dad was always broke between movies. "And your point is?"

"I'm afraid they might have involved you somehow. You need to come home right after the wedding. I'll send the plane, and then you can come with me to the press junket in London I can't get out of. We'll be back home by Christmas Eve."

The last thing she wanted to do was run home to her overprotective mommy. It was one of the reasons Sara was happy she'd moved to California with her father when she'd been thirteen. To gain some degree of independence. "I have to stay here for Christmas Eve. It's our only tradition. Especially because Dad and Veronica will be on their honeymoon." And because Zoila already said she'd miss her if she didn't stay for the dinner.

"Honey, if what I've seen so far is even remotely correct, you might be in trouble."

"How can I be in trouble when I haven't done anything wrong? Well, except maybe I shouldn't have donated my engagement ring right after Scott asked for it back."

"No, Scott deserved *that!*" Her mom huffed out a breath. "I don't like to speak poorly of your father, but..."

"Then don't." Dressed in shorts and a tank again, Sara walked out of the gym doors to the backyard, past the pool, and toward the solarium to sit in her favorite spot. The one in the most secluded corner that looked out over the ocean. "You know I hate it when you talk smack about Dad. Even if he usually deserves it."

"But this time, he might have involved *you*. And I won't have that."

Her mother sounded firm in her position, and she didn't want to fight with her, but Zoila, Justin, and the rest were her family too. "I'll come home right after dinner as usual on Christmas Eve. That's only four days after the wedding. You admitted your dreams weren't making sense when they normally do. It's Gram's and Dani's that tend toward the whacky side."

"True." Her mother was quiet for a moment. "I'm just very worried about you. And I'll continue to be worried until you're here, safe and sound."

Guilt. Great.

"Thank you for your concern, but I'm not sixteen. You had two kids by the time you were my age. If you could juggle a movie career along with Dani and me too, then I can take care of myself just fine."

"You haven't even finished college, much less ventured out into the real world. You've been given a gift to live such a protected life."

Smothered was more like it. "Speaking of gifts, I found the perfect present for the spoiled movie star who has everything. You're going to die when you see it!" Her mom loved gifts. Hopefully, it'd distract her from her worry.

Her mother chuckled. "Nice try, but I'm not changing the subject. Promise me something, will you?"

So much for distracting her with shiny things. "Depends on what it is, worrywart."

"I can't be sure, because I'm seeing just bits and pieces, but trust no one. Except for Brent, but he has some pretty big secrets too. Stay away from your father's business partners at the wedding and call me every morning and evening so I know you're safe. It's not so much to ask."

She closed her eyes and fought the monumental sigh that wanted to escape. "May I point out that it isn't the norm for a twenty-six-year-old to call her mother twice a day? And that some would say your actions border on paranoid?"

"Yes, you may. Right after I point out that using your almost-counseling degree will never trump me and my dreams. Don't make me come out there and drag you with me to London, honey, because it's taking everything in me right now to fight that urge."

Her mom would do it too. "Fine. How about a compromise? I'll send you check-in texts twice a day. But only if you spill about what secrets Brent is keeping."

"I can't. You know the rules. I'm only telling you this much because I need you to listen to Brent if something appears dangerous."

The rules. She'd never been sure who was the gatekeeper for her mother's vision rules, but the one thing her mom claimed she couldn't do was completely change the outcome of future events. It'd risk the balance of the universe or someone's chakras or some such.

Her mother wouldn't tell people what their future held, but she gave vague hints now and again. Annalisa got to pick and choose what she meddled in. "Deal. But give me just one thing. Do you know why Brent never smiles?"

"I do. But taking the time to figure out where people's sadness comes from can enrich your own life greatly. I have faith you'll figure it out on your own."

"Thank you, Confucius. That wasn't helpful in the least. Can't wait to see you Christmas Eve. Love you."

"Love you too, sweetheart. I'll be watching out for you until I see you. *Ciao, bella.*"

"Bye, Mom." Sara punched the icon to disconnect the call and then turned to watch the waves crash against the beach below. What her mom "watching out" for her meant and what kind of trouble she could possibly be in didn't make any sense. But if a bodyguard showed up, it wouldn't be a surprise. Maybe she'd hired Brent to be her bodyguard? He had the body for it.

Her best guess was that the mystery money in her account was the root of the problem. It was "one of these things that just doesn't belong." Money and her dad weren't often together very long. And that would tie Brent in nicely with whatever problems her mother was seeing. Two hundred million dollars was a lot of cash. Maybe she'd better call in some reinforcements to gauge how serious things were.

Sara lifted her phone to video chat with her sister. The fragrances of pink and yellow tropical flowers filling the air made her smile as she drew in a deep calming breath. Being a Botelli was always an adventure.

Dani, who people always said was a taller, curvier version of the two, answered with a big smile. "Hey, kiddo." Then her forehead crumpled with a frown. "Sorry about Scott. What an ass. I want to deck him for you. And Michael says you had every right to do what you did with the ring. He'll help you fight if the scumbag asks to be reimbursed."

"Thank you." Sara's heart filled with warmth. Her sister was the best. Always in her corner no matter what. As was her soon to be lawyerly brother-in-law, Michael. "But I'm calling to see if I've been starring in any of your dreams lately?"

"Oh. Mom must've called." Dani rolled her eyes. "I just spent the last hour talking her out of kidnapping you tonight."

Thank goodness her mother listened to her sister. "Do I need to be worried about this?"

Dani chewed her bottom lip. "I've seen a few odd things too, so yeah. You need to be careful."

Sara's stomach did a quick dive. Her sister wasn't the type to sweat the small stuff like their mom. "What have you seen?" Her sister's visions were usually puzzles that had to be pieced together but in hindsight usually made sense. Not super helpful in the moment, though.

"First..." Dani held up a hand and tucked her finger down as if to tick off the item. "I saw three cactuses, or would that be cacti? I don't know, but they were neon red and green. Then I saw a handgun, diamond ring, blue four-wheel drive, a pay phone, tent, tacos, and Superman, but he had blond highlighted hair." Sara quickly typed the closest icons she could find on her phone, so she'd remember the clues. She had a scary good memory, but visual things stayed in her head forever.

The ring was probably her engagement ring. There wasn't an icon for a superhero, but remembering the way Veronica wanted to lick Brent, she found a vanilla ice cream cone to represent Superman instead. And were there pay phones anymore? No emoji for that either, so she used an old-fashioned handset to remind her.

As she studied the icons, her stomach lurched again. There was no way her sister could know that Sara called Brent Superman. But what was up with the blond hair? Brent had dark hair. More importantly, why was there a gun?

What had she gotten mixed up with?

∞ ∞ ∞

Brent pushed open the heavy wooden door to join his fellow agents for their usual Friday happy hour. The Irish pub was busy and smelled like the nightly special. Corned beef and cabbage mixed with beer.

He drew in a deep breath of the familiar scents and released the stress of his day with a long huff. Was it weird that he felt more at home at a pub with the guys than he did in his own apartment?

Maybe he should get a dog. No, he was gone a lot, and who would he get to feed it? All his buddies had erratic schedules too.

He weaved around the dart players, passed the pool table where some poor schmuck was trying his hardest to impress his date but failing miserably, and sat beside his pal, Rick. The blond surfer boy had a faded bruise by his eye and a still-healing split lip. "Forget to duck again?"

Rick grinned. "Got in the middle of a covert op last Saturday night." He lifted a finger to get the bartender's attention, then twirled it, asking for another round.

"I thought you were stuck in the office until after the inquiry?" That a dirty politician could cry excessive force just because the guy had a platform sucked.

"I'm back in action as of this afternoon." He pointed to his face. "This was an off-duty event."

"Whose wife did you sleep with now?"

"Hey. I didn't know that woman was married." Rick drained his beer. "But this other beautiful woman named Julie asked if I'd dance with her all night to help make her boyfriend jealous. You know I can't resist a damsel in distress. Especially one just looking for something for the night, so I offered to give her the full package and really steam the guy."

A tall college-aged kid dropped a pitcher and some glasses in the middle of the table. He pointed a thumb Rick's direction and said to Brent, "Dude said this was going to be on you. Want to start a tab?"

It was his turn to buy for everyone, so he pulled out three twenties. He never paid for anything on credit. Especially beer. "Keep one for yourself."

"Thanks." The kid snatched the bills and walked away.

Brent refilled Rick's glass, then his own, and held it up. "Here's to lessons learned the hard way."

"Lessons? Parking lot revenge sex is the best. And Julie was really mad." Rick tapped his glass against Brent's and then took a long pull. "She just failed to mention her boyfriend was a marine. He gave me an actual run for my money."

"Dating apps are less painful."

"Yeah. Maybe." He leaned closer and said in a low voice, "I saw the report you filed. Bet if you play your cards right tomorrow, scorned Sara will give you a taste of some fine princess porridge in the parking lot too."

"Sara's not like the women you date." According to Zoila anyway. She said Sara wasn't like her father, who jumped in the sack with any willing woman. She'd always had long-term relationships. Not that he hadn't thought about sleeping with Sara. About a million times.

"No need to get pissy. Some of my best intel has been procured in the sack. Or the backseat of a car. I stop at nothing to close the case." He downed the rest of his beer in three gulps. "You like her, don't you?"

"She's a suspect. I was stating facts." When were the other guys going to get there? The last person he wanted to talk about was Sara.

"Good. Then you won't mind if I ask her to dance tomorrow night? Women like to tell complete strangers things they wouldn't tell acquaintances like you."

Brent's jaw clenched before he could stop it. "I can't get you a wedding invite. I'm just the guy who works in the office paying bills." No way he'd ever let Rick anywhere near Sara. His longest relationship had lasted a weekend.

"Braydon ordered me to attend the wedding. He's even springing for a tux. He's using the dignitaries who'll be there to get me in."

Dammit. He'd declined when their boss had asked if Brent needed some field backup earlier. Braydon warned that screwing up a potentially high-profile case that could include the Russians could end a guy's short career. That guy being him. He needed to show his boss he could handle fieldwork on his own. "Great. Then we can be bored together."

"Not me." Rick lifted his glass in a mock toast. "Ladies love to dance, and blab, to a good-looking guy in a tux."

"Then maybe I'd better do the dancing, because you're pretty ugly." Which was the furthest thing from the truth. Rick's surfer good looks made him blend well in LA crowds. He was a favorite to work dignitary events because of it.

Rick laughed. "Care to make a bet?"

"I have to actually work tomorrow night." Brent finished off his beer then poured another. "Unlike you, whose only job is to look like the waitstaff unless you're needed."

"Says our number-one pencil pusher." Rick smirked. "A hundred bucks says I can talk Sara into a little make out session. Or maybe even some backseat time."

"Stay away from her." His hands clenched under the table. "You even talk to Sara, and I'll pound you ten times harder than that marine did."

"Are you pissed because Braydon is forcing me on you even after you said you didn't need backup? Or do you have it that bad for Sara?"

"It's no skin off mine if you want to hang around tomorrow night. But you need to stay away from my key suspects."

Rick's right brow arched. "You can't let feelings for a suspect get in the way of the job, bro. That's how you get kicked off the team."

He had no intention of getting kicked off the team. "Steer clear tomorrow, and we'll all be fine. I'll let you know if I need your help."

"Yes, sir." Rick gave a snappy salute. "I have an extra ticket to the Lakers game next weekend. Want to go?"

"Sure." Brent took a long drink, forcing himself to calm down. Maybe Rick was right. Maybe he was letting Sara's good looks influence him. Tomorrow, he'd escort her through the press line, work the business partners, and let Sara fend for herself. That was what she'd asked of him, so that was what he'd do. No matter who she danced or talked with, he'd just observe, as were his orders. He'd do his damn job. Nothing more.

Unless Rick tried to leave with Sara, then he'd have to punch the guy's lights out.

Chapter Four

Brent maneuvered his car around clusters of people with cameras pointed at them and pulled up in front of the beachside restaurant where Holden was getting married. He and Sara were exactly forty-five minutes early as per Veronica's instructions. Before he could open his car door, the valet knocked on the window. After Brent rolled it down, the kid said, "You must've missed the signs. We're closed for a wedding today."

Most of Holden's pals probably didn't drive small electric cars. He stuck his thumb in Sara's direction. "I'm with her."

The valet leaned down and peered inside. "Oh. Hello, Ms. Chapman. Your father would like to see you right away." The kid's grin stayed frozen in place like a lovesick puppy. Brent couldn't blame him. Sara looked amazing. As always.

She disconnected her call. "Thank you." She'd been organizing a Christmas party for the kids at the homeless shelter and must've taken ten phone calls on the drive. Which had been fine by him. Less talking that way. Made it easier to keep his cover story intact.

Brent got out and circled the car to open Sara's door for her. He held out a hand. "Ready to do this?"

She placed her small hand in his. "Ready as I'll ever be." She stood on her skyscraper heels and ran a palm down her tight blue dress to smooth it out. "Let's find the bar first, then my father."

"Sounds like a plan." He held out his arm for her to take if she needed the extra balance to offset her ridiculously tall shoes.

Sara slipped her hand on his bicep. "I have a favor to ask before we face the photographers inside." She stopped walking and started fixing his tie. He'd tried to make it look as nice as she'd done before, but clearly, he'd failed.

After she was done she said, "Don't take this the wrong way, but could you look happy to be my date today? Maybe smile just a little bit?"

"Like this?" He let a grin bloom that mirrored the valet's. It wasn't hard to smile at Sara. There was something about her he couldn't put a finger on. She was different from other women he'd known. Hopefully, it wouldn't turn out to be because she was a criminal pretending to be a philanthropic socialite.

She grinned for the first time since he'd picked her up. "You have a sweet smile. Who knew?"

"Sweet?" He'd prefer killer or maybe dazzling.

She tightened her grip on his arm and started walking again. "Zoila told me you had a nice smile, but I've never seen it until now. I'm curious why that is?"

As they approached the front doors, two uniformed men opened them, and the barrage hit, saving him from addressing her question. Cameras whirled and clicked like machine-gun fire as photographers called out, "Who's your date, Sara?" and "Look over here." Mixed with, "Who designed your dress? Love the shoes. How will it feel to see Scott today?"

Brent concentrated on smiling while Sara did all the talking. She was a natural. Polite and patient even with the Scott questions. He had to give her points for that.

It was the slight crinkling around her eyes, like she was fending off a headache, that signaled she'd probably had enough.

He slid his arm around her waist and tugged. "Thanks, guys. Enjoy the wedding." He guided her away from the photographers and farther into the restaurant.

There were people scurrying around, setting glassware on tables as they made their way to the bar. A woman wearing a black vest looked up and smiled. "Hello, Ms. Chapman. What can I get you?"

"Two shots of vodka to start, please."

Sara wasn't kidding about needing a drink. When the bartender looked at him, he said, "Club soda with a twist, thanks."

"You don't drink?" Sara's brows lifted. "I got that second shot for you."

"Not tonight. Driving the boss's daughter. I'd like to stay employed." When the drinks appeared before them, he lifted his glass. "Here's to sweet smiles."

Sara laughed. "That really bugged you didn't it?" She bumped a shot glass against his and then drained it. "It was a compliment, by the way." She downed her second shot and then cringed while she sucked on a lime. "And here's another. You have good taste in music."

"I don't know how you heard any of it with the phone stuck to your ear the whole ride."

"Sorry about that." Sara ordered a glass of white wine and then turned to him again. "I saw Joey Bonner's name pop up on the display just before we got here."

"The lead singer for Dead Pond? You know him?"

"He once asked me to marry him." Sara's wine arrived, so she took a generous sip. "Why do you look so skeptical?"

"I can't see a wild, tattooed guy like him being part of your Rodeo Drive platinum-card-carrying crowd. Doubt he plays polo or owns a fancy yacht either. So, unless you were a groupie, I'm not sure how else your two social circles would ever intersect."

She shook her head. "I don't own a platinum card, never played polo, or been anyone's groupie. And I get seasick just looking at a boat."

"I stand corrected." He lifted his glass in a mock toast. "So how do you know him?"

"Besides going to the same school, I took guitar lessons from Joey's mother. He asked me to marry him while we were in kindergarten. And even though I turned him down, he never gave up. He was the first boy who ever kissed me."

"Too bad he didn't give you your first signed guitar rather than a kiss. At least you could have sold that online for big bucks."

"He did. But a girl never forgets her first kiss, Mr. Cynical." She took a long drink. "Especially when there were braces involved. Do you remember yours?"

"Vividly. Braces with rubber bands were tricky too. Always had to wait for her to take them all out so the serious kissing could happen."

"The serious kissing?" Sara's eyes twinkled with delight. They did that a lot.

"Yeah." He leaned closer, drawing a deep breath of her flowery perfume. "The kind that puts a *sweet* smile on a guy's face. Don't you have to go see your father?"

"I do. And soon after that, Scott and Brandi too, I suppose." She let out a long sigh. "You are officially relieved of your babysitting duties, Brent. So please, feel free to have a real drink to help endure the torture." She turned and walked away.

He called out, "I brought you, so I'll take you home. Text me when you're ready to go."

Sara lifted her glass of wine in acknowledgment and kept walking. Did that mean have a drink, *adios*, or that she'd text him?

No matter which, he'd hurry and hunt down Holden's business partners right after the ceremony and chat them up. If Sara wanted to go home right after the vows, he'd hate to ask Rick to step in for him. That wouldn't win any points with his boss.

He made his way out to the beach where the ceremony would be held and found Rick talking to Bill Miller, one of Holden's business partners, the police commissioner, and his best man. He headed their way to join them. Showboat Rick wasn't going to steal any part of Brent's case.

∞ ∞ ∞

Sara smiled at her dad, grateful he'd chosen to dance with her while Veronica danced with her father. Sinatra's smooth crooning and her father's honed dance skills made her forget her troubles for a few moments.

Her mom's warning still lingered in Sara's mind, though, and she'd done her best to keep her head down and only talk to her friends. And avoid Scott and Brandi. She still couldn't wrap her mind around her father involving her in any of his financial troubles, but maybe she should ask him. "Do we need to have a talk about all the money in my account? Like where it actually came from?"

Her dad frowned. "I told you. Real estate. I'm going to invest in another property again soon too. You need to be sure you don't have to pay Scott back for that ring. Be nice and dance with him now so he'll give you a pass."

Scott appeared and tapped on her father's shoulder. "May I cut in?"

Her father winked at Scott. "You bet." The staccato cadence of cameras clicking started up again from the edges of the dance floor.

Dammit. Her dad had lined up Scott to cut in on their dance and then allowed the press inside the wedding to capture it. She'd been an idiot to think her father had wanted a special dance with her.

The moment her father released her, Scott stepped in and pulled her close. "Smile. Everyone is watching."

She didn't want to smile, she wanted to deck him. "I need my things back."

He whispered, "We're just in town for the weekend. You can stop by anytime next week. I haven't changed the codes. But I was hoping you and I could talk some time."

"Now you want to talk?" Her teeth clenched. "You had your opportunity for that before breaking up with me in the press. And why go after my best friend?" She would not cry. He didn't deserve the satisfaction it'd give him to think he'd hurt her all over again.

Scott grunted. "Maybe to finally get your attention? These days, all you care about is your degree and your precious homeless people. I used to be your top priority. I want to be again."

Seriously? The man was delusional if he thought they'd ever get back together.

Anger boiled her blood, but instead of making a scene that her mother would be upset about seeing in the tabloids, she closed her eyes and counted to ten. When she opened her eyes again, she stopped dancing and took a step back.

After crossing her arms so she wouldn't hit him, she said, "I'm mad at Brandi, but I once loved her too. Don't use her to get back at me."

"I love Brandi too, but I love you even more. Say the word and I'm all yours again."

She poked him in the chest. "Let me say this loud and clear. We. Are. Over!" Raising her voice couldn't be helped.

"You're making a spectacle of yourself." Scott reached out to pull her into his arms again, but Brent beat him to it.

Thank goodness.

He wrapped her up and then quickly and smoothly put distance between her and Scott.

Brent whispered, "You're shaking. Are you okay?" He pulled her closer and held her tight against his hard chest.

She nodded and fought back the tears that burned her eyes. "I just need some air. And maybe another drink. Or three. I've lost count of how many I've had tonight."

"Four. Not counting the two shots at first." Brent maneuvered them to the door that led to a balcony overlooking the beach.

"Thank you for clearing that up." Geez, he really had been babysitting her. Had her mother put him up to it? "Why are you counting my drinks?"

"Not judging. I know tonight is hard for you." He pushed open the door for her to go outside first. "I was watching because I didn't want some guy taking advantage of your love of liquor tonight. Like that blond guy in a tux you were dancing with earlier."

"Rick? He seemed like a nice enough guy at first." She walked to the railing and pulled in a deep breath of salty ocean air. "I shut him down when he got too aggressive." He'd picked the wrong night to mess with her.

Brent smirked. "Yeah. I saw that. Nice move with the ear twist. Want another glass of wine?"

The way he'd been watching probably meant her mother had hired him and sworn him to secrecy. "No, thanks. All your drink counting is taking the fun out of getting drunk."

"Sorry. You ready to go?"

She should stay for the cake for appearances' sake. But after what her father had done, screw it. "Can we sneak out down these steps to the beach? So I don't have to go back through the restaurant?"

Brent leaned over the railing. "Yeah. I see some stairs over there that probably lead up to the street level."

She started for the deck's steps and then stopped. "Wait. My purse is at my table. Be right back."

"I'll get it." Brent walked back inside the restaurant.

She leaned against the railing and watched the moonlit waves crash against the shore while she waited. Playing her discussion with Scott over again in her head, she was glad to be rid of him for good. That he would ask Brandi to marry him out of revenge was such a jerk move. Zoila had been right about Scott and his lack of character. And while Brandi had betrayed her too, maybe a text next week telling her what Scott said would be the decent thing to do. She wasn't in the mood for decency at the moment, though.

And her father? Betraying her, not giving a second thought to her feelings, just for the press he'd generate? She loved him, always would, but he'd changed as his movie career had faded the last few years. A desperation of sorts had made him into a heartless man.

Or maybe she'd just finally gotten old enough to see what her mother often had hinted at. That her father put himself first over everyone else. Even those he claimed to love. Maybe it was time to take her rose-colored glasses off and see him for the man he truly was.

She rubbed a hand over the dull ache in her chest. She'd lost both of the only men she'd trusted in a week's time. But her father's betrayal had been even worse than Scott's. Guarding her heart from both kinds of pain going forward seemed her best plan.

"Here you go." Light-footed Brent returned with her purse, startling her from her thoughts.

"Thanks." That he'd brought the right one impressed her. What guy paid attention to that kind of detail? "Want to get a burger on the way home? Between my 'daughter of the groom' toast and the dance, I never got to eat."

He nodded. "Give me a good burger over sushi any day."

She followed him down the steps. "A man after my own heart."

"What?" He glanced over his shoulder.

Poor choice of words. "Nothing. I just meant I agree. About burgers."

"Oh. I thought you were hitting on me." The corner of his mouth tilted ever so slightly. "Bosses' daughters are off-limits, just so we're clear here."

She snorted. "Men are off-limits for the next five years as far as I'm concerned. They've all turned out to be lying jerks."

When they got to the bottom, she stopped to take off her heels. They'd be impossible in the sand. Brent held out his hand to help her balance and whispered, "Sometimes lies are necessary. We're not all jerks, Sara." He slipped his hand from hers and turned to leave.

She stood and blinked at his retreating back as he started for the steps. Her mother said Brent had secrets. And now she'd probably offended her new bodyguard without even trying.

Way to screw that up too. Just when, according to her mother, she might need him to be her friend.

She caught up with his long strides and then followed him up the steps to the parking lot above. Brent's silence confirmed she'd probably made him mad. She just wanted to go home and pull the covers over her head. And hope she'd wake up to a better day tomorrow.

When they got to the top of the stairs, Brent held out his arm to stop her. He tapped a finger to his lips and pulled her into the shadows, against the building. She'd been so deep in thought, she hadn't heard the men's voices until that moment.

"Kill Brent tonight."

The other man said, "It'll look bad when two people who pay Holden's bills turn up dead."

The other voice replied, "Barker was old. No one will count that. Best case, the brakes fail while they're still in Malibu and he and Sara go over a cliff. Worst case, they're in a fender bender and we have to figure something else out. He's asking way too many questions, and Sara has figured out there's money in the account Barker told us she never looked at. What if she asks for the half million for the ring? We have to get rid of them, or it's you and me who'll end up dead."

She couldn't believe it was real. Who would try to kill them?

The first guy, whose voice she was pretty sure she recognized, said, "Don't take your eyes off them until it's done. And be sure they're taken care of before Holden gets back from his unplugged honeymoon. We can't have him intervening in this and trying to save his kid."

"Already tracking their cells. And I dropped a chip in Brent's glove box. We're good."

Sara's heart rate jumped into overdrive. What the hell was going on?

She was in trouble, just as her mother predicted. And so was Brent.

It was getting hard to breathe. But she had to think. She'd had a ton of classes her mom had made her take to prepare for something like this. She just had to take deep breaths and remember what the instructors had said. And what had her mom told her? To trust only Brent.

Her mom hadn't said to go to the cops, she'd said to come home. So that was what she'd do.

Starting now!

Chapter Five

*B*rent shook his head when Sara tugged on his arm to leave. He needed to see who the men were who were plotting to have them killed. He held up a hand to hold Sara in position as he inched his way to the edge of the building and pulled out his cell. He'd tapped the record button earlier, but he needed more.

He slid just the top of the phone around the corner, hoping the camera would pick up the evidence he needed. Then they'd go back down to the beach and get a decent head start before the men figured out he and Sara had left.

He pulled his phone back and studied the screen. He could only identify one of the men. The police commissioner, Holden's best man. They needed to keep it within the agency until he could confirm who else might be working with the commissioner on the police force.

He tapped out a text to Rick.

Need eyes on Bill Miller. Now. Brakes on my car compromised.

What else might be compromised? It'd been Sara's idea to leave from the beach and go up the steps. Could it have been a setup?

He slowly slid beside her again and took her hand, leading her quietly down the stairs to the beach. When they hit the sand, she whispered, "We have to get to my mother's house in Albuquerque. It's a fortress, and we'll be safe there until we can figure things out."

To test her, he said, "I think we should call the police."

"No. I think I recognized one of the voices. He *is* the police. We can't trust them here. We can call the cops when we get to my mom's. Let's go." She started jogging down the beach, so he had no choice but to catch up with his suspect.

She glanced at him and said, "I'll call us a ride on my phone. We'll have them take us somewhere busy and safe while we figure this out. Those guys said they have trackers on us, so ditch your cell in the water, and as soon as we get a ride, I'll ditch mine."

She seemed to have a plan. Which made him doubt her even more. But he had both a work and personal cell, so he'd play along. Rick would be able to track his movements with their secure work phones. "I think it's better if we hide our phones under one of these parked cars. That way, they'll think we're still nearby. Maybe making out in the parking lot?"

She blinked at him for a moment as they ran, and then nodded. "Yeah. Better idea."

Besides, he'd like to stay alive long enough to solve the case, and that would require a head start, so he followed her up a boat ramp. They crouched behind some cars to wait for their ride. While she put her ridiculously tall shoes back on, he hid his phone under a nearby car. He wouldn't want to hide it in a car and endanger an innocent citizen.

Sara finally wrangled her feet back into her shoes. Those heels could be a lethal weapon if used properly. Her dress looked too tight to conceal a gun, but a knife would still work.

She studied the phone in her hands. "It says the car will be here in two minutes. It's a black Nissan. Guy's name is Carl."

"What did you type in for a destination?"

"The mall. But we need to get off the grid as soon as we can."

"What do you know about staying off the grid?" She was making him doubt her more every time she opened her mouth.

She rolled her eyes. "Haven't you ever seen that show where people try to stay under the radar from ex-military officers, cops, and MI6 agents for like thirty days? They always get caught because they log on to a computer, use a cell or ATM, or by passing highway cameras checking license plates. Or do something as simple as going grocery shopping or getting gas. The ones who win camp in the woods. There are cameras everywhere the police can tap in to when they know who their target is."

Was there really a show like that? He'd have to google that. "Can your mother send her plane?"

"No." Sara worked her bottom lip with her teeth as she watched her phone's screen. "She's in London with her plane. I think we're going to have to take back roads home. The interstate will have cameras."

He glanced at her screen and confirmed the car was really on the way and she wasn't texting with an accomplice. Was Sara leading him into a trap? He'd discovered from their few encounters that she was smart and able. "Why don't you seem more surprised by all of this? It's not every day I overhear someone plotting to kill me."

"I'm freaking out on the inside, believe me. But we need to stay calm and clearheaded." Then she narrowed her eyes at him. "But I think you already know that my mother called yesterday and said she had her suspicions about my dad and his new partners. She hired you to watch out for me, didn't she?"

What the hell? Was her mother involved too? "I don't have a clue what you're talking about. So how do we get to your mother's house?"

She shook her head. "I don't know yet. Driving might be the easiest. They probably have a tracker on my car too, though. And we'd need gas a few times to drive all the way home, so it'd only work if we look different for the cameras."

The car Sara ordered drove up to the parking lot. "I hate not having a phone." She dropped her cell onto the cement and kicked it next to his under the parked car. Then they both kept their heads down and climbed into the backseat.

The surfer-boy driver smiled and headed out. "Sorry about your breakup, Sara. Scott seemed like a cool dude, but that was just wrong, man."

"Thanks, Carl." She leaned close to Brent and whispered, "He's going to post that I was in his car the minute we get out at the mall. Maybe this wasn't the best idea?"

He'd already decided he was going to choose the place they got out long before they got to the mall. Just in case it was a trap.

When he spotted a Mexican fast food chain ahead, he called out, "Hey, Carl? Change of plans. Would you mind pulling over there instead? We're starving."

The driver shrugged. "Sure. You want to drive through?"

"No. We're going inside. You don't have to wait." He glanced at Sara for confirmation. She'd probably never eaten a fast food taco in her life, but she nodded.

Carl replied, "I don't mind waiting. You have to pay for all the way to the mall even if I let you out here." He pulled up and found a parking spot on the side, luckily, off the street.

"That's okay." Brent leaned over the seat and handed him two twenties. "This enough so you won't post Sara's whereabouts for at least an hour? So we can enjoy our meal?"

The kid smiled. "Sure, dude. I'm cool. Have a good one."

"You too." They both got out and waited while Carl backed out. When he was gone, Brent said, "Stay right here so I can see you through the glass. I'll go grab some food, and we'll figure out our next move." And so he could send a text to Rick without Sara seeing.

Sara nodded as she dug through her purse. She found a ten and handed it over. "Get the five-dollar meal box. It's plenty for both of us if you don't mind sharing the drink. We might need to conserve our cash."

He took the ten, stifling a grin. "How would you even know about the five-dollar box?"

"Seriously? You've got me all wrong, Brent. I'm a college student, not Eloise who lives at the Plaza with Weenie and Skipperdee!"

"Who?"

"I'll explain later. Please just go before Carl tattles."

He hated to leave her unsupervised, but he had no choice. She was *way* too recognizable to go inside with him. She didn't have a phone anymore to contact anyone, and he'd picked the stop, so it was probably safe to leave her for a few minutes. He hurried inside to get the food.

After he ordered, he slipped away to the bathroom to text Rick before they called his pickup number over the speaker. He sent the picture and the recording of the men after them too.

Going to her mother's in Albuquerque. Track us. Eyes on Miller? ID the other guy?

He couldn't wait around for a response. He tucked his phone away and went back to the counter to grab their food.

∞ ∞ ∞

Sara rifled through her purse, hoping to find some loose coins. She only had thirty dollars plus the change they'd get back from their meal. Hardly enough to get them both to Albuquerque. If they could change their looks, a bus or a train might work, but not unless she hit an ATM. But that was a surefire way to alert anyone looking for them. They couldn't know if there were other corrupt cops who might be tracking them too.

Her sister could rent a plane and come get them, but what if the men were watching her family's electronics too, like they did on the show she'd watched? No, she couldn't contact anyone. She needed to stay completely off the grid.

Her mom would know there was trouble when she didn't get her twice-daily check-in. But she'd also know Brent was with her, so maybe she was depending on him to help get them home.

She gave up digging in her purse, glancing up to check on Brent's progress in line. He was nowhere to be found.

All the air whooshed from her lungs.

What if they'd found him? Should she go inside to help? Or run for help? But her mom said she couldn't trust anyone but Brent to help her.

"Hope you like iced tea. I don't drink soda." Brent grabbed her arm and tugged her toward a quiet residential street behind the restaurant.

She laid a hand over her chest to contain her pounding heart. "Can you please learn to walk louder? You scared the hell out of me!"

Brent's forehead creased. "I'd think that'd be a desirable trait for your getaway partner to have."

He wasn't wrong. "Right. Anyway, I've been thinking. Those guys might be tracking our families. We're pretty much on our own. And bus stations and train stations have cameras, so the first priority, after food, needs to be our disguises. There's probably a drug store around here."

They passed by a darkened house with tall weeds and a For Sale sign in front. Brent said, "Wonder if that's empty? Let's go on the side and look into the windows."

She followed him up the driveway. They walked along the side, where Brent stopped and handed her the bag and drink. He cupped his hands on the window and leaned close. "Kitchen light is on. No furniture in the house. Let's go."

They opened the gate and circled around to an outdoor fire pit with wood benches surrounding it. They sat and opened up the bag. When she spotted her change, she asked, "How much cash do you have on you?" She put the money into her wallet while he dug out the box.

"About a hundred bucks." Brent held out the opened box for her to choose first. "Dibs on the cinnamon twisty things."

"Forget it. Those are the best part. We'll share." She grabbed a taco and unwrapped it. "Without a phone, we won't be able to check train and bus fares, but I'm guessing we don't have enough for two tickets."

Brent unwrapped the burrito and then poured hot sauce in a neat puddle on the paper. "So you're going to ditch me?"

"No. My mother would kill me. We need to find a car. And hair dye. Clothes, tennis shoes, and hats wouldn't hurt." She finished off her taco, then went for the chalupa. "You want half of this?"

He shook his head. "Do you have any Malibu Barbie friends who live around here?"

In the middle of a deep draw from their shared tea, a thought struck her. "Scott! We can walk from here. I just asked for my things back while we were dancing, and he said he hadn't changed his codes. Let's hurry before they get back from the wedding."

They both stuffed the rest of their food into their mouths and took the cinnamon twists with them. There was an empty trash can beside the house where they dumped the bag and wrappers inside. Her heels were just going to slow them down, so she laid a hand on Brent's broad shoulder and slipped them off. Just as she was about to toss them in the bin, Brent's hand covered hers.

He grabbed the shoes from her and turned them over. "They have red bottoms. That means expensive right?"

"Yeah. Are you thinking we can sell them for cash?"

"Maybe. Best to keep them for now. Especially because I don't want to have to carry you if we have to cross a bunch of stickers." He crammed her shoes in his suit coat pockets as they walked down the drive.

By the time they hit the sidewalk, she was still offended about the "have to carry you" remark. "I think a man who can bench press over two hundred pounds shouldn't be a big baby about having to carry a person who weighs half that."

Brent's eyes cut her way as they walked uphill. "Half of two hundred?"

She lifted her chin. "Half and then a third again. Maybe a smidge more, but only because of the six drinks at the wedding. And then the chalupa."

He patted his flat stomach. "You gotta learn to just say no to those chalupas. You're not twenty-five anymore."

"Very funny." She took both hands and tried to playfully shove him off the curb, but it was like trying to move a brick wall.

"When you're done trying to throw me into oncoming traffic, can you tell me why Scott is going to happily lend us a car?"

A car hadn't passed by them yet on the dark, quiet street. "Scott wants to get back together with me—because apparently *he* doesn't think I'm fat—so maybe we can use that. We'll leave a note so he doesn't call the cops. Cross fingers we don't run into them."

"If we do, you'll have to lose the scowl to be convincing."

She hadn't realized she'd scowled at Scott earlier. "Or, maybe we could just shoot him in the foot with your gun and run?"

Brent's lips twitched, and he almost smiled. "What makes you think I have a gun?"

"It's why you always wear suits to work, isn't it? To cover up the gun? Because you're my *bodyguard*?"

"Maybe I just like to look professional at my job, Nancy Drew."

She smiled at his evasion. And that he'd made another joke. "If you were aiming to look like a professional bodyguard, then you nailed it."

"Whatever you say." He tilted the bag of sweet fried dough toward her as they walked. "Would you like the last one? Or would that just be enabling you? There's a lot of calories in these."

"My mother isn't paying you to abuse me." She snatched the bag and then moaned with pleasure as she took a bite.

He was quiet for a few minutes before he asked, "Do you think they'd be monitoring Scott's electronics too? Maybe we could use his computer to book and pay for train tickets?"

"Since we only broke up a few days ago, I'd say it's possible they're watching Scott's online activity too. Or maybe I'm just being paranoid because of the TV show." She chewed the last of the sweet treat as she pondered. It was uphill to Scott's house, and she had a hard time keeping up with Brent's long strides. "It sort of runs in my family. Being paranoid. I get it from your boss. We need to go this way for a bit and then up."

"You mean your father?"

"It's going to be a long few days if you don't give up this act. My mom said she was going to be looking out for me. She has a history of hiring bodyguards for me and my sister that goes way back."

"Because your sister was kidnapped as a kid?"

She nodded as they walked across the street. She'd enjoy the flat few sidewalks before they had to go uphill again. "I feel like this is all going to turn out fine if we just look for opportunities and keep moving." But mostly because her mother would have kidnapped her for sure if she thought her daughter was going to die. But that didn't mean they could be careless. They needed to look for the clues her sister had already given her.

The ring, and the tacos—that Brent picked, not her— already made sense. And Superman, but the blond hair still didn't work, so maybe that had meant something else. It was good Brent had asked to stop for tacos, so they hadn't gone too far from Scott's house. Even if Carl told the world where he'd dropped them off, it wouldn't necessarily tell anyone where to find them. And both their phones were still near the venue, so maybe they hadn't figured out they'd left yet.

They just needed to look for the three cacti, a tent, a blue four-wheel drive, a pay phone, and the gun. But Brent probably had that.

∞ ∞ ∞

After a few more minutes of Sara trying to get him to admit he was her bodyguard, they finally stood in front of the gates surrounding Scott's massive Mediterranean-style house. There were a few lights on, so it was unclear if Scott and Brandi were back yet. "Does he have staff?"

"No. Not on the weekends." Sara punched a series of numbers into the box by the large iron gate. "We'll go to the garage and count the cars to see if they're in there. Then we'll decide what to do."

"Count the cars? How many does he have?"

"Six." The gates shook and then slowly started to part. Sara squeezed through as soon as she was able, but he was twice as wide and had to wait another few seconds to fit. He caught up with her on the long asphalt drive.

When they got to the garage doors, she punched in another code and one of the doors silently slid open. She grabbed his arm and pulled him inside with her, before she quickly punched in more numbers to close the door behind them. "His Jag is missing. Perfect."

The light from the opener showed five cars standing in the humungous garage. A Mercedes SUV, a BMW sedan, a Porsche, a crossover Alpha Romeo, and a hulking black Hummer. He'd always wanted to drive a Hummer. But the BMW was probably a better choice.

But then he spotted the bikes. Scott had three. Not just one but three Ducati motorcycles. His dream rides. So sleek, powerful, and beautiful, it made him want to sigh as he ran his hand over one of the smooth gas tanks.

Sara moved beside him. "Don't even think about it. Our butts would be numb after the first half hour. And it's cold outside of California this time of year. He never uses the Beemer, it was a gift from a movie studio, so we'll take that."

Too bad. "That's the one I had in mind anyway."

Sara smiled. "Sure it was. I have some workout clothes here. You're more muscle-bound than Scott, but maybe some of his sweats would work for you. He wears them loose."

"Sounds good. Let's hurry before they get home."

He followed behind Sara into the house. It was hard not to stare at all the over-the-top opulence. The art on the walls, the shiny things embedded in the tile on the floor that couldn't be real gold. That'd be such a waste of gold, wouldn't it? But the indoor pool that led to an outdoor pool with a view all the way to the ocean was like nothing he'd ever seen.

When he stopped to figure out if the whole glass wall rose up, Sara grabbed his arm and tugged. She said, "I know that's amazing, but I need to dye your hair red, so hurry up."

"Red?" No way. "That'll stand out too much."

She led him into a room similar to the room she had in her house with makeup chairs and a beauty salon. They stopped in front of a shelf filled with little boxes of dye. They were all blond. "See? Scott wouldn't be caught dead with red hair."

Sara frowned. "He has no imagination, that's all. And I was kidding. Looks like blond it is. I've never cut and dyed my own hair before, so maybe I should experiment on you first. Let me read these instructions on the box. It'll just take me a few minutes. Or maybe I can just use these?" She picked up a pair of electric clippers. "It'd be faster. You might look like a badass totally bald."

Hell no.

He ran his hands down his face, reminding himself that he'd wanted real fieldwork. But he hadn't only gotten thrown into the deep end, he was going to be forced to reveal some of his secret skills to a woman who, for all he knew yet, planned to kill him in his sleep. Or shave his head. His gut said the shaved head was the more likely scenario if he didn't intervene, but still.

They always said at the academy to keep the cover as close to the truth as possible. Easier to maintain the story that way. And time was of the essence, Scott and Brandi would be there soon, and the men at the wedding would figure out they left too if they hadn't already, so Sara's plan made sense.

Besides, he needed to know if Sara's mother was in on the scam too. How else would she have been able to warn Sara? He had to make sure they got the car and changed their looks to have a fighting chance. But it was something he'd never live down with the guys after he filled out his detailed report admitting to the skills his mother had taught him.

"I can dye our hair, Sara. And cut it too. Have a seat."

Chapter Six

ho would've ever guessed a built guy like Brent would know how to cut and dye hair? Sara blinked at her reflection in Scott's makeup room's mirror. She looked really different as a blonde. Better or worse, she wasn't sure.

As much as she hated to lose her long locks, Brent had told her to trust him. Then he shortened her hair, layered it, and gave her sexy spiky bangs too. He was a handy guy to have around.

She said, "Even though you won't tell me who taught you to cut hair. Or admit that my mother hired you to protect me. So far, you're the best bodyguard I've ever had. I'd never trust one of them to touch my hair."

He called out from the sink across the room, "Why'd you let me?"

"Because Zoila said you have character. A guy with character wouldn't say he could cut hair when he couldn't."

"You told me all guys are liars."

"And you told me not all men lied unless it was *necessary*. Maybe I wanted you to prove it. Let me help you rinse, and then we'll get going." He'd dyed his hair and then cut hers while his color set, so she got up from the chair and joined him at the sink.

He laid his head back and closed his eyes as she ran the warm water through his hair with a sprayer. He grumbled, "Make sure you get it all out. It can look funky if you don't."

"Can't have a bodyguard with weird hair." He actually had lovely hair, soft and silky, but it'd already been trimmed shorter, so they'd have to settle for only the color change. But maybe she'd add some gel to give it a different look.

He asked, "What are you going to say in the note you leave for Scott?"

"That we had car trouble and that I'll get the Beemer back to him. But he might be mad enough with me to call the cops. I'll probably have to apologize for raising my voice at him on the dance floor. In front of the press. And tell him I want to talk about getting back together."

"So, you're basically going to lie to him."

"It's one of your *necessary* lies so we don't die. You can thank me later." She turned off the water then rubbed a dab of gel between her palms. As she ran her fingers through his hair, spiking it, his gaze locked with hers and held. It was strangely intimate with her hands in his hair. She should look away, but he seemed to be searching for something. "What?"

"I'm trying to decide if I can trust you."

What the heck would he have not to trust her about? "I'm not the one with all the secrets. You are. So maybe I should ask the same of you?"

He nodded. "You should have before you ran off with me. Now it's too late. Let's get going before Scott gets back. Lead the way."

What was that supposed to mean? Brent was a giant puzzle she felt oddly compelled to solve. She'd have to wear him down on the long drive ahead of them.

She wiped the gel from her hands and headed for Scott's bedroom, where her clothes hopefully still were. As they passed the kitchen, she said, "Why don't you see if there's anything to eat. Something we can take along. And I'll go change."

He shook his head. "We need to stick together. In case they come back."

He really didn't trust her. "Fine. But sticking together doesn't include you watching me change. Just so we're clear."

"Crystal." His eyes shifted toward hers. "But would you be okay if I searched you for weapons? It'd go a long way to help with my trust issues."

"My mother told you about the time I took my bodyguard's gun, didn't she? I just did it to show him how bad he was at his job. I wasn't going to shoot him. And I don't make a habit of carrying weapons with me to my father's weddings!"

He crossed his arms. "Maybe you're incredibly upset that Scott dumped you. Maybe you wanted revenge, so you armed yourself. Maybe that's still your plan if we run into him."

She shook her head and headed upstairs. "I don't have enough feelings left for him to commit a crime of passion like in the movies."

"Then it won't hurt to let me search you."

She stopped on a small landing and slammed her hands on her hips. "If you search me, then do I get to search you for weapons too?" The thought of running her hands all over his hard body should not have put naughty thoughts into her head. But it did. So sue her. She was on a man hiatus, but that didn't mean her hormones were going to stop noticing.

"You wouldn't know what to do with the weapons you find. Could be dangerous."

"Ah! So, you admit you have a gun? And that's why you wore a suit to work every day? To hide it?"

He shook his head. "We don't have time for this. I just told you I have weapons. Do I have permission to search you for any?"

"Fine. Be my guest." She held her arms above her head. "My mother has a big mouth. I was a kid when that gun thing happened."

He frowned as he knelt before her. "This might seem a little intrusive, but it's the only way to be thorough. The touching is necessary."

"There you go again with the *necessary* things in life. You could just trust me, you know."

He winced. "This way is better. I'll be quick." Brent cleared his throat before sliding both of his hands up her right thigh. He lightly brushed against her panties on his way to the other leg, sending a healthy zing of heat racing up her spine.

Next, he ran his hands down her sides, then across her belly and back, stopping his sweet torture just under her breasts. She hoped he wouldn't notice how her breathing had become shallow. She hadn't been touched so intimately in months, and her body was mistaking her bodyguard's hands for those of an eager lover.

Or maybe she was the eager one.

Brent ran the back of his hands along the sides of her breasts and made her heart beat a little faster. Hopefully, her bra would hide the swelling of arousal trying to poke through.

Counting from a hundred backward seemed like a good thing to do to take her mind off his big hands roaming her body. But every time he explored a new place, she had to start over again.

When he was done running his fingers around the hem of her neckline, his knuckles lightly brushing against her chest and leaving her covered in goose bumps, he then inspected the bottom hem of the dress too. Finally, he stood and took a step back. "Sorry I didn't trust you. Let's get moving."

Her fingers were going numb from being over her head, so she let her hands drop and then shook them out. "That made me crave a cigarette. And I don't even smoke."

She could've sworn she heard him mumble behind her, "You and me both."

∞ ∞ ∞

After finding sweats, sneakers, and ball caps for both of them and some water, chips, and fruit to take along on the ride, Brent held out his hand for the keys to the Beemer. "I'll take the first shift, Sara."

"Is your need to drive a male dominance thing or a bodyguard thing?" She looked adorable in her black designer yoga gear that hugged her in just the right places. Even covered with a man's unzipped hoodie, it did nothing to hide how damn sexy she was.

"It's an I've-never-driven-a-six-hundred-horsepower-V12-engine-before thing."

"Oh." Sara blinked at him. "Okay. You can drive first, then." She tossed him the display key fob.

He reached for the car door to open it when one of the garage doors rumbled beside them.

Dammit!

Sara grabbed his arm. "Come with me. Quick." She raced for the rear of the garage to a set of double doors. One side was open, so Sara jumped inside. He followed behind, closing the door behind them just as Scott's Jag pulled into the empty garage stall. Brent was surrounded in pitch black next to Sara in some sort of utility closet.

After her weapons search, and once he could think clearly with the right body part again, he'd taken another step closer to believing Sara wasn't involved with the money laundering. Her relentless insistence that he was her bodyguard had to either be a majorly good act worthy of an Oscar, or sincere. But how could her mother have known to warn her off? Were both her parents involved? Either way, she wanted to get to her mother's house for some reason. He was sticking with her to learn what that reason was.

Amid the closing of car doors, Scott and Brandi talked about a skinny-dip before bed. As their voices faded, Sara grabbed his hand and tugged. "We need to open the garage door while he closes the other if we can."

"No. Wait." He held Sara back. "If they go swimming, they might not hear the interior alerts for the garage door and the gate opening. Let's give them a few minutes."

Sara huffed out a breath. "I still think we should—tell me that's your hand moving up my leg, Brent. Please."

His hand wasn't anywhere near her leg, but she was probably going to scream and give them away if he didn't stop whatever was crawling on her. "Stand still."

"It's moving higher!" She squeaked. "With sharp claws!"

Probably a rat.

He opened one of the doors, letting in a little light from the garage door opener that was still on so he could make a good grab. When a long set of whiskers and two different-colored eyes turned toward him, he let out the breath he held. It was a scrawny little cat. Whose litter box was right beside Sara.

Sara huffed out a huge breath as she lifted the cat to her cheek. "You scared me to death, Mittens. Why did mean old Scott put your box out here? Did he banish you to the garage?" She looked at him. "Scott inherited Mittens when his grandmother died. He never liked her."

The cat meowed loudly as if agreeing with her. Sara said, "Well, you know what, sweet thing? You're coming with us. He won't miss you a bit, the big jerk. You can live at my mom's house in Albuquerque."

Brent withheld a sigh. "That's not a good idea. As a matter of fact, it's stealing."

"He'll think she ran off when the garage door opened. That was always his hope and why he wanted to put her out here, but I wouldn't let him." She grabbed the bag of kibble that was beside the litter box and stepped out of the closet. "Mittens will be no trouble at all. Let's go."

He didn't have time to argue as he and Sara dashed for the car. He powered on the car but didn't start it. Then he pressed the garage opener that lifted the door just as silently as before and put the car in gear and pushed while Sara strapped in with her cat.

It took all his might to push the car out of the garage. Luckily, the driveway tilted toward the street, so the car rolled down the hill while he jumped in. Sara found the buttons on the rearview mirror for the garage door and the gate. By the time they got to the entrance, the gates slowly parted for them. Judging the distance to the house was far enough away, he started the powerful engine and waited until the gates had parted enough to slip out. Once they were on the street, he glanced in the rearview mirror as the gate closed behind them. No lights came on or sirens sounded.

If they were lucky, Scott wouldn't notice the note or the car missing until morning. If not, he was probably calling the cops on them. They had no way to know. Ditching the car for another in the morning was their best plan. Maybe Sara would fall asleep later so he could text Rick and arrange for another vehicle.

He pulled in the intoxicating new-leather car smell into his lungs. Maybe he'd get a Beemer himself one day. It was a sweet ride.

He glanced at Sara, who had the purring cat on her lap. "That's a small cat." But it was cute in a weird way with its different-colored eyes and its random white splotches all over its black body. It was almost polka-dotted.

"She was the runt of her litter back in the day. And is more like a dog than a cat. Where are we going?"

"We need to figure out where they sell paper maps so we can stay off the interstate. Any ideas?"

Sara reached for her purse but stopped. "I was going to google it. It's tough not to have a phone. If I were a paper map, where would I be?"

"While you're thinking, can you look for the car's manual and figure out how to turn the GPS off on this thing? We don't want the police tracking Scott's stolen car."

"Good idea." Sara opened the glove box and dug out the manual. Then she turned the radio on. "If Scott reports that I stole his car, it'll make the news. Guaranteed."

"Let's hope we get a big enough head start tonight before that happens." He stepped on the gas and marveled at how the car jumped to life beneath them. Too bad he couldn't afford to get pulled over, or he'd have punched it on the highway later to see what it could really do. But they still needed a map.

He tried to think back to when he and his mother lived in their car on and off over the years. Gas stations used to have maps, but did they still? His mom used to have an atlas with maps of the whole country. What he wouldn't do to have that now, because he needed to talk to Rick. Figure out where to meet up and exchange cars. Without a map, that was going to be tough. And it was only nine ten. Sara probably wouldn't sleep for hours. How was he going to sneak in a few texts without her catching him?

While Sara poked buttons on the navigation console, he spotted a big discount department store ahead. "Maybe they have maps."

Sara looked up from her task. "Even if they don't, could we use our money to splurge on one thing?"

He pulled into the parking lot and found a space away from the building and hopefully any cameras. "If you're going to ask for makeup, princess, you can forget it."

Sara rolled her eyes. "We don't have toothbrushes. Or toothpaste. I have a thing about clean teeth."

So, did he. "Yeah. I'll grab that. Anything else?"

"Yes. Could you please buy yourself a better attitude while you're in there?"

Ignoring her smart comment because they needed to hurry, he got out and headed for the big sliding doors. Tooth stuff and an atlas then they could get back on the road. But not before he called Rick to get an update. He took out his phone and dialed the number, but it went directly to voicemail. He left a message, quickly updating his friend on what they were going to need, asked him to look into camping to stay off the road during the day and off the grid, and then hung up.

As he headed for the music and book section, Sara's words about his attitude echoed in his brain. And poked at his conscience. Sara hadn't complained once while he'd dyed and cut her long pretty hair or when she'd had to walk barefoot. Or even when she had to eat fast food for dinner.

Her fiancé had just run off with her best friend, and now her father's criminal business partners were trying to kill them. And she'd even subjected herself to a search to satisfy his mistrust.

He'd been too quick to judge her. She wasn't the spoiled princess he'd assumed she was based on social media searches. She'd kept her cool under pressure and was being braver than most would in their situation.

Maybe he *would* get himself a better attitude about Sara. But he'd not allow his attraction to cloud the fact that he might have to arrest both her parents. As much as he was starting to like and respect Sara, she'd hate him at the end of the mission. Better to keep emotional distance for both their sakes. But they needed to operate as a team if they were going to succeed.

He'd google Sara and see if she'd ever mentioned what her favorite candy bar was in one of her many interviews. She'd never know he'd done that, and it might win him some much-needed team points with her.

Chapter Seven

Sara tossed the car's manual back into the glove box. She'd turned off navigation so they couldn't be tracked that way, but there wasn't a way to disable the GPS that she could find. But she did figure out that a person could special order a hidden refrigerator in the backseat behind the armrest with room for champagne bottles to chill. Hardly helpful to their quest, but a pretty fantastic factoid.

Brent, big, hulking, and looking like he was a trainer in a gym rather than her father's estate manager, opened his door and passed her a plastic bag. "Got a map. Why don't you find us the best way to your mom's house in Albuquerque?"

"Okay." She laid the map on the dash and then dug through the bag. She found two little kits filled with travel-sized everything, including deodorant and floss, which she'd thought of right after he'd left. "These are perfect." She kept digging until she found a tiny metal bowl with paw prints on it. "For Mittens?"

He started the car and headed out of the parking lot. "Figured she needed that to drink out of."

That was an incredibly sweet thing for such a gruff guy to do. "Mittens, look. You have your very own bowl. Brent's not mean like Scott. You two might become good friends." Mittens blinked her brown and blue dual-colored eyes open and then went right back to sleep on Sara's lap.

Brent grunted. "I prefer dogs. There's something else in there. I already ate mine."

She stuck her hand inside the bag and felt around until it landed on something wrapped in paper. When she drew it out, she couldn't help her grin. "A peanut butter cup? My favorite. Thanks, Brent."

He nodded and pointed at the map. "Route, please."

"Give me a second here. I'm not Siri." She enjoyed her chocolate-and-peanut-butter treat as she paged through her spiral map of the US. She searched for small roads that led east. "It's going to be hard to stay off bigger roads until we get around Palm Springs. Head that way and look for Highway 62. We'll figure it out from there."

Mittens woke up, stretched, and then hopped over to Brent's lap. Sara was just about to scoop Mittens up and put her back on her lap when Brent's big hand gently stroked the cat stretched out across his legs. "Did you figure out how to turn off the GPS?"

She shook her head. "Short of smashing the console to bits, no. But even if we did that, we might break something we need."

"Let's take our chances for now and hope Scott won't call the cops until the morning. Have you searched your purse and wallet for anything that shouldn't be there? Like a tracking device?"

She hadn't even thought of that. "No. Let me look." She rummaged through her purse and found her watch that she'd taken off because it didn't match her wedding outfit. As she strapped it on, she noted the time. It was nine thirty. It took about twelve to thirteen hours to drive to Albuquerque, but that was on the interstate. Who knew how long it would take on smaller roads.

Brent asked, "So who were Eleanor and Snickerdoodle again?"

She smiled. "You mean Eloise and Skipperdee. Eloise is a fictional little girl who lives on the very top floor of the Plaza Hotel in New York City. With her nanny, her dog, Weenie, and her turtle, Skipperdee. Her mother is always away, so she's close with her nanny and gets into all kinds of mischief. She's a poor little rich girl. I used to love when my mom read those books to me."

Brent was quiet for a few minutes as he seemed to absorb the information. "You said you weren't like Eloise. But maybe you are. You live in a big house with a father who doesn't pay much attention to you. With Zoila and Justin as your surrogate family, maybe taking Weenie and Skipperdee's place, and you don't see your mom very often either. And based on the press, you used to be a mischievous girl who had to serve community service at the homeless shelter once for the trouble you and your friends got into."

Ouch!

"While that's all true, my life is *entirely* different from Eloise's!" Wasn't it? "Actually, it was rumored that Eloise was based on Liza Minnelli. It was her godmother who wrote the books. Liza's dad was a big-time Broadway director and didn't have a lot of time for her, so he dumped her in that hotel. Totally different from my situation!" She huffed out a breath.

"Sorry." Brent petted the purring cat in his lap. "I didn't mean to upset you."

Sara crossed her arms and tried to figure out why his comment had bothered her so much. "My mother loves my sister and me more than anything else in the world. She hated when I went to live with my father. But I needed to— You know what? It's none of your business."

She'd almost told him how she often felt like a third wheel with her mom and sister. They had their unique abilities that bonded them at a deeper level. When she'd ask questions about how their dreams work, they'd pat her on the head and tell her she wouldn't understand. They didn't take her curiosity or intelligence seriously.

Unfortunately, neither did most anyone else. People always assumed she was a spoiled rich kid just breezing through life. Without a care in the world. Not a person working hard to graduate and find a job so the paparazzi would get bored with her and leave her alone. Someone passionate about helping the people at the shelter.

They drove in silence, with only the sounds of passing cars and the pop song on the radio playing softly adding to the thick air of tension between them. Maybe Brent hadn't been all wrong. To an outsider looking in, her life might have seemed a little like Eloise's.

She was just about to concede when he broke their silence and said, "You asked earlier who taught me to cut hair. It was my mother. She was a cosmetologist, when she wasn't a waitress or working in a department store."

Finally, a tidbit of personal information about him. "Then please thank her for me. You did a good job."

As if he didn't hear her, he added, "I'd never heard of Eloise because I didn't have many books growing up. My mom had a hard time keeping jobs, much less a roof over our heads. Because of the drugs. Then she died of an overdose. Don't even know who my father is. Your life sounds pretty great to me. I wasn't mocking it."

She felt like a major jerk for getting angry with him after hearing that. "I'm sorry about your mom, Brent. How old were you when she died?"

He frowned as he stared at the road ahead. "Nineteen."

"That's young to be left on your own."

He shrugged. "I survived. Don't like to talk about it, though."

"Okay." She turned her attention back to her purse, searching for something that didn't belong.

He broke their second awkward silence when he asked, "Ever since that day in my office, I've been wondering something. Where did you learn to solve that Rubik's cube so fast?"

"What you'd really like to know is how an *airhead* like me could solve it so fast. And don't try to deny it. It was written all over your face that day."

He glanced her way. "I'll admit it. I misjudged you. But I was honestly impressed."

"Thank you." She spotted an opportunity to lighten the mood. "So to answer your question, I taught my poor little rich girl self. When I was *all alone*, in my bedroom at the tippy top of the mansion in Malibu with no one to talk to but my nanny Zoila and pet turtle, Justin." She'd added a dramatic flair her mom would have been proud of.

He laughed. For the very first time, he actually laughed. "Guess I deserved that."

He had a great laugh, full-bodied and sincere. It made her smile too. "The truth is, I read how to do that online for a school project. I've always enjoyed school. My friends used to call me google girl."

He turned his head and met her gaze. "Why google girl?"

She wouldn't have customarily shared that, but Brent had opened up to her about his mom. "Ask me something obscure. I have this weird visual memory thing. If I see or read something, it sticks in my head forever."

He laid his hand over the map on her lap. "Name five small towns we'll pass once we're on 62."

She sometimes hated how much of a freak show her brain could be. But it was better than having the curse of prophetic dreams like the other Botelli women had. "White Water, Morongo Valley, Yucca Valley, Joshua Tree, and Twentynine Palms. But the last one looked a little bigger than the rest."

He grabbed the map and squinted at it. "I'll be damned. That's pretty impressive. But two can play this game. I have a weird ability to quickly add, subtract, multiply, and divide huge numbers in my head. I see patterns and designs in numbers no else seems to see."

"When did you know you could do something most others couldn't?"

"I moved around from school to school so much as a kid that no one figured out I was exceptionally good at numbers until college. Including me. I thought it was normal and that everyone could do what I could."

Her too. It had been disconcerting when she'd realized she had her own kind of unique power. And odd at the same time. Like she didn't fit into her own family even more after learning that.

She dug for a pen and something to write on in her purse. "Okay, how much is two hundred ninety-seven times five hundred sixty-two?"

Without hesitation, he said, "One hundred sixty-six thousand nine hundred fourteen."

She had to do the math to check. "That's right. How about division? No one is as fast at dividing as multiplying. How much is two million divided by eighty-five thousand nine hundred nineteen?"

"Twenty-three point two seven eight. I can actually divide much faster than multiply."

"Well then, that just proves you're a total freak." She didn't even bother to check his answer. It would have taken her too long. "How much does the human head weigh?"

He turned and met her gaze again. This time with a ghost of a smile tilting his lips. "That's from the movie about the agent, right?"

"Yeah. It was on the other night when I couldn't sleep. So, do you know?"

He turned his attention back to the road again and nodded. "That kid was off by a bit. He said a human head weighed eight pounds. But the brain weighs about three pounds. The skull and all the rest weigh about seven to eight pounds for a total of ten to eleven pounds."

"Look at that. We've finally found something in common." She raised her hand for a high five. "We're a couple of weirdos."

Brent gently slapped her hand. "Two weirdos whose lives are going to get potentially very complicated when Scott wakes up in the morning. You should get some rest before it's your turn to drive. We need to get as far away as we can tonight."

"Good idea. Mittens and I will climb in the back and stretch out." She grabbed the sleeping limp cat from Brent's lap. "Let me know when you get tired."

"Will do."

She and her new pet cat settled into the buttery leather backseat as she tried to fall asleep. But the gravity of what would happen in the morning crept back into her mind. Those men had been serious about killing them. They'd been lucky so far to get a head start that probably wouldn't last much longer.

She'd learned to put on a good face for the public and to hide all the disappointment her father dished out on a regular basis, but now, alone with her thoughts, it was hard to hold back her worry.

Snuggling the cat closer to her chest, she closed her eyes and hoped she and Brent would make it to her mom's house alive.

∞ ∞ ∞

Brent checked on Sara in the rearview mirror. Sound asleep. He studied the page on the map Sara had left open and then dug out his phone to text Rick.

Status? Heading for 62 now. Need another vehicle without GPS. Meet in Lake Havasu?

Rick responded right away.

About time you checked in. You have company. About ten minutes behind.

Did Scott report the car stolen?

No police activity. Your tail is tracking something else. Boss is concerned for Sara's safety. Brass says abort the road trip.

He didn't want to give up. He wanted to solve the case. Sara wouldn't be safe until they had enough evidence to arrest everyone involved. The information her mother used to warn Sara the day before had to come from somewhere.

If nothing else, they needed to get out of California and away from Miller's jurisdiction if they were going to have a chance at survival.

He glanced at Sara in the mirror again. The cat was curled up against her belly, and her hands were tucked under her cheek. She looked cute sound asleep with her cat and her new blonde haircut.

But where the hell had that smartwatch come from? That was probably what Miller's pal was tracking.

Was she wearing it on purpose?

Doubt about her motives crept back inside his head again. Was there something hidden at her mother's house? Was that why she wanted to get there so badly? Or was she leading him into a trap? Letting the people following know their location until they got somewhere remote. Like when they'd cross the desert in a few hours? Easy enough to lose people there.

But would a woman so worried about a cat that she'd brought it with them be capable of committing a major crime? And why would she wear the watch in plain sight when it'd had to have been in her purse all along? He wasn't ready to concede, so he typed back:

Negative on the abort. Sara's not safe in CA with Miller. Found the tracker. Need a meeting point to hand it off. Take the tail the opposite direction.

Hang on. I'll ck. Boss not happy dude.

While he waited, he called out, "Sara?"

She blinked her eyes open and sat up, annoying the cat enough it grumbled. "My turn to drive?"

He shook his head. "What's that on your wrist?"

"My watch?" She lifted her left hand to show him. "Well, I really use it more for a fitness tracker. Without my phone, it's the only way to know what time it is. Why?"

"Is it synched to the app that finds your lost phone by any chance?"

Sara's eyes widened. "Crap! I set that up when I brought it home. Dammit!" She leaned toward the window and pressed the button to roll it down. "I'll throw it out."

"No. Stop." How was he going to explain his new plan without giving everything away? "If they're tracking us, then let's let them think they're going to catch up while we figure out a way to divert them. Buy us a little more time."

Sara leaned her head between the front seats. "More time for what? We're driving the speed limit. Ten bucks says they aren't. They'll catch up with us soon."

Sara wasn't wrong. He liked how she thought logically. "They might not know what car we're driving, so they'd have to get very close. Close enough for us to see them too. Chances are they'll stay just behind us until we stop, because we have to at some point. Then they'll make a move."

Sara chewed her bottom lip. "Like a shoot-us-with-their-guns move?" She frowned as she grew quiet. After a few minutes, she said, "Maybe we should throw the watch out right before the turnoff to 62. Then they won't know if we went to Palm Springs or took the turn?"

That was his plan B. He wished he could read the text whose alert had just vibrated against his leg. But he worried about something else. "What will happen in the morning when you don't come home? Anyone going to panic at Casa Chapman?"

She sighed. "I didn't think about that. I always let Zoila know if I won't be home. I should have told her I was staying with friends for a few days while I'm on school break. She'll call the cops for sure, if she doesn't hear from me by noon. Like you, I suspect she's on my mother's secret 'babysit Sara' payroll too."

He increased their speed by a few mph. "Zoila loves you regardless of your mom. That's why she'd call the cops." He gave Sara a second to figure out she could send a text from her wrist. The more he let her think things were her idea, the better for his cover.

He needed to stay in character if Sara was going to trust him enough to bring him anywhere near her famous mother.

They were getting close to the point where they'd have to make some decisions. She needed to figure out the watch soon, or he'd do it.

"Wait!" Sara held up her wrist again. "I can send her a text from this. I read it has voice control. Let me figure out how to do that."

She leaned back into the rear seat and started tapping on her wrist. "Maybe I should tell Zoila we were going to the lake but have decided to go to Vegas for a few days instead? The way the roads work, we could've planned to catch a small highway north from Lake Havasu. Then we could go the opposite direction?"

That fell neatly into his plans. "Yeah. Good idea. Then if we ditch the watch right before the turnoff, they'll go the wrong way." Or, not. He wasn't sure what Rick and his boss had in mind yet. It'd fend off an APB brought on by Zoila in the morning. But if Miller didn't get his way, he might file the APB himself on Holden's behalf to make it easier to find them once over state lines.

While Sara figured out her watch, he slid a peek at his phone, keeping it down by his driver's door. Rick had sent a response.

Negative on Lake Havasu. Sara's mother has a house in Palm Springs. Go there and wait for instructions. You'd better be right about the money coming from the Russians. And the political ties. If not, ur ass is grass, bro.

Brent let out a long breath. He could be wrong, but the indicators all pointed to a vast international ring. They needed people in the government and enforcement agencies to operate their laundering scheme. Hence Miller and probably a few others they hadn't identified yet. Brent texted a thumbs-up emoji and slid his phone back into his pocket.

After resisting the boss's orders, Brent had better be right. Or he could probably kiss his beach house goodbye.

Or worse, his and Sara's lives.

Chapter Eight

*I*n the darkened backseat, Sara texted Zoila. Sara was still kicking herself for not realizing her watch could be trackable.

She told Zoila they were going to Vegas for a few days, before flopping into the front seat beside Brent again. Mittens still snored loudly in the backseat. "I'm really sorry about the watch, Brent. Should I throw this thing out now?"

"Let's give it a few more miles. We might have an even bigger problem. If Miller has any cop friends involved, they might have already identified the car as Scott's from highway plate scanning. Know anyone else with a car we can borrow around here?"

She glanced in the side mirror, watching for speeding cars behind. "My mom has a house in Palm Springs. There's no one there right now, but she always has a car in the garage."

Brent nodded. "Then let's go to her house."

"Won't the highway cameras be able to track the car back to my mother? I've been thinking about routes back home, and we can almost stay off the interstate with no cameras all the way except for close to Phoenix and the last stretch into Albuquerque."

Brent frowned at her. "You memorized three state maps that quickly?"

She shook her head. "Not the *whole* maps. Only the parts that pertain to where we want to go."

"That's amazing." He glanced in the rearview mirror. "Change of plan. Time to toss the watch. We have company."

"On it." Her stomach clenched as she fumbled with the button to lower the window. The air had grown dry and the scent of the ocean had disappeared and turned to that of dry desert tundra. After she launched the watch as far as she could, she asked, "Which car?" She started to turn in her seat to look out the back, but Brent laid his arm across her body to stop her.

"Buckle in. Stay down."

"Not yet." The sudden seriousness in his voice made her heart rate and blood pressure spike to stroke levels. However, she wasn't prepared to die. "If you could let the smart driving tech take over for just a few and switch places with me, I'll lose them."

"Negative. Down." Brent pushed her head into her lap and then stepped on the gas. The engine roared to life, pressing her back into the seat and her head harder against his big mitt still covering her skull.

"You don't understand." She pushed his hand away but stayed down. "My mother has made me take kidnapping training, evasive driving classes, hand-to-hand combat, and I can shoot guns. I'm probably more qualified to save our lives than you are!"

Brent smoothly swerved around cars, weaving in and out of traffic, the speedometer reading 120 mph, all while ignoring her. But then maybe he was a little busy. Should she repeat herself or just cross her legs and hope she didn't pee her pants?

A gun appeared in front of her face. "Don't shoot unless I give you permission. Put your seat belt on."

Geez, Brent was a bossy one when under pressure. She fastened her belt, took the gun, and then flipped off the safety. "How close are they? You might want to go a little faster. We must be near the turnoff. If we can make them lose sight of us, they'll think we've gone the other way toward the lake if they were monitoring my email."

He yelled over the screeching of the tires, "Thank you, Captain Obvious. Just waiting for some clear road." He pressed the pedal to the floorboard.

She thought she was being more like Captain Helpful but didn't say so. Best to let him concentrate on not killing them by running into another car.

But she hated not being able to see what was going on. Feeling helpless sucked. "Have we passed the turn-off yet?"

"Yes." Brent's gaze kept zipping back and forth between the road ahead and the rearview mirror.

With her heart still in her throat she said, "Then you'll need help to find my mom's house. Can I sit up now if I stay low?"

"Negative." Brent's eyes cut to the rearview mirror one more time. "Miller might have figured out your mom has a house in Palm Springs too. Someone heavily armed might be waiting to cut us off in case we go that direction."

"Right." She hadn't thought of that. "Want to take the back way to my mom's, then? I could call out the street names."

"Yes." His gaze had grown hard and his jaw clenched while he navigated around a car.

He was like a robot all of a sudden. Maybe she should ask *him* for permission to search his big body for a battery pack. That is, if they made it to her mom's in one piece. The speedometer was showing 150 mph.

She called out the first street to look for and decided that keeping her yap shut was probably the best thing to do. But then she remembered the cat. "Mittens? Are you all right?"

She started to turn around, but a big hand landed on her head again, pinning her face in her lap. "Cat's fine."

Mittens was a tough one. She was probably scared, though. Sara was scared.

The car slowed, and Brent took the first turn. Finally, she knew where they were.

A familiar thumping sounded from above. "Is that a helicopter? Are the cops up there?" Dammit. They weren't a match for policemen in a helicopter.

Brent kept his eyes on the road ahead. "We'll know in just a few seconds." He'd slowed considerably, so they were sitting ducks.

As the sound of the rotors thumping slowly faded, she let out the breath she'd been holding. Must not have been the cops. She called out the next two streets for Brent to take.

His gaze never stopped scanning in all directions. "When we get there, you need to stay in the car. I'll check things out first."

"Negative, right back atcha. You need me to get in. My mom uses retina scanning on all her homes now. It's her latest thing."

"Seriously?" Brent's forehead scrunched. "That's *way* over-the-top."

"Then you obviously haven't met my mother yet. She's the queen of crazy when it comes to protecting her family." Sara couldn't help but love her mom even more for it in their current predicament, though. Thank goodness she'd hired Brent to protect her. He was an amazing driver. None of her past bodyguards had ever come close to Brent's skills.

Brent's jaw worked back and forth as they drove in silence.

She examined the gun in her hand. Brent would have had to have something that big tucked behind his back. Must've been uncomfortable riding in the car.

She glanced his way. The hardened look on his face was almost scary. "It's the next left. Past a grove of palm trees. All my mom's houses have back entrances."

He made the turn and then headed for the plain gate at the rear. As they moved slowly toward her mom's house, Brent's eyes scanned the area. "For deliveries and gardeners?"

"No. For escape. My mother has an arsenal of weapons in a safe inside for the same reason. After Dani was kidnapped, we actually had intruder drills, like some families do in case of fire. It's a wonder Dani and I didn't turn out to be scared of our own shadows."

He nodded as he cut the headlights a few feet before the gate, and then they parked at the curb. He held out his hand. "Gun."

She turned to check on the cat, who was crouching on the floorboard in back. "I'd rather keep it since I'm the one who has to get out and stick my face into the box."

"While your face is in the box, who'll be looking out for your fine rear end?"

He thought her rear end was fine?

Flattery always gets the gun in her book, and he had a point, so she handed it over. "I used to feel so stupid doing that zigzag run during the drills, but maybe I should do it now?"

"Couldn't hurt." One side of Brent's mouth lifted. "And here I left my phone behind. I could've sold that video and be set for life."

"Very funny." She shook her head and opened the car door. At least his sense of humor seemed to be back. The scary Brent was sort of...scary. She preferred the Brent who looked at her like she was an alien, albeit one with a nice butt. "Let's hope they read my text and are all heading for Vegas. Not hiding with guns in the bushes." She was freaking herself out with the possibilities as she got out and crouched beside the car looking inside, waiting for him.

Brent pulled up his hood, motioning for her to do the same, then got out and took a position with his back to the twelve-foot stucco wall. "Go!"

She did the zigzag run, feeling like an idiot, but an alive one. When she got to the gate that was just like the one at home, she lifted the lid on the security panel. She tapped in her code and quickly scanned the display, searching for any trouble lights on the estate. All lights were green, so she poked the button and then leaned her face in for the scan.

Her mom recorded all the individual greetings with her sexy-movie-star voice. She updated them often, so Sara never knew what to expect, but they were usually very mom-like. "Do my eyes deceive me? Is it really my wayward child who never writes, never calls... Welcome home, sweetheart."

She smiled as she waited for the gates to slowly part. If she lived through this, she'd call her mom every Sunday for the rest of her life.

Brent started the car and slid past the open gates. She tapped the button on the other side to be sure they closed right behind them before she opened the passenger door and slid inside. Brent's shoulders were shaking with his restrained laughter.

"Shut up. No one looks normal doing the zigzag run."

∞ ∞ ∞

Brent quickly scanned the area in front of the house on the lush estate filled with palm trees and flowers. No sign of activity. Yet. Looked like they were alone. He returned to the car and opened Sara's door. "All clear."

"I told you that already. The security system was all in the green." Sara grabbed the cat and got out of the car.

He shut the door behind her. "Eyes are more reliable than electronics sometimes."

"Not at one of Annalisa's properties." Sara entered a code to let them in a side door of the pink stucco mansion.

He scanned the perimeter again. Where were the other agents? He needed to have a look at his phone to see what the current plan was.

After a beep sounded, Sara opened the door and put the cat down. "The security team is going to call any second. They'll have gotten an alert and know it's me by the scan, but they'll check anyway."

"Are they here in town?" Maybe he could use that. Have an agent pose as one of them.

She shrugged. "I have no idea." The phone sitting on the desk in the big chef's kitchen rang as she'd predicted. "Should I ask them for help or not?"

"If they call the local police, we're screwed. Better not. Where's the bathroom?"

She pointed down a hallway as she picked up the phone.

He jogged down the short hall. A motion sensor turned the overhead lights on as he closed the bathroom door behind him. After he'd used the facilities and washed his hands, he dug the phone out of his sweatshirt's pocket.

Arrived. What's the next move?

Only a few seconds passed before Brent got a response from Rick.

Boss ordered a chopper to pick you guys up. Holding for orders overhead.

Dammit! Probably the same chopper that had passed over earlier.

Blow my cover and we might never get to Annalisa with her army of lawyers. She knows something. She tried to warn Sara. Need to stay undercover. Sara's my ticket in.

Dude. You're pissing the bossman off. Hold for instructions.

The only thing Brent intended to hold was his curse as he shoved the phone into his pocket. If they blew his cover, he'd be off the case. They'd have no one on the inside anymore. And he didn't have enough evidence yet to get the players at the very top. Why didn't Braydon see that? Could he be protecting someone?

It'd been unusual to be placed inside Holden's house when he could have gotten the banking records without any trouble. Taking the old guy's place after he died gave the FBI an excellent opportunity to see what was going on from the inside. They already had enough to bring Holden and Miller in for questioning, but that might cause the operation to shut down before they could gather enough evidence to convict. Brent's assignment was to figure out who was at the top. Maybe finding out a dirty cop was involved changed something? He'd proceed as if the mission was on, even though every second that passed without instructions dimmed his hope.

He walked back to the kitchen. Sara, bent over at the waist, made for an enticing view of her rear end as she rummaged through a cupboard. With her hands full, she turned around and let out a yelp. "Geez, Brent. You've got to stop sneaking up on me like that!"

He lifted his hands. "Sorry. Which way to the garage? We need to get going."

Sara shook her head as she filled a paper bag with the cans and jars she'd found. "I'll show you as soon as I find a can opener. Can you please look for Mittens? I think she headed for the dining room. She used to like to hide under the furniture at Scott's."

Great. His boss wanted to scrub the mission, and now he'd been relegated to cat-finding duty. Staying in character sucked sometimes.

He found the dining room with a long wooden table all set as if company would arrive any second. He glanced underneath and found the sleeping cat. "Time to go, kitty." He lifted the polka-dotted feline and held it against his chest. Mittens snuggled her face under his chin. The sleepy little cat was sort of growing on him.

Filled with defeat now that their mission was probably over and he'd failed to solve the case before being booted off it when his cover was blown, he walked into the kitchen. Sara was nowhere to be found.

The sound of a toilet flushing down the hall signaled where she'd gone. How mad was she going to be when she found out he was an agent in a few minutes? And why did he feel guilty for deceiving her even though he'd only been doing his job?

He'd probably never see her again after they took her into custody. The thought sent a surprising pang to his heart. Sara was growing on him just like Mittens.

Sara reappeared and grabbed the bag off the counter. "Let's go see what we have to drive."

He followed behind her down another long hall, past a laundry room the size of his apartment and then into a big closet. Inside was a panel with a set of car keys, a control panel for the security system, and a huge gun safe. Sara typed in the code and cranked open the safe, revealing the arsenal she'd said was there earlier. "Which do we want?"

If they were going to call off the mission, they'd be better off leaving Annalisa's guns behind. Otherwise, they'd get confiscated. "We're good with what I have on me."

Sara glanced over her shoulder. "Which is still a secret to me. But fine. I'm taking this for myself." She chose a .38 and grabbed some ammo. She slapped the safe closed and then swept the car keys off the hook.

He listened for the thump of copter blades while he followed her to the garage. Should they take the car and make a run for it? He hadn't gotten an official answer yet. If the mission was still on, the farther away they got before morning, the better. It was already past one a.m.

He asked, "Since we can't call the police for help, what if we called the FBI? I'm sure they could keep us safe from Miller." He'd feel better knowing he'd offered her an out once she found out who he really was.

"Nope." Sara opened the door that led to the garage. "Besides, I think you have to cross state lines or something for the FBI to get involved. And like you said earlier, how do we know the FBI wouldn't get the local cops involved and therefore Miller?"

He wasn't going to explain jurisdiction to her. "Why are you so sure your mom can protect you?"

"She'll protect you too." The big garage was empty except for a sleek black Mercedes. Sara opened the car's back door and tossed the grocery bag inside. "It's hard to explain, but my mom sort of has this sixth sense about things. She's never wrong. She told me to trust only you and to come home."

Sixth sense? That sounded like a crock of crap. There had to be another reason she wanted to go to her mother's so badly. And he was going to find out what that reason was. They'd get back on the road, and he'd risk his boss's wrath and claim ignorance. After all, it was his first real field assignment.

He added Mittens to the backseat with the food and shut the door. Then he rounded the car and studied the front license plate. The number ended in two threes. "Do you think there'd be any paint or a marker around that'd match the color of these numbers? We can make these threes eights."

Sara joined him and placed her hands on her hips. "Would nail polish work? My mother must have every color under the sun."

He nodded. "Whatever you can find will have to do. I'll go get our things from Scott's car while you look."

Sara nodded and then headed back into the house. He took out his phone. Rick still hadn't answered, so maybe they were reconsidering. He shoved the phone back in place and then went outside to Scott's car. The faint sound of a chopper filled the air as he grabbed their stuff. He placed Scott's key fob in the glove box and then shut the car's door. Interesting that the chopper wasn't getting any closer.

Before he went back inside, he typed a message to Rick.

Can you confirm our tail's 20?

Rick replied. We have visual on your tail. Heading north toward Vegas. You're clear.

Brent typed, THX. Contain Scott so he doesn't report Sara for stealing the car.

Done. Boss says he'll give you 72 hrs. Sara gets a scratch and you're a dead man.

Yes! He couldn't help his grin. He was going to get a chance to prove he was right about Annalisa and the Russians. But they were going to need just a bit more help to be sure he could keep Sara safe.

Can you arrange vehicle swap in AZ? Somewhere along Hwy 60. No GPS.

10-4.

Brent wiped the smile off his face and went back inside to doctor up the license plate. If they stayed off the major roads and could keep Sara's face hidden, they had a fighting chance to make it to Annalisa's house in Albuquerque now.

He returned to the garage to find Sara admiring the numbers she'd just painted. "That looks great." When she looked up and smiled at him, it made his stomach do a flip and roll.

She said, "Painting my own nails all these years came in handy. Ready to go?"

"Yep." He started for the driver's side, but she slipped by him and placed herself uncomfortably close between him and the car.

"My turn to drive, Brent. You can get some rest now."

Since they'd lost their tail, he didn't see why not. They'd have to drive the speed limit anyway. "Only because you've been to evasive driving school. And it'll give me time to study our route." Her pretty face, with her brows arched in silent challenge, was just inches from his. It took everything inside not to close the gap and kiss her. Instead, he opened the car door for her.

"Thank you." With a smug smile, Sara slipped behind the wheel while he rounded to the passenger side. She opened the garage door and then started the powerful car.

After closing the door behind them, she got out of the car and typed a code into the panel on the house. Afterward, they headed for the back gate. When they were on the small highway that would take them to Arizona, she flipped on the radio. "What kind of music are you in the mood for, Brent?"

He shrugged as he studied the map. "Anything but country."

"What?" Sara's face flipped his way. "But country music tells stories we can all relate to. I mean, don't all of your exes live in Texas too?"

God, he liked her.

"Hearing about some achy breaky heart just ain't my thang darlin'."

Sara laughed. "Do you have a girlfriend who makes your heart achy for her?"

"No." He went back to studying the map, looking for a good place to make a car swap.

Sara tuned into a classic rock channel, while Mittens decided she didn't want to be in the back and jumped into his lap.

"You and your one-word answers. Have you ever had an achy heart over any woman?"

"Nope." He didn't want to look her in the eyes when he lied to her, so he kept his gaze glued to the map while he petted the cat. He had a feeling his heart would never be the same after the mission was over. She'd wormed her way in there like no other woman ever had. But no way could he act on it.

"Well, that's just sad. Maybe when this is all over—"

The radio announcer interrupted the song with a news bulletin. "Police are looking for Sara Chapman, daughter of Annalisa Botelli and Holden Chapman. She disappeared from her father's wedding earlier, along with a man who works for Sara's father named Brent Jackson. Police fear Jackson has kidnapped Sara and ask for your help if you have any information. They were last seen in a late-model dark BMW heading west just outside Palm Springs."

Sara's forehead creased. "Why would they accuse you of that? And who would've reported me missing already? It's only been a few hours since we left."

"Miller, probably. By implying I kidnapped you, it'll get more people's attention."

Why didn't Rick share that information? It hadn't been fifteen minutes since they communicated. Surely the FBI would have known it before a radio DJ. He trusted Rick like a brother, had known him for years.

Something didn't feel right.

Chapter Nine

*A*s they headed east, the sun, just rising over the hills, hit Sara in the face. She slipped on her sunglasses as they drove on the mostly deserted little highway. Brent had suggested they stop a while back, but Sara was still driving because she hadn't been able to sleep with all the adrenaline pumping through her veins. Now, she regretted not stopping because she had to go to the bathroom. Bad.

She glanced at Brent. His eyes were still closed, so she made an executive decision and turned off onto an even smaller road. They'd made good progress, but much more slowly than if they'd taken the interstate.

Mittens, lounging on Brent's lap, nodded her approval. The cat probably needed to go too.

Sara's worry had increased with each hour they'd driven. Zoila and Justin had surely heard the news that Brent had supposedly kidnapped her. She hated to worry them, but with the California police after them, she had to stay away from the internet if they were going to make it to her mom's house in Albuquerque. And avoid people who might recognize her now that the whole world thought she'd been kidnapped.

Sara glanced at Brent again. Spiky blond hair, a face and body chiseled as if out of stone, and a smile, when he used it, that did something tingly and nice to her insides. She'd always found him attractive. Who wouldn't want to run her hands all over a body with muscles and abs like his?

Just the day before, if someone had asked if she thought she and Brent would ever be friends, she would've said no. Mostly because it'd seemed like he couldn't stand her. But not anymore. They were two people working together toward the same goal: to save their lives. Sort of a forced friendship, but it felt like a genuine one.

He wasn't at all like other guys she knew. Most of them were spoiled overgrown boys who took more time getting ready in the morning than she did. Fun to party with, but not the ones she'd call when her life needed saving.

"Why do you keep looking at me?" Brent asked and scared the crap out of her.

"Your eyes are closed. How would you even know?"

"I can feel it." He blinked his eyes open and sat up. "Where are we?"

"Just west of Phoenix. I took a little detour. There were signs for a campground and recreation area with full amenities just a few miles ahead. Before you say a word, I need to use the ladies' room and do things I'm not doing on the side of the road."

He smiled. "Okay, princess."

"Oh, please." His grin had given him away. "Like you're going to turn down a toilet right now? Admit it. This is a good idea."

He shrugged. "It'd be nice to heat whatever is in the cans you brought for breakfast. And a stretch of the legs is prudent. So, yeah. It's a good idea."

Great. Why had she even mentioned her bathroom needs? And why was it she always felt embarrassed around him? The way he'd shaken his head when she hadn't known how much money should be in her account. Then her pathetic need for a last-minute wedding date, getting stuck on the stationary bike, forgetting her watch had GPS, and now he had graphic details of what her bathroom routine would include. She could just crawl under a rock and stay there until this was all over.

He drew her out of her funk when he asked, "So, why *were* you staring at me?"

Busted for that now too. "I was just thinking I like your dark hair better than the blond," she lied. He looked hot with spiky blond hair. And the dark scruff that had appeared on his face overnight made him look even more rough-and-tumble.

"Noted."

Him and his short answers.

"And maybe I was wondering why a good-looking guy like you is single?"

He turned and met her gaze. "You're beautiful and single."

She shook her head. "I'm only single because—oh. Did you get dumped recently too?"

"No."

"Well, it couldn't be because of your scintillating conversation skills, that's for sure."

He grinned. "I just moved to California a few months ago. Everyone I've met have all been kind of fake, needy, and way into themselves. Not my type."

"So, he does speak in full sentences." Geez. It was about time. "Describe your type, and I bet I can find you just the right woman after this is all over."

"I'm good, thanks." He turned and stared out the window.

"Now you're forcing me to guess. Let's see. You don't like fake and into themselves, so maybe you like women who don't wear makeup, because that would make them a princess like me. And probably someone who doesn't shave her legs? And not needy because she can kill her own dinner, arm wrestle, and start fires?"

He shook his head. "Just look for the turnoff, please."

"Wait!" She held up a finger. "I know. We'll find you a cavewoman who can grunt back at you. You'll never have to utter a full sentence again. See? I'm a good matchmaker." She smiled at the irritation etched on his face.

He gazed silently ahead while he petted the cat on his lap, so she poked his arm. "Or you could tell me who your type really is. Then I could find you someone nice, albeit quiet, so your heart has somewhere to deposit all that love I'm sure must be somewhere locked inside." And she could squelch her curiosity about who his type was. Oddly, she really wanted to know.

He closed his eyes. "Has it ever occurred to you that I might be gay?"

Oh, crap! What the heck had she just done? How freakin' insensitive could she be?

"Brent, I apologize. I made an assumption. That was wrong of me." She was an idiot!

He burst out laughing. "I was just kidding. The look on your face was priceless."

She fought the grin that threatened. "Have I mentioned I think you're annoying?"

"Nope." His smiled hadn't faded. "But I'm pretty sure you like me, but don't want to."

"Why do you think that?" He was right, but probably not for the reasons he thought.

"Because I confuse you. You're used to men whose rich daddies set them up for life, not someone who really works for a living." He poked her arm like she'd just done to him. "Do you want to know what kind of woman I *don't* want?"

More than she wanted her next breath. "Only to pass the time."

He shook his head at her flip answer. "I don't want a woman who can't stand on her own two feet. Who needs to be told she's beautiful constantly to feed her ego. And who cares more about herself than her own family. Or who talks about all the material things she wants and needs and expects a man to give to her. Someone who can't appreciate a beautiful sunset more than those damned shoes with the red bottoms."

Sara slowly nodded. "So, because my mother pays my tuition and insists I wear shoes with red bottoms, that makes me weak and materialistic?"

"No." He frowned before turning his attention out the window again. "I wasn't talking about you. I was talking about my mother. She was like Marilyn Monroe. Beautiful, fragile, and men dropped at her feet, but none of them took her seriously. She'd do just about anything for a pair of red-soled shoes. More than she cared about feeding her kid. I loved her, but I want to be with someone who is an equal partner, not a grown-up child."

"Makes sense." Sara's heart ached for the childhood he must've had. She'd never gone without food, shelter, or her mother's love. "But I can relate to not being taken seriously."

"It's the press." He scratched the stubble on his chin. "They make you out to be someone you're not. But you handle them better than most."

She shook her head. "All I want is for the press to leave me alone. Stop popping out of bushes and poking lenses in my face. They're like vultures just waiting for me to screw up again. That's why I'm going to get my degree and work at the shelter. Nine to five every day. They'll get bored with me, and then maybe I can have my life back."

"Maybe dating someone who isn't famous next time would help too," he pointed out.

"Yeah. And I'm sure you'll find the right person for you too." She gave his hand lying on his thigh a sympathetic pat.

"Maybe." He slid his hand out from under hers and pointed ahead. "There's the turn. On the right."

"I see it." She slowed and put her hand back on the wheel as she made the turn into the recreation area, feeling like something had just passed between them, but she wasn't sure what exactly. "Just so we're clear, here, I don't hate that I like you, Brent. I'm just fine with liking you. And it's okay if you don't like me."

"I never said I didn't like you." He placed Mittens in the backseat and started the scanning-all-around-with-his-eyes thing again. "I said you'd never like a guy like me. Probably because I'd never tell you you're beautiful or buy you red-soled shoes. And because I grunt out one-word answers like a caveman."

"Well, there is that. Except you just called me beautiful before you so kindly pointed out my single status. So, thanks."

"Just stating the obvious." He continued his surveillance. "And I meant what I said. You're very good with the press. That you held it together at the shelter the other day was impressive."

That he thought she was attractive in her workout clothes and with her new boyish haircut made her smile inside. But that he'd taken her seriously, complimented her public speaking skills made her heart smile.

She followed weathered wood signs down a long dirt road surrounded by cactuses, the tall ones looking like headless people with bent arms scattered among rocks and boulders, and felt compelled to ask, "So, are we done fighting?"

"Didn't realize we were."

"Oh. Okay." Maybe it had been her own internal fight against falling for anyone new for a while. Because there was something about Brent that made her feel safe, challenged, and attracted to him all at the same time. She'd never felt like that before.

A sign at a fork in the road pointed to camping one way, and the other to the day recreation area.

Brent tilted his thumb to the left. "Let's avoid the camping people. Go for the day option."

"Sounds good." She turned to the left, eager to find those full amenities.

Empty covered picnic areas with grills and tables spread out before them and had pretty views of a canyon just beyond. Signs pointed to different trailheads. One even said there was a waterfall. In the desert? Weird.

She headed for the most remote picnic site that wasn't too far away from the facilities.

"Dibs if there's only one bathroom." She threw the car in Park and didn't wait for his answer.

As soon as Sara disappeared inside the brick structure, Brent dug out his phone. The display read:

Car in place by 0800. Map attached. Parked on the street. Older 4x4. Supplies in glove box.

He was still confused about Rick's lack of information earlier about what he and Sara had heard on the radio. 10-4. Any new chatter?

PD searching from above. They haven't ID'd Annalisa's car yet. Matter of time. What's your plan?

Why wouldn't Rick mention the APB? It made no sense. He replied,

Switch cars and drive until we have to stop for gas. Make ABQ tonight.

Still confused by Rick's lack of communication, Brent tapped on the map pdf and found the recreation area they were at. The new car wasn't far. They'd have to wait until the car was in place at the pickup location, but how was he going to convince Sara to go along with taking it? She'd think they were stealing it. But first, where could they hide Annalisa's car until they could take off? It was only six thirty.

The hilly desert terrain covered with cactuses and low scrub brush wouldn't provide any cover from above. And not a tree in sight. The black Mercedes stood out in the empty picnic area like a shining beacon from above. He needed to check out the camping area, see if there was some shelter there where they could hide the car until it was time to go.

Mittens meowed loudly from the backseat, so he tucked his phone away and grabbed her bowl. He found some bottled water and a can of sardines in the bag Sara had packed. He opened the door and let the cat out, hoping it knew what to do without a litter box. Then he opened her sardines and found an apple for himself.

After a few minutes, Sara reappeared, looking like she needed a nap. "Thanks for feeding Mittens." Her eyes had dark circles under them and they lacked their usual sparkle. "The bathroom wasn't nearly as bad as I had imagined."

He nodded as he finished his apple. "I'll go see for myself." He headed for the bathroom while trying to decide if it'd be safer for them to drive to the town where the car was going to be delivered or stay put at the rec area and off the streets. The police might be concentrating on the roads rather than a state park. It was Sunday morning. Maybe more people would show up soon, so the car wouldn't stand out so badly.

After he was done, he joined Sara and the cat in the car again and then picked up Mittens. "Why don't you get some rest? I'm going to walk over to the camp area and see if there's any better shelter in case they have choppers looking for us."

Sara opened a box of breakfast pastries. "Why are you taking Mittens and not me?"

"Because she talks less and listens better."

"Such a comedian today." Sara handed him a pack of toaster pastries. "Thank goodness for Mrs. Wilson. She always has these on hand in case I visit."

He opened up the kids' treat and took a bite. "Who is Mrs. Wilson?" Raspberry and sugar sweetness exploded in his mouth. It wasn't half-bad.

"My mom's chef. She's like a second mother to me and Dani."

Thinking of the way Zoila treated Sara, he said, "Seems you have a few second moms. Stay inside the car, please." He grabbed the empty water bottle, opened the door, and stepped out.

"Wait." Sara leaned over the seat to peer up at his face. "Seriously, why are you taking the cat? You aren't ditching me, are you?" Her features scrunched with concern.

He leaned his head in the car so she wouldn't have to crane her neck. "I'm not going to ditch you, Sara. Ever. I'm taking Mittens, so I look trustworthy. I'm a big guy with this cute cat looking to fill up a water bottle for her. How nefarious can I be?"

Sara's tempting lips formed a slow smile. "I don't know. You sure aren't the quiet accountant I thought you were when we first met. I have a feeling you might just be a little nefarious."

He wanted to kiss her, so he leaned away before he did. "Get some rest, Eloise."

She rolled her eyes at him right before he closed the door. He pointed to the locks and waited until she was secure, then he headed out toward the camping area.

The December air was crisp but would warm to about sixty-five according to the weather report he'd called up on his phone while he walked along the dirt road. He'd hoped for low clouds, but no such luck. Looked like it was going to be a sunny day. Making it easier for cops with eyes in the sky to see them.

After a short walk, he spotted the camping area. There were a few people mulling around the half-empty campground. And no shade structures to hide the car. Looked like most of the campers had awnings on their units or brought their own shade.

He made his way near the bathroom where there was a place to get water to fill the bottle for Mittens. Nearby, an older couple looked as though they were packing up to leave. The woman was cleaning up their breakfast dishes, and the man was storing blocks he'd just removed from behind the tires.

Brent put Mittens down. "Go look hungry and make some friends."

There were only two ways to leave from the park, and one was through the town they needed to be at by 0800 to pick up their new ride. They were sitting ducks in the nearly empty picnic area as it was. And maybe if they found a ride, left the car in the parking lot, a ranger might not notice it until closing time, giving them a head start before they figured out they'd switched cars. Besides, he really wanted to use someone else's phone and text Rick on his private cell to see what was going on at HQ. Everything on their work phones was monitored.

Brent killed time by washing his hands and face. Mittens had failed at her mission. She'd walked about ten feet and then flopped onto a patch of grass to groom herself.

He sighed and filled the bottle. A dog would've gone in hunt for scraps for sure. Mittens seemed to have her own agenda.

He called out, "Mittens?" and turned in a circle as if he didn't know exactly where she was.

The lady called out, "I think she's right over there."

Brent turned around and forced a big grin on his face. "Thank you." He walked over to where Mittens sat licking her paws and lifted her up. "My girlfriend would kill me if I'd lost her cat."

The woman cocked her head. "You brought a cat along to camp?"

He smiled and moved a little closer. "No. We're just using the facilities on the day parking side. Passing through on our way to Sun City. Got a call in the middle of the night that her dad was taken to the hospital with chest pains."

The woman's face wrinkled with concern. She appeared to be in her late seventies. "I'm sorry to hear that. I hope he'll be okay."

"Yeah. Us too. But then we ran over something and have two flat tires." He slowly walked closer and held out a hand for a shake while his mind raced for a believable story. "Name's Randal Mason. You wouldn't have a cell phone I could borrow, would you? We left in such a hurry last night, our phones weren't all the way charged and they died. I need to see if I can get a tow truck to come save us."

The woman reached out and shook Brent's hand. "Esther Kincaid. My husband, Will, has our cell phone. Be right back." She walked to the big RV and disappeared inside. Brent sat at the picnic table with Mittens while he figured his next move to get him and Sara a ride out of there and away from Annalisa's traceable car.

Will, who looked like he'd been a pro football player in his prime, rumbled down the steps. "The wife says your phone died and you need to borrow ours?"

Brent stood and held out his hand. "Hi, Mr. Kincaid. Yes, please, to call for a tow."

The old man's grip was surprisingly strong as he returned the handshake. "You can use my cell, but it isn't a fancy one with internet. It just makes calls."

Not good for contacting Rick, but now Brent wouldn't have to lie and say they couldn't get any help on a Sunday in such a small town.

Brent frowned as if thinking. "Well then, I guess I'll have to call the police for help. That is, unless you'd happen to know the number of someone nearby who could help us out?"

"Nope. We're from California. Going to Texas to visit the kids." Will pinned Brent with a steady gaze. As if measuring Brent up. "Your girlfriend's back at your vehicle?" Esther quietly slipped beside her husband.

Brent nodded. "Taking a nap. She drove the last few hours."

"And where was it you told Esther you were headed?"

It was an interrogation all of a sudden. "Sun City. Eloise's dad had to be rushed to the hospital." Brent glanced up and spotted a satellite antenna on top of the RV's roof. They had to have posted his and Sara's pictures on the news. Did this guy suspect it was Brent?

Will crossed his big arms and angled his head. Just as he opened his mouth to speak, Esther said, "He's an ex-cop. He can't help himself." She held out the phone. "Go ahead. Make your call."

An ex-cop? Crap. If he'd seen his and Sara's pictures on TV, they might be screwed.

Chapter Ten

*L*oud banging on the car's window woke Sara from a deep sleep in the backseat. Had Miller or the police found her? Her eyes flew open, and she spotted Brent. Relief slowed her pounding heart.

She sat up and opened the door for him. "You scared the crap out of me. Again."

Brent handed her the cat and then started packing up their things. "I got us a ride. Your name is Eloise, and mine is Randal. You're my girlfriend, and your father was taken to the hospital last night with chest pains. Your parents live in Sun City. Will and Esther will be here to pick us up with their RV any second."

Sara blinked at Brent. "Have you hit your head or something? Why would you even talk to anyone?"

Brent stopped his gathering and rubbed the back of his neck. "Because we have two flat tires. I noticed they were low when we left, but now they're flat."

What? She hadn't noticed that.

She got out to see for herself. How had two tires on the same side gone so flat while she'd slept? "So, your new friends are taking us where?"

He grabbed Mittens' bowl and tossed it into the grocery bag. "To the next town. For a tow truck."

That was going to slow them down. "What if they recognize me? Should I stay here?"

"They're older. I doubt they'd know who you are. Will is a retired cop. We need to look like we're in a relationship. Don't forget to call me Randal."

Brent had gone back into robot mode. And the tire thing wasn't adding up. The car had driven just fine. "What aren't you telling me? Because getting a ride from an ex-cop seems just plain stupid, and that's something you're not."

Brent frowned as he slapped the car door closed. "I didn't know he was a cop. That was just bad luck. You need to trust me."

She crossed her arms. "I don't think I can trust a person who would let the air out of our tires when bad guys and the cops are chasing us!"

"Pipe down." He stuffed the map into the bag with their travel kits. "I did that so Esther and Will would believe us. And so you'd go along with my new plan. I don't think you're going to like it."

"What's not to like?" She lifted her chin, upset and a little hurt that he'd made plans without her. It was her life in danger too.

A big RV blasted its horn as it pulled up nearby. Moments later, the door swung open and a big man waved them inside.

Brent said, "Follow my lead. Pretend to like Randal and be concerned for your dad."

Sara mumbled under her breath, "I like Randal a whole lot better than Brent at the moment." But she plastered on a smile and followed Brent to the big RV all decked out for Christmas with tinsel and garland strewn everywhere. As they stepped inside, Brent did the introductions and then nudged her and Mittens onto a couch. Brent said, "Thanks again for the ride, guys."

Esther turned in her big copilot seat and smiled. "You're welcome. Where do you two live, Eloise?"

Sara returned the older woman's smile. "Malibu."

Will sat behind the wheel and started up the behemoth vehicle with a loud rumble. His eyes found hers in the mirror above his head, and he squinted. "Randal said you'd come from Lake Havasu."

Crap! She cut her eyes Brent's way and hoped he could save them.

Brent slid his arm around her shoulder and pulled her against his hard body. "Eloise has been going to school at Pepperdine. She's getting her master's in counseling come spring. We've just come from my parents' house in Havasu. We were staying with them over Sara's winter school break. But we live in Malibu."

Phew. He'd saved that one. It was stressful lying to a cop. Damn Brent for making her do that!

Esther nodded. "Lake Havasu is very nice. What do you do, Randal?" Will continued to look suspicious in the front seat. Or maybe it was her imagination.

"I'm an accountant." Brent stroked the cat in Sara's lap, looking fresh as a cucumber, while sweat dripped between her breasts.

Will called out, "So what's going on with the RV and second-home tax laws?"

Sara held her breath. It had to be a test. Was he onto them? Was he taking them to the police?

Brent gave her shoulder a reassuring squeeze and then spouted off a bunch of mumbo-jumbo tax stuff that had Will nodding. Thank goodness Brent really was an accountant. And a bodyguard? Were her parents working together to protect her?

Grateful that Brent seemed to have things under control, Sara laid her head on his shoulder to make it look like they were a couple and closed her eyes. It'd be easier not to speak if they thought she was asleep.

After the men finished up their conversation, Will said, "Hope you don't mind if I switch this on. Helps us avoid traffic problems."

It wasn't a traffic report that came through the speakers. It was police scanner news, with all sorts of squawks and numbers that made no sense. Brent tensed ever so slightly beside her, causing her to open her eyes to gauge how worried he seemed.

He mouthed, *Kiss me?*

What? Kiss him?

While she stared into his earnest eyes, it dawned on her why he'd ask. They might report about Brent kidnapping her. She needed to initiate the kiss while eagle-eyed Will watched.

She said loud enough for Will and Esther to hear, "Thank you for coming along to visit my parents. I would've been stranded alone without you, babe."

Brent nodded his head ever so slightly with approval.

Strangely nervous about a fake kiss, she laid her lips on his. And boom. All thoughts about cops, Miller, and their broken car flew out of her mind. Replaced by pheromones or hormones or whatever the things were that made her entire body ignite, eager for more.

He slowly slid his large hand around the back of her neck, pulled her closer, then added his tongue to their kiss. Heat flew straight to all the right places, making her moan a little. Or he did. She couldn't be sure. Didn't matter, though. She'd never been kissed like *that*.

Brent leaned away first, his face lit with one of his rare, huge grins. No longer was he the robot, he was the guy who teased her but also promised he'd never ditch her. Ever. It sent a jolt straight to her heavily guarded heart.

Will cleared his throat and ended her and Brent's stupid-smiles-on-their-faces staring match. "Looks like they're having random roadblock checks around Phoenix. Luckily, you're not too far from your parents' house, Eloise, so it shouldn't bother you two too much."

She tore her gaze from Brent's. "That's good news. My mom sounded upset when she'd called. My dad's health has been declining the past few years."

Will nodded as he navigated the RV as big as a Greyhound bus around a corner. "Would you like us to take you all the way to Sun City? It's not too far out of our way."

Brent and Sara both said "No!" at the same time.

"But thanks." Brent's face lit with a fake smile. "That's nice of you to offer, but we might need the car to run back and forth to the hospital. Eloise's mom doesn't drive anymore."

Esther nodded. "That must be hard for your mom, Eloise. We'll drop you at the nearest police station, then."

Police station?

Panic made her heart pound again. She tried to keep her face impassive while she freaked out a little inside. Brent slowly ran his hand up and down her arm, probably to keep her from losing it. How could he seem so damn calm?

She glanced out the window. Little houses alongside the road started appearing. Mailboxes wrapped like Christmas presents and little trees with ornaments lined the road. Must be close to the town they headed toward. What would they do if Will insisted he go inside the station with them? Put in a good word, one ex-cop to another brother in blue? There was no way they'd get out of town if the cops asked for Brent's ID.

When they turned a corner, a small main street lay before them. Then she saw it. A diner. With a neon sign with three cactuses lit. Just like the one her sister had seen in her dreams. "Hey, Will? Can you drop us off at that café ahead?"

Will looked up in his mirror and frowned. "Are you sure you wouldn't rather go to the station? It's a few miles from here yet."

Sara stared into Brent's eyes. "We've eaten there before." She suddenly couldn't remember what Brent's name was supposed to be. "Remember, babe? The lady who ran it was really nice. I'm sure she'd help us." She pleaded with her eyes. It was where they were supposed to go, but she had no idea how to explain it if asked. She whispered, "Trust me. Please?"

Brent's eyes cut toward the diner, then back to Will's. "Eloise is right. We can grab a bite and then get a tow. A two-for-one deal. We'll even buy you guys breakfast for the help if you'd like."

What the heck was Brent thinking? Inviting them to have breakfast?

She gave him a sharp jab with her elbow. "I'm sure Will and Esther are eager to see their grandkids, honey."

Esther's face lit with a grin. "We are. Haven't seen them in almost a year. Besides, we just ate before we left, but thank you for the kind offer, Randal."

Randal. Right. That was his name. She repeated it in her mind a few times to make it stick this time. Her nerves and all the lies were giving her a headache.

Will pulled the big rig to the curb and cut the engine. Then he slowly turned around and stood. Sara's heart beat triple time, making it hard to draw a deep breath. This was it. If he'd recognized them, he'd pull out his cell to call the police.

Will stuck out his big palm. "Good luck, you two."

Relief whooshed through her as Brent stood and shook Will's hand. "Thanks for the ride. We appreciate it."

Will slapped Brent on the back. "No worries. Good luck with the car." He held out his hand to her too. "And best wishes for your father, Eloise."

She wiped her palm, damp with nerves, on her yoga pants before returning the shake. "You guys are the best. Safe travels." She waved to Esther, hugged Mittens closer, and then high-tailed it to the door. She opened it, and the steps slowly lowered so they could make their escape. Brent grabbed their bags then wrapped a hand around her arm and tugged to slow her down. Her rush might make them look guilty, but she couldn't get out of the RV fast enough.

Once on the curb, Brent whispered, "Smile and wave goodbye, Eloise."

All her instincts screamed for them to run, but she stood beside Brent and fake smiled, waving as they drove away. When they were out of sight, she said, "Why did you ask them to have breakfast with us? Are you crazy?"

He laid his free hand on her lower back and led her across the street and toward the diner. "Makes us look less guilty. I knew they weren't going to accept. I saw her packing up their breakfast stuff earlier."

"Yeah, well. Will looked like he could eat anytime. That was a big risk, buddy."

His jaw clenched. "As big a risk as asking him to pull over in the middle of town where everyone can see us? Will told me the station was on the other edge of town. Much safer than here for two strangers walking down the main street with a cat. So, what's your plan?"

She didn't have a plan, just knew they were supposed to go to the diner. How to explain that escaped her. "What were you going to do if he dragged you into the police station? We'd have been busted and sent back to Miller for sure."

"I had a plan." He stopped walking. "Tell me I didn't make a mistake by trusting you."

She quickly ran through her clues again. Maybe the pay phone was inside the diner? "You also said I wasn't going to like your plan, but before you could tell me why, the RV drove up. So, what wasn't I going to like?"

"The part where we steal a car."

She opened her mouth to object, and he held up a hand to stop her and said, "We'll return it. But for now, we needed to ditch your mom's car and find another way to get to Albuquerque."

That was it. She needed to find that pay phone. She wasn't going to take some innocent person's car. She drew the line at stealing. She'd call her ex-brother-in-law. No one would be monitoring him, hopefully, and he'd know what to do. "Let me go inside and see if they have a pay phone. Do you have any change?"

"Nope. Who are you going to call?"

"Jake, who used to be married to my sister. He's an ex-cop and currently in charge of my mother's security. He'll know what we should do."

Brent scratched the stubble on his chin while considering her plan. "You can trust him not to turn us over to the cops? One hundred percent?"

"Yeah. We need some help here, Brent. And I draw the line at car thievery."

"What if we made a trade for your mom's car for an older one without GPS?"

She laughed. "My mother would kill me. Do you know how much that car is worth?"

He shrugged. "I'm guessing a whole lot less than your life."

That was true. Her mom had more money than she could ever spend. "Who'd do that without a title?"

Brent smiled. "The fewer details you know, the better if we get caught. I'll take the heat. It's probably a good idea to split up anyway. I'll meet you in that park over there in a half hour or so?"

She glanced down the street. The park had picnic tables and a playground with a few kids playing. She could sit nearby and blend in. "Maybe I should talk to Jake before you swap the car?"

He shook his head. "Ask Jake to meet us somewhere before we hit Albuquerque. He can drive us the rest of the way in so we avoid the cameras."

She nodded, still uneasy with the plan. She didn't want to be any part of an illegal car swap, but then, she wanted to live.

She glanced at the diner. Her sister said it was part of her dreams, so Sara hoped there'd be a pay phone in there or at least a phone she could borrow. "Do you think I look different enough so that no one will recognize me?"

"Out of context. But can you add a slight Southern accent? That might help."

She smiled and added some twang when she said, "Brent, darlin', actin' runs through these veins like beer through a honkytonk's taps." Occasionally listening to country music might prove to be handy.

Brent leaned down and whispered, "Slow that roll a bit, Eloise, and you'll be perfect." He laid a quick kiss on her lips. "But then, you were already pretty perfect. Be careful, okay?"

She was so thrown off by his kiss, she said, "Too you, Brent."

A slow grin lit his face before he turned and walked away.

Too you?

She slapped a hand across her eyes. What an idiot. She was falling for Brent at the worst possible time in her life. She needed to pull it together and find a phone so they could get the hell out of Dodge. And stop thinking about her hot bodyguard who kissed her like he meant it.

∞ ∞ ∞

Brent, carrying Mittens, walked across the street, resisting the urge to check on Sara one last time. He hated to leave her alone to find a phone. But it was for the best. People were looking for the two of them. Splitting up made the most sense, even though it had taken everything inside him to leave her.

He shouldn't have kissed her like that. It just seemed like the best way to reassure her that he had her best interests in mind.

Who was he trying to fool? He'd kissed her because he cared what happened to her. More than he had any business caring, but he hadn't ever felt the need to protect anyone as much as he wanted to protect Sara.

When she'd kissed him in the camper, it'd felt so...right. Like he'd finally found the soulmate he didn't even realize he'd been looking for. At the same time, he might have found the one woman who could hurt him even more than his mother had. Losing Sara too when the case was over was going to hurt. Bad.

She was kind, and good, and surprisingly sweet for someone who grew up with the Hollywood brat pack. She wasn't one of them anymore.

The real Sara was a woman who made him feel things he couldn't quite put his finger on. Good things.

But her dad was going to be locked up for sure, and Sara might never be able to forgive the agent who put him there. Namely him.

He hoped to God that Sara wouldn't have to see both her parents go to jail, though, because Sara's face lit up whenever she spoke about Annalisa. Sara's love for her mom was apparent.

An errant thought came and went. It was stupid to want Sara's face to light up like that when she saw him too.

As he started across the park, the kids' joyful voices as they asked to be pushed higher on the swings and their begging to go faster on the merry-go-round sent a familiar pang to his heart. He'd always hoped he'd have a kid one day but vowed he'd never be a parent like his mother had been. But then, age-old doubts always crept back in and whispered warnings that maybe bad parenting was genetic and he'd be a crappy parent too. He'd never want to ruin some poor kid's life.

He needed to stop thinking about kids and Sara. Get his mind back on track. Mission focused. He had a major case to crack and less than sixty-five hours left now to do it. Hopefully, the car would be at the drop point early so they could get back on the road. Sitting still felt like being fish in a barrel waiting to be shot. And

Sara wasn't a trained agent but doing something that'd be hard even for someone who was. Holding a cover and staying calm when under duress was stressful.

Sara could handle herself, though. He was sure of it.

But he couldn't shake the fear that something could go very, very wrong in that diner.

Chapter Eleven

ara sucked in a deep breath, told herself she could do it, and opened the diner's glass door. Blasted instantly with the enticing aroma of bacon, eggs, waffles—and was that apple pie and caramel she smelled too? Her mouth watered like one of Pavlov's dogs when hearing its bell. She did love a hearty breakfast.

Her stomach quickly forgot about that sweet pastry she'd had earlier and grumbled its message that a few pancakes never hurt anyone. Especially like the ones the man had who sat at the first booth, with apples, caramel, and whipped cream piled high on top. Like breakfast and dessert all rolled up in one.

The diner was decorated for the holidays with life-sized elves in one corner and a tree with presents in another. The windows all had snow scenes, kind of ironic but adorable in the desert. And the stools at the soda counter had garland wrapped around the poles. It made her heart happy. Christmas always did.

But she had a job to do, so she stepped farther into the festive diner, half-full at the early hour, and headed for the hallway that led to the bathrooms. A small TV in the corner quietly played an old movie her mother had starred in. The banner running below said the station was going to run all of her mom's movies until Sara was found.

It sent a wave of pride to her heart that her mom was so beloved they'd do something so sweet. But it also was a reminder of how many people outside of California knew of her supposed kidnapping.

Was the movie playing a good omen? Or a bad one, since she looked like a tiny, less voluptuous version of her mom. Usually. Maybe not so much with blonde hair and no makeup after she'd washed her face at the rec area.

A female voice called out, "Want some coffee to get you started?"

It'd look bad if she didn't stop.

Sara turned and headed toward the counter where a young blonde girl, probably high school aged, flipped over a coffee cup atop a paper placemat. Sara's feet wanted to run again, but she forced herself to stroll to the rows of red stools lined up and sat. Working up a softer version of the accent she'd laid on Brent earlier, she said, "Thank you. Just black please."

"You got it." As the girl poured, she studied Sara. "You seem familiar. Have we met?"

Bile rose in Sara's throat as she shook her head. "Nope. Just passing through for the first time." She cleared the blockage away from her throat and pointed to the sign above the restrooms. "Does there happen to be a pay phone back there? My cell died."

The girl, whose nametag read "Rayne," shook her head. Her long earrings hanging from multiple piercings dinged like wind chimes as they crashed against each other. "I don't think we have any of those in town. The only phone we have here is locked in the owner's office. He's not due in today."

Sara's hopes crashed. Why else was she supposed to be in the diner? Maybe there were more diners with three neon cactuses along the way? Before Sara could figure out what to do, the waitress said, "I'd loan you my cell, but my dad caught me texting a guy late last night and took it away. For an *undetermined* period." The kid rolled her eyes.

"Sorry. It's nice you'd offer, though," Sara twanged in response as her mind whirled with possibilities. Surely someone else in the diner had a cell she could borrow. But then, they'd have Jake's number. If her cover got blown, she didn't want to get Jake in trouble.

When the front door opened, Rayne glanced toward it and scowled. "Well, look who's here. It's as if just by speaking of my poor phone, we conjured him up."

Expecting to see the boy Rayne had been texting, Sara glanced over her shoulder. Her heart skipped a beat. Not in a wow-he's-a-handsome-guy kind of way, though.

An older, tall, thin cop walked toward her. Had Will and Ester stopped off at the police station and turned them in after all?

Might be the perfect time to use the restroom. Maybe she could sneak out the window like people always did in the movies.

She threw a five-dollar bill down first, though. She didn't want to stiff the kid, especially with her cop daddy approaching fast.

Just as Sara slipped off her stool to make a run for it, Rayne said, "Keep your money. The coffee's always free. Wait! My dad will know if there's a pay phone in town."

Rayne's dad, the cop, made steady eye contact with Sara. His gaze laser-focused on her face as his eyes scanned her features.

She could practically hear his mind filing away her stats. Five-four, brown on blonde. Caucasian, sloppy dresser.

Would her disguise hold up under direct scrutiny?

Her heart pounded so hard, Sara was sure Rayne and her father could see her pulse pumping at the base of her throat. Cops were trained to spot liars, and she was a big fat one at the moment.

Hearing her mom's voice on the television, Sara glanced up in time to see her mother smile. It wasn't the smile she beamed whenever she saw one of her kids. Those were exclusively for Sara and Dani. Instead, it was her *I'm an enchantress, and I can make anyone do my bidding* smile.

Sara had learned the craft of acting pretty much by osmosis, living her whole life with two of the best. Helping them run lines when no one else would.

Time to grow a pair and look confident. Like her mother always did no matter how nervous she felt.

Channeling the great Annalisa Botelli, and her best Southern belle character, Sara lifted her chin, threw her shoulders back, and slowly stuck out her hand to the cop. "Nice to meet you, sir. Eloise Jackson. Would you know if there are any pay phones nearby?"

The officer's forehead crumpled as he shook her hand. "Let me think for a second." He dropped her hand and laid both of his on his utility belt. One that packed a radio, pepper spray, handcuffs, and a super-intimidating .45 Glock.

She wished she'd left her .38 somewhere else other than on her person. Could complicate things if he apprehended her.

The policeman snapped his fingers. "There is one. At the Quick and Go." He threw a thumb over his shoulder. "'Bout two blocks behind us. On Third Street."

"Thank you both so much. Have a good day." Sara smiled and slowly glided as gracefully as her mom would have toward the door. Although, her mom would never be caught dead in public wearing yoga pants and a man's hoodie. Or with a .38 tucked behind at her lower back. Sara hoped the cop wouldn't notice that the most.

Just as her hand landed on the door and she was seconds from making her run for it, the cop called out, "Hold on a second, miss."

Crap. Had he made her?

She could run. But to where? At least Brent would have a chance to get away if she said she was alone. It was the right thing to do. He'd do the same for her.

She just hoped to God she'd get her one phone call to her mother before they turned her over to the California cops. That was where the pay phone probably was. The police station.

She was going to need some help to convince the California police that their top man was crooked.

Resigned, Sara slowly turned around to face her fate.

The cop stood a foot away. "Hold out your hands for me."

To put the handcuffs on. Dammit. Would he believe her if she told him the whole story? He had kind eyes, so maybe?

She slowly lifted her hands, both palms up, waiting for the cold slap of metal on her wrists.

The cop took both her wrists in his big hand and then dropped a pile of quarters into her palms. "Rayne changed out your five. You'll need these to make your call. Have a good one."

Sara nearly cried tears of joy as she stared at the stacks of quarters in her hand. Pulling herself together was a monumental task, but she finally said in a whispery voice, "You've both been so very kind. Thank you."

Just as she turned to go, the radio on the cop's belt squawked. The dispatcher said, "Mitch, Sam wants you to head out to the campgrounds. Check out a Mercedes on the day side. CA PD's looking at it for the Chapman kidnapping."

Sara didn't wait to hear what the cop replied. She strolled through the door and across the street, forcing herself to walk. Not to break out in a full run until she was out of sight of the diner. Then she ran like hell to find Brent. No time to call Jake anymore.

∞ ∞ ∞

Brent parked the older blue Jeep Rick had left for them at the park near the playground, grateful the car had been in place at the drop-off point earlier than planned. That Rick had filled the glovebox with condoms showed his pal still had a sick sense of humor. He'd also stocked the Jeep with camping supplies, water, and some food for the trip.

Everything they'd need if they had to stop for the day like Rick suggested to avoid detection from the air, but that wasn't what Brent wanted to do. The clock hadn't stopped ticking closer to the deadline his boss had imposed, so he hoped to drive straight through to Albuquerque.

He drummed his fingers on the steering wheel of the beat-up 4x4 with a faded hard top, impatient to get going again. It took all his willpower to stay put. He wanted to check on Sara, but it was best if they weren't seen together.

He glanced at the kids playing across the park, closely observed by their parents. He couldn't stay long without looking like a creepy guy spying on little kids, so he scooped Mittens up and found a bottle of water. "Time to stretch your legs, kitty."

He found her bowl and walked with the cat to a bench. He filled her water bowl then set the cat on the wooden seat beside him. Mittens ignored the bowl of water and headed straight for the playing children. He couldn't afford to let anyone else see his face, so he caught up with the cat and lifted her up again. "No, you don't."

He sat on the bench again to wait, glancing toward the diner down the street every minute or so while he petted the cat. The next time he glanced up, Sara was running toward him at full speed.

Dammit. Something must have gone wrong.

He slowly stood, stretched, and picked up Mittens' water bowl. Strolling to the car with the cat tucked under an arm, he glanced Sara's way again. She tilted her head toward the Jeep in a "hurry up" gesture. But he wasn't going to appear alarmed, even if she looked as though she'd just stepped on a venomous snake.

He opened the car door, placed Mittens in the back, and then sat and started the engine. When the passenger side door flew open, Sara said, "Go! Now!"

"Is someone chasing us?"

"Not yet. Just go. Please, Brent."

"So, someone *will* be chasing us?" He put the car in gear and headed toward the highway, mindful of the speed limit.

"They might. I can't believe how many freakin' cops are around here. It's unnatural!" Sara swiveled her body to check behind them.

He wanted to ask a million questions but needed her to calm down enough to tell him the threat level first. "Deep breaths. Did someone recognize you?"

Sara turned toward the front again and closed her eyes. "Not per se."

She recounted what happened in the diner. Not good. The police would run the plates and figure out the Mercedes was Annalisa's car. They maybe had an hour head start if they were lucky. Should they stop at a campground and wait until dark to travel?

Sara sighed. "I started out walking calmly, but then... I screwed up by running, didn't I?"

He laid his hand on her thigh and gave it a reassuring pat. "We're good. Don't sweat it." Although the chances the cop would realize he'd been talking to Sara had significantly risen. Especially after he found out the car just a few miles away was Annalisa's.

Sara closed her eyes again and shook her head. "I thought the cop had recognized me for sure. My first instinct was to run. But then I didn't want to lead them to you. I was going to tell them I was alone, then maybe you'd have a chance. If we get separated and one of us gets caught, that should be the plan. Right?" She intertwined her fingers through his.

It moved him that she would've lied to the cops for him. As far as she knew, he was in as much danger as she was. It was a selfless act. No one had ever done anything so heroic for him. Sara had put a crack in what his buddies called his "cynical nature."

But he still had a job to do. "If I get caught, then you should keep moving. But if you get caught, I need for you to tell them where I am."

She frowned at him. "Why would you want that?"

He wanted to confess who he was so bad. Especially when she clasped his hand tight, her complete trust in him evident. He'd never hurt Sara on purpose. But it couldn't be helped—she was going to feel betrayed when she found out the truth. "Because your mom would want me by your side if we have to deal with Miller and his men. You said she's never wrong, right?" He hated to use Sara's misconception about his role, but it was for the best.

"I guess." Sara slipped her hand from his. "Let's just hope we don't get separated." She pulled out a pile of quarters from her jacket pocket and reached for the glovebox.

Before he could stop her, she flipped it open. A slow smile lit her face as she dumped the quarters inside. "My mother will be so proud when I tell her we traded her ninety-thousand-dollar car for this beat-up old Jeep and a glovebox full of condoms. That's a deal no one in their right mind would ever pass up."

He'd kill Rick when he saw him next. "And camping gear, water, MREs and a ten-gallon extra can of gas strapped to the back. I drive a hard bargain."

"Clearly." Sara turned around and scanned the contents of the rear while she petted Mittens. "What are MREs?"

"Meal, Ready-to-Eat. Just add water. They're not bad."

Sara squeezed between the seats to investigate, her rear end level with his eyes, so he forced himself to concentrate on the road ahead. After rummaging around, she sat in her seat again and studied the plastic package in her hands. "No way. This pack has individually wrapped meatloaf, mashed potatoes, garlic bread, peach cobbler, a spork, napkin, wet towelette, gum—because of the garlic bread, no doubt—and even a flameless ration heater. You must've made a deal with a horny survivalist."

He smiled. If Sara only knew that it had been her amorous dance partner at the wedding who'd ordered up the stocked Jeep. "We aren't going to talk details about the car swap, remember?"

"Right." Sara tossed the package onto the backseat. "We still need to find a pay phone to call Jake. Will we have to stop for gas now that you so expertly negotiated the extra can of it back there?"

"Maybe not. We'll see. It'll be close."

She nodded then glanced behind them again as if expecting to see a police cruiser closing in. "Did you ask for all that camping gear, or did it just come with the car?"

"I asked. We need to decide if we'll find a campsite for the day and travel at night, or if we want to drive straight through. Now that they'll find your mom's car soon, it might be better to lay low just outside Phoenix."

Sara chewed her thumbnail as she pondered. "Can I ask just one question about the car swap?"

"Negative." He took the exit that would take them to the freeway to cross Phoenix the fastest. The plate scanners wouldn't be a problem anymore, but if the cop figured out he'd been speaking with Sara and he asked the people in the park to describe their ride, they might be in trouble. "What do you think about the campground? Do we stop, or do we risk it and keep driving?"

"The waitress thought I looked familiar. And the television station she's watching was running a marathon of my mother's movies. If they show my picture during the break and Rayne recognizes me, she'll tell her father for sure."

"Stopping could go either way, but no one would expect us to do that." He reminded himself he was supposed to be part of a team, so he asked, "What do you think?"

"I don't know." She glanced over her shoulder again. "There's only one sleeping bag back there. Is that your lame attempt to get me to have sex with you on the hard floor of a tent?"

"No." Damn Rick. Payback was going to be a bitch. "The guy only had one bag, but if you'd *like* to have sex with me, I could be on the bottom. More comfortable for you that way," he teased.

"Well, if you make love to a woman as well as you kiss..." She turned and stared out her window. "Maybe I'll think about it."

Was she serious? Really considering sleeping with him? Or just joking?

He shouldn't consider it. She was involved in his case. He was an agent, not allowed to sleep with witnesses. He'd lose his job. And the house on the water. He'd never give up his dreams for a quick roll in a tent.

But would he risk it to be with Sara? Even if it was only just one time?

Below his belt screamed yes, but above his shoulders advised to cool his jets.

It'd been a while since he'd been with a woman.

The jet noise was deafening.

Chapter Twelve

Sara stared out the window as she and Brent drove in silence on a congested highway through Phoenix. He stayed exactly the speed limit, ignoring the cars zooming past them.

That the car Brent traded her mother's for was a blue Jeep jibed with her sister's dreams. Hopefully, whoever made the trade would keep his yap shut. At least until they got to her mom's house.

Well, that and after Brent's sleeping-on-the-bottom comment, she needed to decide if she wanted to take Brent and her relationship to the next level once they were safe at her mom's home. Their kiss earlier had been off-the-charts fantastic. And running her hands over his hard muscles while he made love to her would probably be as amazing as she'd imagined a few times since.

Thinking about his hot body wasn't remotely appropriate at the moment, though. They were running for their lives.

She turned on the radio, surprised when it worked. Maybe there'd be an update about her so-called kidnapping. "Will's police scanner said they were doing random roadblocks all around Phoenix. Why would they do that?"

Brent shrugged. "Could be checking that insurance, registration are up-to-date, things like that. Bad timing for us, though."

She opened the glovebox and moved the condoms around, searching for the paperwork. "I don't see any of that in here. If we get stopped, we're dead."

He stared straight ahead as he replied, "I have the paperwork on me. If we get stopped, we'll say it's my cousin's car. We borrowed the Jeep to go camping."

She slid a condom into her pocket, just in case she decided to sleep with him. She didn't worry about him seeing her do that because he hadn't looked at her the last twenty minutes.

Brent was acting weird. Or maybe it was her. She couldn't tell if he'd been joking about sleeping with her or not. She couldn't take another man's rejection.

She forced herself to stop thinking about Brent and asked, "You're sure the car hasn't been stolen, right?"

Brent nodded but didn't elaborate. As usual.

Pop music filled the uneasy silence between them for a few minutes until he said, "I was joking earlier about being on the bottom. I'm sorry if I made you uncomfortable."

Geez. Way to make a girl's ego deflate instantly. "So you don't want to sleep with me?"

Brent smiled. "I've never wanted to sleep with any woman as much as I'd like to with you." His grin faded into a grimace. "But you're off-limits to me, remember?"

"That's ridiculous." She shook her head. "I can date whomever I choose. My parents don't get to dictate that too."

Brent's right brow arched. "To quote your father, 'Receiving a paycheck is contingent on keeping your hands off Sara. And that goes for Veronica too.'"

"He should've told Veronica to keep her paws off you." Thinking about the way Veronica flirted with Brent in the dressing room boiled Sara's blood. "I'm the only one in charge of permitting people to put their hands on me."

"Do you think we'd ever have been together if not for our situation?" Brent frowned as he changed freeways. "If you'd seen me sitting in a bar, would you have given me a second glance? Face it. I'm not, and never will be, in your league, Sara."

Him saying something so dumb just made her more determined to prove him wrong. "I would have given you lots of glances if you'd smile instead of scowl at me like you used to do at home."

He nodded.

Then remained silent as he drove.

That was more infuriating than him saying he wasn't in her league.

She crossed her arms and stared out her window again. If he wasn't going to fight with her, or for her, she'd be better off keeping her distance.

After leaving her to stew in her own juices for a solid ten minutes, he finally said, "Why did you choose to be with Scott?"

Great. Now she was going to have to rehash all that pain. "You probably think it's because he's handsome, rich, dense, and spoiled. Like you thought I was when you first met me. Right?"

Brent's jaw clenched. The first sign he'd shown of irritation. "It's the obvious reason. But that's not what I was getting at. You don't have one-night stands." When she opened her mouth to protest his assumption, he held up a finger to stop her. "Zoila told me."

Zoila had a big mouth. "Maybe I'd like one for a change. I just got dumped in front of the entire world. I don't want another real relationship right now. But I like having sex now and again."

His brows furrowed. "So I'd just be quick revenge sex in a tent to you?"

"No." Dammit! She'd hurt his feelings. She hated that. "I actually like you. A lot. I feel like this whole thing about me being off-limits is you saying you hate my lifestyle, don't want to come live in my fishbowl. Or maybe you aren't attracted to me, but you don't want to hurt my feelings by telling the truth."

He crossed three lanes of traffic, pulled the car to the shoulder, and parked. Then he laid his hands on her shoulders, turning her so they were eye to eye. His rough palms slid to her cheeks, and he pulled her face close to his. "I'm so attracted to you, it scares me." Then he kissed her. Slow, sweet, and deep. Like a man who wanted her as much as she wanted him.

He held her tight while his tongue made love to hers. Being held by Brent was as sexy as his kiss.

When he slowly leaned away, she whispered, "You're confusing me."

He closed his eyes and nodded. "I know. I'm sorry, Sara. If circumstances were different, I'd..."

With her arms still around him, and how that had happened, she had no idea, she asked, "You'd what?" She searched his eyes for the truth. He seemed truly conflicted.

He pulled away and put the Jeep in gear again. "Nothing can happen between us. Because I don't want to hurt you. I had a rough past, and I have secrets I can't share with you. We're too different. That's what I was trying to point out about why you picked Scott."

Her mom had warned about Brent's secrets. And yet she still told Sara to trust him. That went a long way with her.

She laid a hand on his arm as he searched his mirror for an opportunity to rejoin the morning traffic. "I obviously made a bad choice by being with Scott. Maybe I need to try someone the exact opposite of him. Like you." There. She'd said it. If he rejected her, she'd live with it. She'd lived through all the times her dad had made her feel unimportant. Like at the wedding when he'd used her for a photo op. She could take one more rejection.

Brent pulled back onto the highway. "I think you were with Scott because being in the public eye and growing up the child of famous people isn't as easy as it looks. Scott's parents are actors too, and then he became one. The two of you probably connected at some deep level because of your mutual upbringings. An understanding that you might not ever be able to have with another man, especially one like me."

He *did* understand about Scott.

It made her eyes burn with tears. "True about Scott. But now I want to know what it'd be like to be normal. Go to work every day without people following me everywhere. And to help people who need it. Like you do in your job."

"I don't want to be the guy you sleep with because I'm *normal*." His jaw clenched again as he negotiated another lane change. "I want to be the guy you sleep with because I'm... It doesn't matter."

"It does matter." She squeezed his forearm. "I want to sleep with you because I'm attracted to who you are as a person. And because it'd make Zoila happy. She says you're the kind of man I need."

"Time out." He shook his head. "Bringing Zoila into the discussion is playing dirty."

"Because you care what Zoila thinks too?" She mothered him like she did Sara. Zoila mothered everyone in her dad's house. Except Veronica.

There was something about Brent's childhood growing up with a flawed mother, combined with his hard-bodied outer shell, that made her want to hug him, but he wouldn't want to hear her say that.

He took her hand. "How about we table this discussion until after Miller and company are behind bars?" The music stopped, and the weather report came on. Brent released her hand to turn up the volume.

After a few minutes, the station finally teased more news on her kidnapping after a commercial break. "I bet they found my mom's car by now."

When the anchor's voice returned, she said, "Authorities report that a car owned by Sara Chapman's mother, Annalisa Botelli, was found abandoned at a state park west of Phoenix. According to witnesses, a woman fitting Sara Chapman's description was seen in a nearby town dressed in workout clothes and asking to use a pay phone. Sara's hair had been cut short and dyed blonde since her father's wedding on Saturday. There was no sign of Brent Jackson, the man believed to have kidnapped Sara, but police still believe Sara is in danger and asked to be contacted with any relevant information. Keep it right here for all the latest news and weather on the top of the hour."

Brent turned down the volume again. "Only a description of you. None of the Jeep. Get in the back and stay down. They're looking for two people."

Sara joined Mittens on the small rear seat. "So do we lay low and travel later tonight still?"

"We can't risk anyone recognizing you. I'll take the exit coming up that'll take us north to Show Low, and then we'll grab I-40 all the way in. It's the fastest from here. But we might still need Jake's help. If Miller has figured out we're headed for your mother's house, he'll have people waiting."

"Maybe we can find a phone in one of the smaller towns we'll pass through before we hit 40." Jake would know what to do. He'd keep them safe. Hopefully.

Brent let out a string of curse words under his breath as the vehicle slowed down. "There's a roadblock ahead. Get under the sleeping bag on the floor. Drag some things on top of you. Hurry."

Sara grabbed the sleeping bag, two grocery bags of food, and the tent from the rear. The Jeep was small, so she crammed as much of herself as she could under the backseat and then laid the sleeping bag over her legs. She put the tent on her calves and the bags of food near her middle.

Her heartbeat picked up speed again, making her breaths too shallow. She had to calm down or she'd be a heaving mess under the fabric. "Should I keep my gun on me if we get pulled over?"

"No. Stuff it under the seat if we have to get out. And let me do all the talking." He placed Mittens on top of her, then his jacket. "Stay as still as you can. They're picking people at random, letting others pass through, so we might not get searched."

She drew a deep breath and then pulled the sleeping bag over her head. With her eyes closed, like that was going to help anything, she forced herself to draw air into her lungs while she counted to seven. She let her breath out to the same count.

Visualizing calm blue waters, she used her meditation training to help her calm the hell down.

Brent was good at lying. He'd been amazing at it with Will in the camper. Much better than she'd ever be at it. He'd do fine with the cops at the roadblock if she could do her part. And be still.

But was being a good liar a positive trait for a man she was falling for?

$$\infty \; \infty \; \infty$$

Brent tapped his fingers on the Jeep's steering wheel as they slowly moved forward in line at the roadblock. If they were busted, he'd have to blow his cover and arrange to take Sara into custody immediately, so Miller wouldn't have a chance to touch her.

While Sara was hiding, he pulled out his phone to check on things from Rick's end. No new activity since his last text. Odd, because they'd found Annalisa's car. And ID'd Sara. Something was wrong. There was no denying it anymore.

Any update on Miller?

As the cars slowly inched ahead, his phone remained quiet. Brent scrolled through Rick's last text looking for anything to help him understand what was going on. Then he reread the text about supplies in the glovebox of the Jeep.

He leaned over and opened the glovebox. Pushing the condoms aside, he lifted the piece of carpet on the bottom. His fingers landed on a cutout, so he lifted it up. Inside was a burner cell phone. He quickly powered it on.

It showed an outstanding text message, so he navigated the unfamiliar screens until he found it. Sent just a few minutes prior.

Dude. They took all of us off the case. Said you're a suspect now along with Sara so it's an internal affairs issue. By noon today, everyone will be looking for you guys.

Dammit. Had he been sent undercover just to be set up? His boss had been surprised how quickly Brent had figured out the investment patterns, but then that was one of the things his numbers gift gave him. Had he been sent undercover to test how tight the scam was?

He tapped out a reply to Rick's personal phone, hoping he'd be online.

Go to my apartment. Grab my bag with thumb drives on the kitchen counter. Evidence to prove I'm innocent is in there.

Rick replied, Your apartment was raided while you were at the wedding yesterday. They sent Cramer. He came to my house this a.m., he was so freaked. Says orders came from way at the top. He wasn't even supposed to tell Braydon about taking the drives. They took your and Braydon's equipment at the office too.

Cramer, part of their Friday-night drinking group, was a friend and one of the most decorated field agents in their office. But things still weren't adding up. Why would the raid be kept from their boss if the top command legitimately thought Brent was on the take? And why let him and Sara run? They could've sent the chopper after them and ended it all last night.

Why not detain us at the wedding?

Rick typed back: ??? Time to Dr. the data to get the arrest warrant?

Maybe. Who dropped off the Jeep? Can u be sure the new cell won't be tracked?

Yep. Called in a favor from the Phoenix office. You remember agent Morales from the academy? She thinks I'm handsome even if u don't. You're paying for her plane fare out here next week, btw.

Rick and all his womanizing might have finally paid off. You got it. Appreciate the assist.

Me and Cramer know you're clean, bro. I tried your personal cell to warn you, but you must've ditched it. We'll do what we can to help.

Thx.

Good luck.

He and Sara were screwed. Miller probably ordered the hit on their lives so he could pin a small part of the scam on Sara and the new bookkeeper, and then pocket the rest from past operations while walking away a hero.

Brent had suspected but hadn't been able to prove that the millions in Sara's bank account was probably just a fraction of the overall take.

He'd told Braydon with the file in the dressing room that'd been photographed, Brent was close to breaking open the case. Braydon probably told the same to his superiors. Getting closer must've set off alarms to whomever the higher-ranking dirty agent was. By throwing Sara and Brent under the bus, the traitor agent hoped to end the investigation that only Brent had been able to make headway on in the past five years. Braydon said they'd both get significant promotions if Brent could crack the case.

But that meant staying alive to do it.

He searched different radio stations to hear any further news about him and Sara as they crawled forward occasionally in line at the roadblock. It was almost nine, so they had a few hours before noon to figure out how to get a new ride. They might have to legit steal a car this time.

If they could get through the roadblock, that was. Busting out of line was a sure way to get chased.

They were on their own now, operating blind.

He needed help from someone he could trust. Zach, his mentor and former instructor from the academy, the one who promised him the house on the water if Brent could afford it one day, was the only person he fully trusted. But Zach often went deep-sea fishing for days in his retirement.

Brent sent his mentor a text:

Hey. It's Brent. Caught up in the middle of the Sara Chapman investigation. Insiders warned I'm being framed. Need your help.

After he sent the text, Brent debated telling Sara he'd found the burner phone. But they were close to the roadblock, so he tucked it into his pocket. Then he pried open his FBI-issued phone and ripped out the battery and yanked out its guts to leave it disabled. He'd toss the mangled mess out right after the roadblock but slid the parts under the seat until it was safe to do so.

He called out to Sara, "Just about there. I'll let you know when we're clear."

A muffled "'Kay" sounded from the rear.

If they got past the roadblock, they couldn't go to Annalisa's. If Rick was right, whoever was in charge at his office had probably been letting the chase go on until they could tamper with the evidence to show he and Sara were the ones laundering the cash. Miller apparently planned a dramatic end to the chase. One that would play out on national television to make him and his partners look like heroes.

But only if he and Sara were too dead to testify.

Chapter Thirteen

Sara, still buried under the mound of camping equipment, drew in another long breath, held it, and then let it go. What was taking so damn long? They had to be close to the checkpoint.

Brent's quiet voice called out, "They're talking to the people in the car in front of us. We're next." Sounds of the rickety old window cranked open, and unfamiliar voices made her close her eyes again to concentrate on being still.

If someone recognized Brent, it might all be over soon. Undoubtedly, by now, the press had shown the pictures of her and Brent at the wedding. The cops might be looking for out-of-date car registrations, but they had to also be on the lookout for her and Brent.

Brent had spiky blond hair and sexy chin stubble now, so that was something. And the cops would be looking for two people, not a guy with a cat. Those facts didn't do a thing to stop her heart from pounding like a bass drum, though.

The car inched forward, and Sara tried her best to go limp. What would happen to them if the police busted them? Would they be sent right back to Miller to be killed?

Brent's voice called out, "Thanks! Have a good day." And then the Jeep picked up speed.

After a few minutes and some rustling around under his seat, Brent cranked up the groaning window. "Stay down, but you can take all that crap off you. The backup of cars got so bad that they flagged us by and the car behind us too."

"Thank God." Sara flung the material off her face. Mittens mewed and then snuggled on the floor beside her. "Look for a pay phone. I need to call Jake. My heart can't take much more of this."

"Will do."

Sara threw the rest of the things that had been covering her into the back and then crawled up on the backseat to lie with her cat on something more comfortable. After her heart rate returned to normal, she said, "While I was lying under all that stuff, freaking out, my mind raced with all sorts of dark thoughts."

Brent reached back through the seats and gave her thigh a quick pat. "We'll figure this out. I promise."

Hopefully. "I was thinking earlier that if I died today, I'd never be able to fulfill my dreams. No one wants to die without some sort of legacy." She scooted over so she could see his eyes in the rearview mirror.

His reflected gaze cut to hers. "You mean like both your parents? So famous, their legacy will live on years after they're gone?"

She hadn't thought about it like that. "Fame is a plague I can't wait to shed. My parents pay an even bigger price for theirs. Especially my mom. I just want to privately help people. Even though I'll never get rich doing that. You're not going to believe this, but money doesn't matter to me."

Brent's right brow arched in the reflection. "Says the girl who has always had plenty of it. Not having it sucks."

She nodded. "My work at the homeless shelter made me acutely aware of how fortunate I've been so far. And how hard your life must have been at times. But the satisfaction of knowing I've helped people who struggled to care for themselves or their kids makes me feel..."

His gaze switched from the road to hers again. "Like a benevolent rich person? It took lots of money for you to save that shelter. It takes money to have security."

"I was going to say it made me feel like I'd made a difference. That maybe I helped a kid like you were to know that there's hope for him or her too."

Brent shook his head. "I never sat around *hoping* someone like you would save me. I always knew I couldn't depend on anyone but myself."

"Of course. But didn't anyone have a positive influence on your life growing up?"

He shifted gears as he prepared to pass a slow-moving truck on the two-lane road. "One of my professors, Zach Walters, who saw my gift of seeing trends in numbers, challenged me to learn how to invest money. He promised he'd sell me his house on the ocean if I could save five million by the time he's ready to go live on his boat and sail the world. The house has got to be worth ten times that."

"Sounds like a great investment." She scooted closer with interest. "What would you buy with the money you made after you sold it?"

"I'd never sell it." He shook his head. "My mother once dated a rich guy who had a house on a lake. We lived with him for a year or so, and it was the best year of my life. I swore then that I'd have a house like that. Paid for in full so no one could ever take it away from me."

She hated that he still feared losing another home. "Why do you think Zach offered you that opportunity?"

Brent shrugged. "I guess because he didn't want the house in Malibu anyway. He inherited it from his parents. He's from a rich family like yours."

"I think it's because he saw potential in you and wanted to give you *hope* for the future. Zach helped you see that you have a gift, and by using it, you'll never go hungry or be homeless again. Sometimes having people believe in us gives us the courage to try new things."

"Maybe." A small grin tugged at his lips. "But I'd pay big money to see you try to live on forty K a year."

She poked him in the arm. "Maybe I'll hire that freaky brain of yours. You can invest my measly savings for me, and we can both have a house in Malibu."

Brent smiled. "If you're still talking to me after all this is over, you've got a deal."

A little pang struck her heart at the thought of never seeing Brent again. He'd definitely grown on her. "You're sort of bossy sometimes, but you're an interesting guy. Why wouldn't I talk to you?" Something was wrong. She could feel it and found herself holding her breath as she waited for his answer.

His smile slowly faded in the reflection of the mirror. "Because I'm an undercover FBI agent." He reached into his pocket and pulled out a cell phone. "And I've just gone dark because Miller and his FBI cohort, whoever that might be, have stolen my evidence against them and changed it to look like you and I are guilty of money laundering. We need help. Call Jake on this burner phone."

Gut punch.

With a capital G!

It was hard to breathe as she accepted the phone. "You're an agent. And had a phone all this time?"

"Yes." Brent's knuckles turned white as he gripped the wheel tighter. "I'm sorry I had to lie to you. I'd never hurt you on purpose, Sara."

An FBI agent? Brent? Not her bodyguard.

Her mother's words when they spoke last started to make sense. The money in her account was dirty money. Her father managed it and was friends with Miller, so that made her dad guilty by association? "You've been spying on my family for weeks." Her stomach roiled at the violation. Like that time she found a paparazzi's hidden camera in her hotel bathroom. But worse. Because it was Brent. And she'd come to care for him.

"Just doing my job, Sara. Trying to keep you safe."

She closed her eyes and pinched the bridge of her nose. She would not cry. "You don't think my father is guilty, do you?" Her dad could be insensitive and uninterested in her life, but who the hell would use their daughter to launder money? Then it dawned on her. "It was my account with all the money. You've been investigating me too."

He nodded.

"I haven't done anything wrong."

"Then why run to your mom's house? Not take me up on my offer to go to the FBI?" His eyes begged her for an answer she couldn't fully give him. People would never believe her mother could see things in the future with her dreams.

"Because I knew we'd be safe at my mother's house. With the police commissioner trying to kill us, it made the most sense to be with someone the media gives a voice to like no other. She could shine light on Miller's corruption."

"But how did your mother know to warn you?"

Tears burned her eyes. "My mother has nothing to do with this. It was just her motherly sixth sense thing like I told you. Nothing more." That was all she could say without betraying her mom.

Brent's jaw clenched. "That's the part that's hard to believe."

"Oh, I see. So you only kissed the suspected criminal to keep your cover intact?" Just when she'd thought she'd found a decent guy, he'd been lying to her like all the rest.

"The first time. In the RV. Yes." He huffed out a breath. "I kissed you the other times because I wanted to kiss you. I shouldn't have. Technically, you're still a suspect."

Anger instantly replaced betrayal. "Even better. You kissed me, maybe planned to sleep with me, and then you were going to arrest me?" How had she been so stupid to fall for a guy who could lie right to her face? Again.

"I know you're not guilty." He found a pullout and stopped the car. Then he got out of the Jeep and yanked the front seat up to make room for him to slide in the small backseat beside her. "Let me explain. Please."

When he reached for her hand, she crossed her arms. "It doesn't matter. This is where we part ways, pal." It hurt even worse to think that he was just with her to gain evidence against her parents.

"If you try to escape, I'll have to arrest you. For your own safety."

Not if she was quicker than him. She was smaller, could jump into the front easier. "I'll give you two minutes to explain. Starting now," she said, even as she planned how to catch him off guard.

But he caught her off guard first by scooping her up and placing her on his lap, trapping her against his hard chest, and forcing her to look him in the eye.

Sadness and remorse swam in his gaze. It softened her urge to hit him. Slightly. "Please just let me go, Brent. You go your way, and I'll go mine."

"I can't. We're both in danger." He closed his eyes and winced as if in pain. "Besides that, I don't want to let you go, Sara. I have feelings for you I've never felt before." He slowly opened his eyes and met her gaze again. "I would have never slept with you under false pretenses."

He cared for her too? But how could she trust what he was saying?

Thinking back to their many conversations, Brent *had* insisted she'd been off-limits. He'd told her that more than once. And she was the one who chose to kiss *him* in the camper. But was he still lying to her? Telling her things just to make her stay with him? "Tell me the part about how much you care for me again. But with your eyes open this time."

Please let that part be real. Please.

He slid his rough hands along the sides of her face, staring intensely into her eyes. "I care for you more than I have ever cared for anyone. Please let me protect you. I couldn't bear it if anything happened to you."

Brent was a trained liar. She'd seen how easily he'd lied to the RV people. But not with the sincerity his eyes currently held.

And she couldn't deny her body's physical reaction to Brent. No other man's smile had warmed her heart as Brent's did.

She should *hate* him for lying to her, but apparently in his case, she was incapable of it.

It was so damned hard to stay mad at him when he looked at her like that. With nervous expectation in his eyes, as if she rejected him, he'd die right on the spot. No one could fake that. Not even her Oscar award-winning parents, some of the best thespians in the world.

She laid her forehead on his shoulder and whispered, "I have an overwhelming urge to punch you, but at the same time, I still want to kiss you. It makes no sense. What the hell is wrong with me?"

"Nothing. Punch me as hard as you'd like." His arms tightened around her, pulling her closer. "Then kiss me as long as you want."

She shook her head. "I'd never hit you, but I'm still too hurt to kiss you."

"Fair enough." He gave her a quick squeeze. "Maybe one day, you'll forgive me."

"Maybe. But only after you invest my whopping thousand bucks in savings so I can have a house in Malibu next to yours. It'll be the only way I'd ever be able to afford it on a counselor's salary."

He released his hold on her and smiled, thawing the coating of ice around her heart a bit more. "You actually have almost eleven hundred. And forty thousand a year won't even pay the taxes and upkeep on a house in Malibu, so I'll make you plenty more. We need to keep moving. Will you please call Jake now?"

"Geez. Do you know my bra size too, Mr. Nosey?"

"I'd be happy to gues—"

She gave him a look that cut off his almost stupid answer, then lifted the phone still clutched in her hand and dialed Jake's number. Her freaky ability to recall anything written was even better than having a contact list in her cell. Numbers got lost when system updates occurred on her phone, but never in her head.

While the phone rang, she asked, "Is Brent even your real name?" She found the speaker button so Brent or whatever his name was could hear too.

"Yes. But my last name is Keiser, not Jackson."

"And all the stuff about your childhood and mom? Is any of that real?"

"All of it. I avoided lying to you as much as I could."

At least he'd told the truth about his family. "And this Jeep filled with condoms?"

Brent smiled. "That was Rick's idea. You twisted his ear while you danced with him at the wedding. He's an agent too. That was his form of torture. Reminding me I couldn't be with you."

"Rick deserved to have his ear twisted. His hands were all over me." After the fourth ring, she said, "Jake won't recognize the number. He'll probably let it go to voicemail."

Then a gravelly "Morris" sounded.

"Jake? It's, Sara."

"Hey, kid. 'Bout time you checked in. Your mom is about to lose her mind. Where are you and the kidnapper now?"

Kidnapper? She chuckled. Jake was the best. He'd be sure they were safe. Without *lying* to her. "Heading toward Show Low."

"That works. But you can't come here. The place is swarming with cops. Mario's got a plane on standby. I'll call you back with the details in a few."

"Thanks, Jake. Maybe you're not such a bad guy after all," she teased. She'd always love Jake like a brother even though he wasn't married to her sister anymore.

"You can buy me a beer and tell me all about it later." He hung up.

Brent asked, "Who is Mario?"

"Mario Giovanni. He owns a casino in Las Vegas. He's also my sister's father, but Dani didn't know that until recently."

Brent's brows shot up. "The Giovannis are mobsters, Sara. His family is one of the most notorious there is."

"Mario isn't a mobster... Anymore. He's a legitimate businessman now."

"Perfect." Brent ran a hand down his face. "Crooked police, bankers, FBI agents, Russians, and now mobsters? It can't get much more complicated than this."

Sara smiled inwardly. Brent hadn't met the Botelli women yet, or he'd know that wasn't true. Things would definitely get a lot more complicated than Brent could even imagine once her mother and sister with their dreams and visions got involved. If her grandmother joined them too, it'd officially be chaos.

∞ ∞ ∞

With Mittens tucked under his arm, Brent followed Sara into the mobster's luxurious Gulfstream jet. Luckily, Show Low had a medium-sized airport. He'd leave the Jeep in long-term parking and hope no one noticed it for a bit. When the FBI found the Jeep, it'd be doubtful they'd make the connection between them and the mob guy's plane right away. Maybe it'd buy them some time. He really needed to talk to Zach. He'd know what to do. They couldn't trust anyone in law enforcement.

Even more, he hoped Sara would smile at him again. She'd been quiet the whole drive.

A man with olive skin and with a touch of gray at the temples folded Sara up in his arms, blocking the aisle. Brent had no choice but to wait behind them.

Mario said, "*Bella.* Your mother is just sick with worry. She's on her way back from London. I'll keep you safe now."

"Thank you for coming for us, Mario." Sara closed her eyes and hung on to the man as if he were a life raft in the middle of the ocean. The relieved tears that slid down her cheeks revealed Sara wasn't as tough as she liked him to think.

It hurt a little that she didn't feel as safe with him as she did with the mob guy. But then, maybe she didn't feel the same for him as he did for her. She'd never said how she felt after he'd spilled his guts all over the backseat of that damned Jeep. Other than how much she wanted to hit him.

Maybe he'd been an idiot to confess his feelings for her. He'd said things to her he'd never told anyone else.

Sara, as if suddenly realizing Brent was there, said, "Oh. Sorry." She wiped away her tears and held out a hand. "Mario, I'd like you to meet my very own personal undercover FBI agent, Brent. And Mittens, our stowaway cat."

He appreciated she'd left his last name out of the intros but wasn't as happy about revealing his FBI status. It could get him kicked off the plane, or worse. And even though he was tempted, he refused to read more into Sara's comment about the cat being "ours" and not "hers."

He stuck his hand out. "Appreciate the ride."

The mob guy's eyes gleamed with amusement. "I suspect you'll be the first and only FBI agent I ever welcome on my plane. Especially one holding a cat."

Brent forced a smile at the little dig. "Sara loves the cat. I think we can both agree that Sara's safety and happiness is the first priority here?"

"Well said." Mario shook Brent's hand. "Shall we get going, then? You two can take a seat here, next to me." Mario motioned to the flight attendant to close the hatch and then took a seat in a big club chair.

Relieved at not being kicked to the curb, he sat beside her in one of the club chairs and settled in. Four other seats in the rear were occupied with men who looked like "muscle." All wearing dark suits. Scowling at him as if he had the plague. Their massive shoulders were all wider than the seats they sat in. The nonverbal vibes they sent out said they'd be happy to shoot him for sport.

Could he and Sara trust the mob guy, or was he committing career suicide by conspiring with possible felons? Or maybe he'd end up swimming with the fishes in cement shoes.

Chapter Fourteen

Sara stood with her arms crossed in Mario's penthouse atop his old Chicago-themed casino, staring at the Vegas skyline. The hotels were decked out for Christmas, with gold and silver everywhere, but things were too shiny, too gold, and lacked that homey charm the diner in Arizona had with its silly elves and sweet hand-painted window displays.

The setting sun outside cast long shadows across the busy street below. Tourists in colorful tops, scantily dressed women handing out fliers for burlesque shows, and men in suits swarmed the sidewalks. Like race cars battling for pole positions, eager to get on with all the fun Vegas had to offer. Fun she and Brent weren't allowed to partake in or risk being arrested.

Still a little hurt because of Brent's "necessary" lies, and with her mom for not telling her who Brent really was, and mostly with her father for dragging her into his mess, she reminded herself that she couldn't choose whom she loved. She had to accept the ones she loved for who they were, flaws and all. Even the stubborn Agent Keiser, with whom she was currently having a frustrating conversation.

She glanced over her shoulder for one more attempt at reason.

Brent still tapped away on the secure laptop Mario had provided, so she said, "I don't get it. You trust Mario enough to believe that the computer is secure, but not enough to let him help us?"

Brent's fingers continued to fly across the keys. "He'd probably be in jail if he didn't have top-notch security on his computers. That's what I trust."

She rolled her eyes. "He gave up the only woman he'd ever loved, my mom, to keep Dani safe until he could be released from his family's hold. It took almost thirty years. Bad people don't do selfless things like that."

"Yes, they do. Mobsters are super protective of their families. Until someone displeases them. Then they kill them. Haven't you ever seen *The Godfather*?"

"No. But we need help. I vote we let Mario do that."

Brent's response was a loud grunt as he continued to type.

"I get it. You're the dictator, and I'm the dictor-ee, or whatever you call those poor people whose opinions are meaningless." She glanced at Mittens, who stopped grooming her paws atop Mario's silk couch. The cat could probably feel the tension in the air too.

Brent smiled. "Once I get responses to some inquiries, we'll talk about what we want to do next. We're still a team, but someone needs to run the plays if we want to win. That's why ships and sports teams have captains."

She gave him a snappy salute. "Aye, aye, Captain Dictator."

He ignored her sarcasm and continued working.

While she studied Brent's earnest, handsome face bent close to the screen, her heart warmed for him despite their disagreement. He was a good—but incredibly stubborn—man.

Instead of working on the ups and downs of Wall Street, he chose the steady government paycheck and a guaranteed retirement plan because what he needed most was security in his life. Something he'd never had as a child. Something he gave others by being in law enforcement and helping keep the country safe.

He'd finally admitted to Mario that three agents before Brent had made zero headway on the case that took him a few weeks to crack. How could she still feel hurt and betrayed by Brent? He'd been doing his job. And part of his job had been to lie to her to protect her.

If only he'd trust Mario as she did. But that was probably like the cat guarding the mouse hole in Brent's mind. She'd just have to be persistent and change his views.

She turned back to the skyline and let out a long, frustrated, sigh. They were both prisoners, albeit in the most excellent jail cell in the world. She hated waiting for fate to do what it would with them. She wanted action. To do something to clear their names. What, she wasn't sure, though.

A big set of arms wrapped her up in a hug from behind before Brent whispered, "What's wrong? That was a pretty dramatic sigh."

"I come from a dramatic family. It's in my blood. You'll see for yourself. My mom and sister will be here in a few minutes."

"I thought maybe you realized that your life is now exactly like Eloise's. Stuck on the top floor of the hotel. Maybe you should change Mittens' name to Snickerdee."

"You mean Skipperdee. And please don't say that in front of my mom. She's sensitive about having been away so often filming movies when Dani and I were growing up."

"Got it." He hugged her tighter. "Anything else I should know before I meet your mom?"

She laughed. "No. She's a normal person like anyone else. She just has an extraordinary job." And an extraordinary ability to see the future in dreams. But she couldn't tell him that. "And she's super stubborn, so the two of you should get along just fine."

"But is she a dictator like me?" He nibbled on her ear, sending a delightful shiver up her spine.

"At times. But she's a lovable one. You, the jury's still out on."

"I'll have to work on my closing argument, then." His lips moved to her neck, making her pulse kick into overdrive. "I apologize for being a little star-struck. I used to watch your mom in movies and think she was the prettiest woman I'd ever seen. I read recently that men half her age still line up for dates."

Sara leaned her head back on his shoulder. "She is beautiful. Even without makeup, but you'll never see her like that. She's always camera ready." Her mom had been voted the most beautiful woman in Hollywood and even in the world a few times. "What people don't know is how hard she's worked to maintain her looks. All the daily skin routines and fake smiling so her eyes don't crease. I haven't seen her eat anything with carbs in like fifteen years. Me? I'm happy to eat lasagna and cheesy bread now and then and be average looking."

"Average looking?" He stopped making her knees weak with his kisses and slowly turned her around. With a frown creasing his forehead, he said, "You don't really believe that, do you?"

She shrugged. "All my life, the press has pointed out that my nose is slightly crooked, and that my lips aren't as full as my mother's and sister's. Oh, and a so-called beauty expert decided that my eyes are a tad too widely spaced."

"Yeah. I'd noticed that too but didn't want to mention it."

She jabbed her finger into his gut and got a satisfying grunt.

"I'm kidding. That person needs to get a life. Your eyes are perfectly spaced."

"Well, thanks, but as if that wasn't rude enough, they'd say it's a shame I didn't get the Botelli curves. Like it's a crime to have an average bra size these days."

Between kisses on her collarbone, he whispered, "Actually, you have a larger than—"

"I'm going to pretend you're just guessing you know what size my bra is, and that it's not documented in an FBI file somewhere." She pondered how embarrassing that'd be. "Is it?"

He laid a quick kiss on her lips. "Can't tell you or I'd have to kill you. Go on."

Brother. It probably *was* in his stupid file on her. "Then these so-called experts would wonder aloud why I didn't get all my flaws fixed so that I could follow in my genetically perfect parents' footsteps to the big screen. Like they were both born looking like they do? Please. I'm perfectly happy with the original version of me."

"I wouldn't change a thing about you either, Sara." He slid his hands along her cheeks and lifted her chin. "Don't tell your mom, but she got bumped to second place for the prettiest woman I'd ever seen once I met you. More than that, I respect what you're made of. Kindness, compassion, and courage. I've never met anyone I admire more."

Wow. That made her heart turn to a big puddle of goo. "Careful. Remember what you said earlier? That you'd never be the kind of guy who'd tell me I'm beautiful?"

"Because it's a given." He laid his lips on hers and kissed her. When his tongue joined the party, it made her sigh again.

Man, Brent could kiss. And make her feel like the most desired woman in the world.

She wrapped her arms around his neck, pressed her body against his solid one, and kissed him back. Hard. To show him how much she wanted him.

He softly groaned as his hands slid to her rear end. Brent gave a quick squeeze right before a cleared throat from behind them put a stop to things before they got R-rated.

Brent slowly ended their kiss, but the desire lingering in his eyes promised more where that'd come from. She looked forward to seeing just how much more.

Her mom called out, "It's my turn for a hug."

At the sight of her mom, Sara had to blink back the tears that threatened. There'd been moments in the past days she wondered if she'd ever see her mother again. Now she looked photo-shoot ready as always, even though she'd just stepped off an overseas flight. "I've never been happier to see you, Mom."

Annalisa swept Sara into her arms with all the dramatic flair she was known for in Hollywood. "Hi, sweetheart. I'm glad to see you in one piece too. And I love your new hair!" After a long hug and a kiss to the forehead, her mom continued, "I haven't slept, I was so worried about my beautiful, far-from-average-looking daughter."

How long had her mom been standing there? Had she seen Brent's hands wander? Sara was twenty-six, but her mom had a way of making her feel like she was sixteen sometimes.

Before Sara could answer, her mom turned to Brent. "Funny story about Sara's nose, Brent. It's exactly what mine looked like before my agent made me change it. I think it suits Sara better than it ever suited me."

"It looks perfect to me. And it's an honor to meet her nose donor." Brent smiled and held out a hand for a shake.

Her mom ignored his outstretched hand and gathered him up in a bear hug that turned his cheeks an adorable shade of red. "Thank you for keeping Sara safe. If there's ever anything I can do to return the favor, it's yours. I'm even willing to forgive you for bumping me off my pedestal when you met my gorgeous daughter."

Her mother had been standing there for some time, apparently. Eavesdropping. "Brent did us a favor, Mom. Someone has to keep that huge ego of yours in check. Where's Dani?"

Annalisa kept an arm slung around Brent's shoulders. "She's waiting for you in the den. Run and see her while Brent and I have a chat."

Alarm bells clanged. Her mother was up to something. "I think I'd rather stay and protect Brent from the interrogation."

Her mom's grin turned mischievous. "Brent will be fine. Your sister would like to talk to you about something important. Now, go!"

Sara glanced at Brent. The expression on his face was somewhere between sheer panic and pure joy at the prospect of talking to one of his idols. "You'll be okay?"

He nodded. "I've had extensive interrogation training. I think I can handle your mom."

"Training in traditional methods, like waterboarding and sleep deprivation. She can be worse. Don't say I didn't warn you." Sara shook her head as she made her way toward the private elevator that would take her to the den level. "Behave, Mother. I know Brent's cute, but he's mine!"

Despite her mother's reputation for dating younger men—one that the publicist falsely had spun to keep her real relationship with Mario private—her mom would never cross a line with Brent. But it was fun to make him squirm a bit.

Sara poked the button to summon the elevator and then turned to gauge Brent's reaction. With a mile-wide grin, he mouthed, *Thank you.*

She wasn't sure if his gratitude was for forgiving his dictator ways or declaring him off-limits. Maybe both.

He was hers, all right.

And she intended to keep him.

∞ ∞ ∞

Brent studied Annalisa as she poured them both a glass of wine. She'd been compared with the classical good looks of Sophia Loren. Modern-day beauties competed for that top spot, but the press always declared Sara's mom the winner hands down. He had to agree.

But never in his wildest dreams did he imagine he'd ever be in the same room as Annalisa Botelli, much less served a glass of wine by her. Her man-eating reputation and fame were almost intimidating, but her obvious love and concern for her daughter made her approachable and real.

She held out a glass. "I imagine you have some questions for me?" Her eyes never left his as she sipped her wine. As if searching for something.

She'd pored her drink from the same bottle, so one sip couldn't hurt.

"I do. Have questions." He took a sip, and his mouth exploded with notes of aged wood and fruit. Must be what expensive wine tasted like. "Wow. That's amazing. Thank you."

"My pleasure. Let's sit." She swept a hand out toward the couches that were so nice, he hadn't wanted to sit on them while still wearing Scott's ratty sweats. He grabbed his borrowed laptop to take notes.

Brent sat on the very edge of the cushion while Annalisa arranged herself on the sofa across from him with all the grace of a princess. After she smoothed her skirt in a way he'd seen Sara do, Annalisa set her glass down and folded her hands. "You'd like to know how I'm involved in this, I imagine?" Mittens decided Annalisa's shimmery dress would make an excellent place for a nap and jumped onto the actress's lap.

"Sorry. I'll take her." He started to rise, but Annalisa lifted a hand to stop him.

"The cat is fine. Mario told me Sara had taken in another stray. Believe me, this is better than the mangy roadrunner she brought home when she was ten."

Cute, and so typically Sara. But could a person catch a roadrunner? He'd have to ask Sara about that later.

He laid his glass down on a coaster made of something gold on the coffee table and then got back to finding out precisely what Annalisa knew about the money laundering. "Sara said something about motherly instincts made you warn her about Holden, but that can't be the whole story."

Annalisa shook her head. "Sara's father has had money issues since I've known him. I don't talk about that with Sara often, because she loves him. But when a few weeks ago he asked if I'd like to invest in a "sure thing" he found, I listened and then asked him to send me more information. When he said I had to promise to keep the details to myself, that raised red flags."

Brent tapped notes into the laptop as he asked, "Has he asked to borrow money or to invest in his projects in the past?"

"Yes. Often. And he never hesitated to use Sara's well-being as the reason, preying on my desire to protect her." She leaned closer. "Holden is charming, but he isn't a good man, Brent. I think maybe now Sara will finally see that for herself."

Says the woman involved with a guy who used to be a mobster. "What happened next?"

"I told Holden I'd think about it, and then forwarded the emails to Mario for him to look into." She reached into a purse at her feet and pulled out a cell phone. After she unlocked it and found what she searched for, she handed the phone to him. "You're welcome to read the emails if you wish. Make copies if you'd like."

Brent accepted the phone, scrolled through the emails, then forwarded them to the new laptop and Zach. After he handed the phone back, he said, "That still doesn't explain how you knew about me."

Annalisa put the cat down then stood and walked to the windows. With her arms crossed and staring out the windows at the bright lights of the strip, mirroring Sara's stance a few moments before, Annalisa said, "That's where things get a little tricky. Things that could hurt Sara if she finds out. I hate to risk it. Can we skip that part for now?"

"Sara can handle it. But I doubt you'd fare as well in jail." Annalisa was like his mother, pampered and spoiled. A jail cell would be Annalisa's worst nightmare. His best bet to get her to spill.

"Is that a threat, Agent Keiser?"

Agent Keiser? His stomach clenched.

How could she possibly know his real last name? The media had all reported his last name as Jackson. And he'd been with Sara the whole time. She hadn't told Mario or her mother what his real name was.

It made trusting no one but Zach his only option going forward. He hoped Rick hadn't been involved too, but wouldn't risk finding out. He'd cut off contact with his best friend also. "No threat. A fact. Miller and his men know you know something. A jail cell might be best for your protection."

"And yet Miller's men, who've been guarding my house and my plane night and day, have no idea I slipped out right underneath their noses." Annalisa turned and raised a brow. "After Dani's kidnapping as a child, I made sure my family and I could disappear at a moment's notice, never to be found. You, on the other hand, can be arrested with one phone call. You might want to reconsider your tone, Brent."

Time to change tactics. He'd underestimated Annalisa's fortitude. Maybe that was where Sara got hers from.

"I apologize." He went back into the archives in his mind to Negotiation 101 class. "Why don't we start over? Please know that my chief concern right now is clearing Sara's name and keeping her safe. Help me do that. In return, you'll have my word I'll do my best to shield Sara from any testimony that could be hurtful to her if I possibly can."

Annalisa turned her back on him and peered out the windows again. "Let's skip the part about how I know you're an agent and focus on why I told her to trust you."

It'd be disturbing if Mario was her source when it came to Brent's identity, but for now, he'd take what he could get. "Fine. I'm all ears."

"You're all hands from what I saw earlier with Sara, but we'll get to that part in a bit." She turned around and returned to her place on the couch. "Many years ago, Holden informed me that he could no longer afford to keep Zoila and Justin employed. The two people who Sara loved like family during the parade of women Holden dated and married. So I gave them both a raise and told them they reported to me going forward and I expected regular updates about my daughter. Sara was never to know."

"Like spies? Who reported Sara's actions to you?" No wonder Annalisa didn't want Sara to know about that. Sara loved them both. It'd be a massive betrayal to her. Although Sara had said earlier she'd guessed Zoila was on her mom's payroll.

"You don't understand. Sara moved to LA as a restless teenager, claiming she wanted to be a bigger part of her father's life. The daughter of two famous parents, no less." Annalisa lifted her hands in clear frustration. "She gives people the benefit of the doubt. Always. Until they prove themselves to be untrustworthy, she trusts. She's been hurt badly because of that. Worse, Holden wasn't supervising her, and she got into some trouble. Zoila and Justin have always had her best interests at heart. They're the ones who both told me you seemed trustworthy. I simply repeated their sentiments to Sara in case there was trouble."

"How did you know to warn her that she was going to be in danger at the wedding? Did Holden warn you? Or perhaps Mario knew?" He watched her for a reaction. Some sign of where the information had originated.

She shook her head. "Neither of them told me. I just had a bad feeling. I'd asked Sara to come home a little early for Christmas so I'd know she'd be safe and away from whatever her father was up to."

A bad feeling? Seriously? Did she really expect him to believe that? Sara had been warned; she'd told him that right after the wedding. That was why she thought he was a bodyguard. "You need to come clean. For Sara's sake. Otherwise, it could look to a jury like you were both involved with the money laundering too."

Annalisa huffed out a breath. "I suspect at some point, I'll have no choice. But first, I have a few things I need to share with you. Mario asked a relative who shall remain nameless if he'd heard anything about Miller and his crew. Mario's family isn't afraid to make a quick and dirty buck, but never again with Miller."

Brent sat down again. "Why not?"

"Because Miller burned members of Mario's family before. Lives were lost, and relatives went to jail. Miller came off looking like a hero. He wants the same results this time with you and Sara."

"Yeah. But it won't be enough for Sara and me to be arrested. We'd have to be dead to be sure his scam stays operational. He knows I know how they're getting away with cleaning up millions in dirty money."

Annalisa nodded. "I'm glad you understand the severity of the situation. This group has connections in high places. You and Sara won't be safe until Miller and his inner circle are all dead. Mario's family has an ax to grind and might be your best solution to making the problem go away."

Brent shook his head. "I'll find a legal way to solve this. I just need a little time to figure out who I can trust."

"Time is something we don't have." Annalisa drained her wineglass and then walked back to the bar to refill it. "Miller and his men will figure out where you two are if you stay here. Mario's plane can be traced, and Miller has the full cooperation of the police and FBI. I have a place I can take you both to ensure your safety."

He'd love to let Annalisa take Sara away to keep her safe, but he couldn't let that happen. She was a witness who was under his protection. He knew how to keep her safe, albeit not in as swanky conditions as her mother would probably provide. Besides, he'd lose his job if he let her disappear, and Miller and company might get away with attempted murder, and that wasn't going to happen. Couldn't happen. "Sara and I will be fine. And as soon as I hear back from a friend, we'll be sure Miller and his people are all arrested. We have to do it by the book so that they stay in jail forever."

"You're so determined to follow rules that you'd endanger my daughter's life?"

"I care deeply for your daughter. I'd never let anything happen to her."

"Yes, I know you believe that." Annalisa closed her eyes and pinched the bridge of her nose. "Trust your gift, Brent. Use it for the good of others, and you'll find the happiness that's eluded you. But only after you prove it by taking that leap of faith. Trust me, I know. I hate the path you'll choose to figure it all out, though."

What the hell was she talking about? And how could she know about his gift? Was his identity as an agent known in

Mario's circle? Would he ever get an undercover assignment again?

Didn't matter. He needed to keep Sara safe. He'd deal with the rest later.

Chapter Fifteen

Sara walked into Mario's den and smiled. Her situation must've made her grandmother, Eva, decide to leave her home in Taos. She rarely did but had a few times recently when Dani had found herself in a mess. Not as big a mess as Sara was currently in, but close.

Her beautiful grandmother had a fantastic figure, fit still at seventy, with sexy curves that her mom and Dani had inherited. Dani and Grams had the same light brown curls that Sara formerly had until Brent had turned her blonde, and both were her favorite women in the entire world.

Sara leaned over the back of the leather couch and slid her arms around Dani and Grams' shoulders. "Hey, guys! Merry almost Christmas."

Dani and Grams stopped their hushed conversation and hugged Sara back. Grams said, "There's my favorite smarty-pants. And blonde now, no less. I love it, Sara!"

Dani frowned. "I thought I was your favorite."

Grams shook her head and patted the couch beside her, inviting Sara to sit. "You're my favorite smartass. Sara's still the sweeter version of you."

"True." Dani shrugged. "Hey, kid. Dying to meet Brent."

Before Sara could reply, Grams said, "He's one hot kidnapper. Have you nailed him yet?"

Geez. Leave it to her grandmother to cut to the chase. "Not yet. How's your love life?"

"Much better than yours." Her grandmother chuckled and patted Sara's leg. "Mario says you're safe here, so let's talk about the happy parts of your life."

Dani's voice was overly bright and happy when she said, "Yes, let's hear all about your sexy kidnapper." She rose and grabbed a bottle of wine and a tray of snacks. Hummus, cheese, crackers and Sara's favorite thing in the world, chocolate dipped strawberries. Dani laid the goods on the coffee table. "Feel free to ruin your dinner."

"Don't mind if I do." Sara bit into a strawberry and moaned. "God, this is good. But it's still not enough to distract me. What are you two up to? Spill."

Dani poured out the wine. "Nothing. Have another strawberry."

She finished off her strawberry and then reached for another. "Please don't make plans behind my back like I'm a child. Besides, you know you can't change the future. It's against the rules, right?" She glanced at her grandmother for confirmation.

Grams took a long drink from her wineglass before she said, "That's true. But sometimes it's tempting."

Sara's stomach tightened. "Did you see something bad in a dream?"

Grams shrugged. "I saw many things last night. But the best thing I saw was you and your sister, blue ocean in the background, and a minister asking—"

"Grams!" Dani laid her glass down with a thump. "I'd like to talk to Sara about that myself, if you don't mind." Her sister turned to her and smiled. "But first, tell us all about Brent."

Sara forced a smile. A sharp pang pierced her heart at a memory. When she'd been younger, her sister had laughed when Sara had declared that Dani was the only person in the world she'd ever ask to be her maid of honor. Dani had explained that job went to a person's best friend. Sara had always thought *they* were each other's best friends until that day. Dani would choose her friend Zoe to be her MOH, and if Sara were lucky, she'd be a bridesmaid at best. "Why don't you tell me about your wedding first? I'm excited to hear the details."

Grams said, "And *we're* both dying to hear about Brent. Did he make you want to rip his clothes off when he kissed you?"

They probably both knew more about how she felt about Brent than she did. It was so annoying living with a bunch of people whose dreams kept nothing of hers secret.

But she'd push her embarrassment aside and play along to make the most of it. "Kissing Brent doesn't only make me want to rip his clothes off, he makes me forget my name, Grams. And his abs? Drool-worthy. I dream of tracing them with my tongue. And don't get me started on his fine ass. Rock hard, baby. He puts that Mr. Universe you dated before Grandpa to shame! It's been difficult to keep my hands off him."

Dani laughed, while Grams rubbed her hands together with glee. "Now we're talking. Why *have* you kept your hands off him?"

Sara glanced at her sister. "He's an FBI agent, and I'm involved in his case. Cut to the chase. I can see by the gleam in your eyes you're both just dying to give me some advice. Unsolicited, I might add. What are you guys trying to tell me about Brent?"

Dani stood then sat on the other side of Sara, making her the middle of the family sandwich. "You and I aren't like Grams and Mom. We don't sleep with people for sport."

Grams grunted. "Maybe you both should. Sex relieves stress, you know. And there's nothing wrong with fulfilling natural urges."

"Seriously?" Sara threw her hands over her face and moaned. "Please don't talk about urges. Ever again."

"My little prude." Grams patted Sara's leg again. "Go on, Dani. But only if you're going to tell Sara to jump Brent's bones. Otherwise, I'll take it from here."

The elevator dinged, and her mom stepped out. Saved by the bell.

Annalisa glided across the room and settled in the big leather chair Mario always sat in. "Ladies. What are we talking about?"

"Nothing," Sara answered. "Is Brent still alive? Or did you gobble him up?"

Her mom laughed. "He's speaking with Mario about something. They'll both be down for dinner in a few minutes." Her mom leaned over and snagged Sara's full wineglass. "He's nice, honey. I like him. And he cares deeply for you."

Dani stood to get another glass. "I was just about to point out that Sara has a history of picking idiot men who she thankfully never fully commits to. Like she expects them to disappoint her, so why bother?"

Sara took offense to that. "No, I don't. Scott and I had lots in common. And we were both committed. Even friends before we dated." But every guy she'd been with *had* disappointed her. They were all like her father. Cheaters.

Her mom lifted a finger. "But was the sex with any of them mind-blowing? Or just okay?"

Please, just shoot me now.

"The sex was fine. Thanks for asking. Can we change the subject, please? Like, Dani's wedding? That'd be a fun topic."

All three Botellis smirked as they exchanged smug glances.

Dani handed over a full replacement wineglass. None too soon. Then her sister said, "Sex that's just fine is far from it. Be honest, have you had any better than just fine?"

Sara took a long drink of the excellent wine as she formulated her response. Maybe it was better to concede and get it over with. "I might've had it. Define mind-blowing?"

"Sweet, sweet Sara." Grams chuckled. "You'd know if you'd had it. Frankly, it doesn't happen as often as it should. I've never let that stop me from searching for it, though."

"Clearly," her mom mumbled into her wineglass. "Honey, what they're trying to tell you is that Brent isn't like the other men you've dated. He's the kind worth truly committing to."

Zoila had said the same thing. "So I'll have better sex if I fully commit?" That made no sense.

Dani bundled Sara up in a hug. "Sex is better when you're in love. Mario told us you look at Brent like he looks at Mom. Mario did some boneheaded things, and his family didn't make it any easier, but in the end, he never stopped loving Mom."

She was NOT asking her mom if she and Mario had mind-blowing sex.

183

But the smirk on her mom's face told it was true. TMI.

They all knew something they weren't saying. Because nothing changes what's to come. But sometimes it helps to hear that things will be okay in the end. "So all I have to do is sleep with Brent, and I'll finally have mind-blowing sex? Is that a guarantee from the Botelli woo-woo department?"

Grams nodded. "Those rock-hard abs and his butt don't hurt either." Everyone laughed, including Sara. They knew she hated talking about sex and were giving her a hard time. The genuine joy on their faces showed they were enjoying every minute of their torture too.

Dani, with her arms still wrapped around Sara, whispered, "I promise, you won't regret sleeping with him. But I have a question I'd like to ask you. As much as I don't want a full-blown wedding, Michael does, so I'm going to give in this time. Will you be my maid of honor?"

Sara's heart started to leap for joy until reality hit. Dani would rather have her best friend. She was just being polite. "I'm sure you'd rather have Zoe do it. You've been planning that since you were in high school and I was in middle school, remember? That's why you eloped last time, right? So you wouldn't hurt my feelings?"

"No! I eloped because I didn't want all the fuss." Dani hugged her tighter. "Since high school, I've learned that friends can come and go. And while Zoe is still an amazing pal, I'll always have my best friend, and that'll always be you. Please say you'll do it."

Tears blurred her vision as she hugged her sister back. "Yes. I'd love to be your MOH. Thank you."

"No. *Thank you.* You're the one who has an eye for flowers and design and all that's pretty. And this way, we can gang up on Mom when she's being unreasonable."

"Deal!" Sara smiled, feeling like a true Botelli for the first time in a long time. And it felt great.

Maybe her family didn't know anything specific about her future or what would happen with Brent in the long run. Maybe Mario had merely said that she looked at Brent a certain way and they were trying to take her mind off her worries. Well, it'd worked. And she loved them for it.

Now her thoughts were about how fun it'd be to help with her sister's wedding, but more immediately, how she'd get Brent to agree to sleep with her so she could see what she'd been missing out on.

∞ ∞ ∞

After a fun and amazing dinner with Sara's family, Brent lay in bed with his hands behind his head, reviewing Mario's advice. He'd also offered to "take care" of things while he and Sara were sent away to a safe place. It tempted. For Sara's sake. But it'd be wrong. The right thing to do was to let the justice system fairly "take care" of Miller and his cohorts.

Brent believed in the system, or what would the point be of what he did to keep people safe? Not to mention if it came out that he had anything to do with ordering hits on people like Mario's family wanted to do, Brent's job would be toast. He could even go to jail. Not going to happen.

Zach was on the case now, so it'd be fine. His mentor had finally texted back and said he'd go all the way to the top in DC. To wait for instructions before making any more moves. Zach understood the need to move quickly and would find a safe place for Sara. Then Brent could go back to his job and help take Miller down. It was a good, solid plan where no one would die. Hopefully. And it made the most sense.

But without his missing data, it could take some time to clear Sara's name. Zach had mentioned that Miller had put all the blame on her. Which meant Brent was Miller's number one kill target while he sent Sara to jail. Sara needed to be as far away from him as soon as possible.

It made him long for the quiet days at Holden's house when just a glimpse of Sara made him smile inside. When she'd remembered his name, then sat at his desk looking so pretty and solved that Rubik's cube with ease might have been the day he'd officially fallen for her. And realized she was genuinely kind, smart, and more than just a pretty face, even though he hadn't wanted to believe it or acknowledge his feelings for her. Mostly because Sara ran with a different crowd. When the case was closed, would she give him the time of day?

Thinking of that day in his office, he was struck by a thought. Sara had seen the computer screen with all the deposit and withdrawal transactions when she'd asked how much money was in her account. Could she possibly recreate what she'd seen the way she'd memorized the small towns on the map? It'd speed things up considerably. Help them trace all the involved parties faster. Arrest all the players, even the ones at the top. Then Sara would truly be safe.

He threw the covers back and stepped into a borrowed pair of Mario's silk pajamas. Not bothering to button the shirt in his haste, he opened his bedroom door and stepped into the hall. He nodded to the guard seated outside their rooms and then knocked on the room across the hall. "Sara? It's Brent."

Her voice called out, "Come in."

He opened the door and then pulled up short. Sara was slipping into a robe, but not fast enough for him to miss the lacy black number she had on underneath. "Wow. That's... You look... Amazing."

"Thanks." She grinned as she tied her robe. "My sister, who wears football shirts and shorts to bed, brought this for me to wear. It's a little much."

Thank you, Dani! "I think it's great." What a dumb thing to say. He should've told her how beautiful she looked, but his resolve not to sleep with her teetered as it was.

What had he come across the hall for again?

Evidence. Right.

"Hey, so do you remember in my office that day? When you looked at the computer and saw the details of your account?"

Her gaze had drifted from his face to his midsection. "I'm sorry, what?" Her eyes lifted and locked with his again. "You should probably button your shirt." She splayed her hand and moved it in a circle in front of his belly. "All that is way too distracting."

"Sorry." He slowly buttoned up his shirt, loving the way she bit her lower lip as she watched his every movement. Sara had the sexiest mouth.

Please let her remember my name after the trial.

Finished buttoning, he said, "Can you recreate what you saw on my computer that day?"

"Yes." Sara's grin turned mischievous. "But it'll cost you, Agent Keiser."

Why was Sara playing games at a time like this? "It's evidence that'll crack the case quicker. So you'll be safe."

Sara circled her arms around his neck. "Sounds vitally important that you get this evidence out of me, then. But I won't give it to you unless you sleep with me."

He blinked at her while his mind caught up. "What are you doing? You know we can't sleep together until the case is closed. Even then it could be frowned on."

"I know." She stood on her tiptoes and kissed him. Sweetly, teasingly, temptingly.

Then she added a little nip to his bottom lip that sent a zap of desire to his groin. Hard to resist her. But he had to.

Pushing her gently away before he hauled her to the bed and made love to her, he said, "Sara. Please. I'm barely hanging on here."

"I just googled it. You're allowed to sleep with a suspect if you think not doing so will blow your cover or impede the investigation. I'm not going to give you what you want unless you sleep with me. I'll testify to that."

That wasn't exactly how the regs read, but the spirit was close. Maybe. It was hard to think straight. "So you're stating, for the record, the only way I will get that vital piece of evidence is for me to sleep with you?"

Sara's eyes sparkled with amusement. "Yep. Not budging."

Thank God for Google. "And you understand that this evidence might be the key piece of data that will absolve you of all guilt? Thereby ensuring that you'd not serve jail time and that it could save your life? And yet you still stand by this requirement, Ms. Chapman?"

She laughed. "I do, Agent Keiser. I've been in here since we said good night trying to find a loophole. My plan B was to sneak into your bed later and beg."

"Really?" He pulled her into a hug. "I love that, but I'm still not sure."

She laid her small hand over his heart and looked up at him with the most earnest expression he'd seen from her. "My family gave you the stamp of approval, said I'd experience mind-blowing sex because I have real feelings for you. Feelings I've never had before."

His heart wanted to jump out of his chest and into her hand. "I feel the same for you."

"And for the record, my buttinski family also informed me that I hadn't had mind-blowing sex before or I'd know it. I'd like to experience that, just in case Miller gets to me first and I die. You wouldn't deny me that, would you?"

Knife to the heart.

He'd not deny her anything if he could help it. Why the hell hadn't he memorized the fraternization part of the manual better? There was something close to what she'd said, but with all the blood in his body pumping somewhere other than his mind, he wasn't sure. "Would you consider giving me the data first? And then we'll sleep together?" That'd give his blood time to return to where it was supposed to be so that he could think more clearly.

"Not a chance. Because then your boss would say you could've walked away. I'm not exactly the size of that guy sitting out in the hallway. You could overpower me. Instead, sleep with me first, and then you'll get your data."

"You drive a hard bargain, but I won't sleep with you, Sara."

"Seriously?" Her expression turned from confident to devastated in an instant. "I could promise never to tell. Would that be better?"

"No. I learned growing up with a drug addict that lying is always wrong. But it's what they do best." He kissed her forehead. "What I'd meant was that I wasn't going to sleep with you. I intend to make love to you. Blowing your mind will be the secondary objective of the mission."

Her face lit up again. "And you don't like to fail. Do you?" She took his hand and led him to her bed.

"Haven't failed a mission yet. Don't intend to now."

"Perfect. Because I saved a condom from the Jeep." When they stood by the edge of the bed, Sara started in on his buttons. "Thanks for not making me beg."

He swept her up and laid her on the mattress. "I'm still going to make you beg, Sara. Guaranteed."

She smiled. "I love a guarantee."

He kissed her, then nibbled on her neck, before he whispered, "Hopefully, this one will last a lifetime.

Chapter Sixteen

Sara was still processing his lifetime guarantee comment as she stared into Brent's eyes. He had her pinned to the bed under his weight, already needy and ready for him. But she wanted to tell him something first. "You don't have to say that. We have a crazy shared experience that will probably bond us forever. But please don't feel like you have to make promises you can't keep."

Brent dipped his head and ran his tongue along her collarbone. "Does it scare you to think of being with someone like me forever?" His lips tugged the string that held her flimsy negligée together.

He was making it difficult to concentrate. "No. I just wanted you to know that it's okay to make love and then go our separate ways, if that's what you want to do." Though it wasn't what she'd want.

With the flimsy material between his teeth, he tugged open the top, exposing her blatantly aroused breasts. "Anything off-limits? Like a gag?"

"A gag?" She lifted her lower half up off the bed so he could tug the whole getup she wore down her body. He took his time sliding it down her legs, his warm breath teasing between her thighs on the way by. Then he kissed her toes before he tossed the whole thing aside. It took all her concentration to finish her question. "Who'd want to be... Oh, you want me to stop talking now?"

"Mmmmhmmm." He couldn't speak because his mouth had traveled back north and was busy pleasing her breasts again. He was making her mind turn to mush, so she closed her eyes and let all the thoughts about promises and the future go. When he used his teeth to apply pressure, her back arched off the bed. "Please tell me you don't need complete silence to work. I might not make it."

"Nope." He chuckled. "Anything in particular you'd like me to do to you?"

With her eyes still closed and her body heating up at a dangerous rate, she weakly managed a hand wave. "You're doing fine." Better than fine, but now talking seemed like too much work. Sharp darts and quick zaps of pleasure made her hips writhe for him. Against him.

He slowly moved up her body, his mouth hovering above hers so close, his warm breath tickled her lips. "I love kissing you, Sara."

She opened her eyes and stared into his deep blue ones. All she could do was nod her agreement. The desire in his gaze was enough to make her self-combust. No guy had ever looked at her like that. As if she was the most desirable woman in the world. And pleasing her was his number one goal in life.

Brent rolled halfway off her, his gaze lowered to take in her naked body. Why had she left the lights on? That chalupa probably hadn't been her friend the other day.

"Even better than I'd imagined." His fingers danced along her collarbone, then his warm palm flattened, and he ran it down her chest, across her belly to her thighs, and then he circled her calf before starting back up again. "So soft. So perfect."

So aroused, she was going to go off like a rocket in about two seconds, but she didn't say so. With all self-consciousness suddenly gone, she ran her fingers through his spiked silky hair and pulled his face toward hers again. She *needed* to kiss him.

His gaze met hers again, his desire so blatant, she licked her lips. When she couldn't take the anticipation any longer, she lifted her mouth to meet his warm, soft one. He had plump, full lips that made her want to settle into them and stay awhile.

Brent kissed her back just long enough, deep enough, to get her engines revved up to overdrive. Then he left her humming with need when he lifted his mouth from hers and used his incredible lips on her neck. He made all sorts of foreign kind of magic happen there, so she let her head drift all the way back onto the pillow with a moan. Her mind wasn't blown yet, but things looked promising at the rate he was going. Even if some mysterious thing didn't happen, Brent was already the most considerate lover she'd ever had. Every soft touch of his hands and mouth left her skin hot and aching for more. Her heart was melting for him right along with the rest of her body. Was she falling in love with Brent?

Wanting to be even closer to him, she ran her hands up his back, needing his hot skin against hers, but her palms filled with silk fabric instead. As soft and sensual as it was, it was in the way.

She'd unbuttoned his shirt earlier, so she parted the material and dragged it down his big arms. He sat up and straddled her. After a little help from him, she managed to get the shirt all the way off, and she tossed it to the floor.

And then his tempting abs were right in front of her face with all their glory. Her fingers had to touch, so she reached out and traced all six of the hard muscles that quivered under her touch. It wasn't enough.

She leaned forward as the heat between her legs grew from a bonfire to an inferno. She glanced up at his face, his eyes closed in ecstasy, and whispered, "I've dreamed about touching you like this."

"Me too." He groaned. "It's been hell not being able to make love to you."

She smiled while she caressed his abs with her tongue. But now she wanted to see more. She slipped her fingers under his waistband to tug his pajama bottoms off, but his large hands stopped her.

Confused, because no guy had ever turned down the chance to have her please him, she glanced up in time to see his sexy grin.

He said, "I have other plans for you first."

The naughty gleam in his eyes made her lean back and place her hands behind her head. "Can't wait." "Other plans" sounded like more pleasure for her to reach. Maybe she'd achieve her goal of experiencing the best sex ever yet. It wouldn't take much, it already had been better than any before, but she was more than eager to let him show her how much more it could be.

∞ ∞ ∞

That Sara lay before him, offering up her body for him to do as he pleased, tested his limits. He wanted her so badly, but he wanted to please her even more.

He kissed her again while he slipped his hand between her thighs. She was ready for him, but he wanted to watch her come undone first, so he slid two fingers inside. Using his thumb, he matched the cadence her hips set. He leaned away to better concentrate on her beautiful face.

Sara's hand searched the nightstand while her teeth dug into her lower lip. "Condom," she panted out as she lifted the wrapper. "Hurry, please. I'm going with or without you here in about ten seconds."

"What was that?" He'd promised to make her beg.

Sara's head thrashed from left to right on the pillow. "Not funny, Brent." Then she grimaced, and her insides tightened around his fingers. "Okay. Fine. I'm begging. Now hurry up and put that on!"

He wanted nothing more than to slip into that condom and pound away the weeks of relentless desire he'd suffered for her, but instead, he pressed his thumb harder, moved his fingers deeper and faster until her hands dug into the sheets. Her back arched off the bed, and she let out a moan so deep, so full of desperate desire, it reverberated in his groin.

He wanted to be buried deep inside when she came, so he reached for the condom, but the way her body convulsed and then clamped down hard around his fingers signaled it was too late. She was going over the first edge without him.

He slowly moved his hand away, giving her time to recover and for him to cool his jets or he'd go off like a schoolboy soon. But Sara's smug smile and the lazy stretch of her arms above her head that did amazing things to her breasts snapped the last cable of control left within him.

Her eyes were still closed as he settled between her legs. "Ready for the mind-blowing part now?"

Her eyes opened, and she focused on his. "I'm pretty good right now, actually."

She might as well have thrown a bucket of freezing water in his face. Seriously? He should have joined her when she'd asked. He was an idiot.

He nodded and rolled off Sara, headed for a cold shower to put him out of his misery, but her hands slipped around his waist from behind and tugged. "I was kidding, Brent." She laid a soft kiss on his neck as her hand slid under his pants and circled him. Her small hand stroked him while she nibbled on his earlobe.

He wasn't sure he could take much more "kidding."

She whispered, "Let's get rid of these pants—"

He was out of his pants and on top of her so fast that she yelped. Then Sara grinned at him and cupped the back of his neck, drawing his mouth to hers again. When she kissed him, long, slow and deep, his control teetered on the edge again. He ended the kiss on a frustrated growl and searched for the condom that was somewhere on the sheets where Sara had dropped it.

"Looking for this?" Sara slowly ripped the package open. "I'd be happy to do—"

He grabbed the condom and quickly rolled it on. He didn't want to wait another painful minute to be inside her.

Sara must've felt the same, because she reached down and guided him to just where she'd like him to be. Then she whispered in his ear exactly how hard and fast she'd like it. God, he loved that, but instead, he took his time. Slowly filling her all the way up before moving out at the same pace. Sara's body resisted when he'd pull away, clenching around him, encouraging him to fill her back up again.

Like the ocean tide, back and forth, he kept the slow and steady pace until he thought his head might explode from the pressure built up inside him. But the way Sara's body throbbed for him, around him, tighter and harder, was something he might have missed had he not slowed the pace.

He'd never make that mistake again. It was *his* mind blown now.

Sara's hands moved lower, grabbed his butt, encouraging a faster pace. He took her cue and opened his eyes to find her staring into his. Then she kissed him, and all his resolve was gone. He couldn't hold back any longer, and his body took over.

With his mouth still on hers, he reached down and wrapped one of Sara's legs around his back to go even deeper for her. She followed suit with the other leg, so he placed both hands on the mattress and breathed out her name with every thrust. Harder, faster, and deeper, until Sara cried out and her body clamped down on him like a vise, making him lose all control.

He closed his eyes and succumbed to a powerful wave he'd never experienced before. It stole his breath, his strength, and his mind. He felt as if he'd been hit by a dump truck. But in the best way.

Careful not to crush Sara, he wrapped an arm around her waist and rolled onto his back, taking her with him. She rested on top of his chest while he panted for air and tried to work up a coherent sentence. He wanted to tell Sara how amazing that had been, but it'd take a bit.

Sara crawled up his body and slipped her face into the crook of his neck. Then she laid a sweet kiss on his cheek. "I'll go write those transactions down for you and send them to your laptop."

He tightened his hold on her. "What's the rush?" Maybe she hadn't enjoyed the sex as much as he had? The thought made his stomach ache a little.

She shrugged. "Most guys don't like to snuggle after sex. I don't want you to feel like you have to."

"Or maybe the sex didn't meet your expectations, so you'd like to get away as fast as you can?" Didn't she have a fantastic time like he did?

She lifted her head and looked him square in the eyes. "That's a ridiculous assumption. I liked it so much that you made me beg." She poked him in the chest. "And it wasn't very nice of you."

Relief that she'd liked it too made him smile. "You weren't so nice yourself. I thought I was going to have to take an ice bath."

Sara laid a quick kiss on his lips. "So you can dish it out, but you can't take it?"

He rolled Sara under him again. "The better question is can you take any more?"

"I only grabbed one condom. Unfortunately." She sweetly smiled as she ran her hands through his hair. He loved when she did that.

"Lucky for us, I grabbed a handful. But they're in my room." He kissed her, taking his time about it, amazed that he was ready for round two so fast. "Be right back."

"Wait." He started to leave, but Sara's arms snaked around his waist again, nudging him back on top of her. "The real reason I was going to leave so fast was that I'm a little freaked out."

His stomach clenched. Was she going to cut him loose? Like so many other women had because he wasn't an excellent communicator or an attentive enough boyfriend? He was afraid to ask, but he whispered anyway, "What's wrong?"

"Please don't feel like you have to respond if you don't want to, but…" She closed her eyes and scrunched up her nose. "I think I'm falling in love with you."

Thank God.

She opened just one eye. "I know it's quick. It's stupid quick. And maybe it's just adrenaline or lack of sex or lack of having a real man in my life, but—"

"Stop." He laid his hand over her mouth. "I feel the same, Sara. But I'll bring a gag back anyway before you talk either of us out of our feelings."

Her smile bloomed under his palm, so he lifted his hand. She whispered, "Really?"

"Yes." He leaned down and kissed her. "Be right back." He found his pants and slipped into them, while Sara made her way to the bathroom.

Just as his hand landed on the knob, Sara called out, "Just for clarity's sake, you meant you feel the same about me too, not that you're really bringing a gag back, right?"

"You'll just have to wait and see," he said with an eyebrow hitch.

After dodging the baby bar of soap Sara threw at him, he jogged across the hall, the happiest he'd been in his life.

Chapter Seventeen

S ara glanced at the bedside clock while she waited for Brent to return from her bathroom. Would he kiss her good night and then go back to his room now that they'd had their fill of each other? It was after one in the morning, so he must be tired. She wasn't, though. Her blood hummed with energy and an excitement she'd never experienced after sex before. Heck, she'd never had sex that many times in a row before. Maybe that explained her restlessness.

Brent returned and slid under the covers next to her. "I don't know how to ask this without seeming like a jerk, but...did you...was it better than..."

The nervous anticipation in his eyes warmed her heart. "You want to know if my mind was blown as promised?"

He swallowed hard and nodded. "Because mine was. I'm pretty sure I'm falling in love with you too, Sara. And I can't wait to see where this relationship can go."

A hallelujah choir sounded in her head. And in her heart. "Being with you was better than I could've ever imagined. I hate that we'll have to wait until my name's cleared to be together."

"Same here." He leaned forward and kissed her. "But it'll be worth the wait."

She was sure of it.

He grinned. "But now I'm starving. How about you?"

"Let's go raid Mario's fridge!" She threw the covers back, relieved he hadn't told her he'd rather be alone. She was too wired up to be alone. "Or we can order a pizza from room service. Mario's hotel delivers twenty-four seven."

"Pizza sounds amazing." Brent plumped up their pillows against the headboard. "What do you like on yours?"

She had weird taste in pizza, but if they were going to be together, he might as well know that sooner rather than later. While slipping into her robe, she said, "I like anchovies and black olives."

He blinked at her. "You're kidding, right?"

"Nope." She found the button on the panel beside an old-fashioned dial phone to order and lifted the receiver. "We'll just get two different halves. What do you want on yours?"

"Chicken and barbeque sauce."

"Funny. Seriously, what do you want?"

He held up his palms. "That's seriously what I like."

"Gross. I think we'd better order two separate pizzas. I don't think my anchovies could bear touching your barbeque sauce." And she thought she had weird taste in pizza toppings. Who put barbeque sauce on pizza?

He grinned. "Then I don't think I can kiss a mouth that's had anchovies in it."

She rolled her eyes and ordered the pizzas.

After she hung up, she walked to the door and stuck her head out. The goon in the hall raised a brow in question. "We ordered pizzas. They should be here in a half hour. We'll share if you intercept the room service person at the elevator so they don't wake my mom and Mario."

"Can't leave my post, but I'm starving. Let me get someone else to do it." He took out his cell and tapped a text. "Done. I'll knock when it's here. What kind we got?"

When she told him, his face puckered up as though he'd just sucked a lemon. "Yeah. No thanks. I just lost my appetite."

"Suit yourself." She shut the door and then padded across the thick carpet back to the bed. Her guest room was decorated with a '30s décor, tasseled lampshades, red velvet bedspread, and antique fixtures in the bath matching the rest of the hotel's décor. It should be tacky, but it was sort of cool. She crawled into bed and sat next to Brent against the headboard. Then she lifted the receiver and ordered a pepperoni pizza for the guard.

After she hung up, she said, "The dude in the hall thinks you have terrible taste in pizza."

"But never in women." He wrapped an arm around her shoulder, pulling her close. "I feel bad that I don't have a Christmas present for you. I'd buy you your own Rubik's cube, but I can't use my online account and give our location away. How about a rain check?"

"That'd be great." She'd almost forgotten all about Christmas. And it was so late that it was officially Christmas Eve. She'd miss Zoila's dinner later. She hated that. And the worries Zoila must have. "I bought *you* a gift. I got it just in case you showed up for Zoila's dinner."

"That was nice." He laid a kiss on the top of her head. "No one has bought me a Christmas gift in a very long time."

That broke her heart. "Which reminds me. Why don't you celebrate holidays?"

He huffed out a breath. "Because those were the days my mom would be the saddest. She'd drink, do drugs, and pass out, leaving me to fend for myself."

"I'm sorry. No kid should have to deal with that. You don't have any other family?" She couldn't imagine a little boy spending Christmas alone like that.

"Not that I know of. When does school start again for you? Maybe after all of this is over, we can get away for a long weekend. I have tons of vacation I've never used."

"That sounds nice, but way to change the subject." She snuggled closer, laying her head on his big shoulder and her hand over his heart. It beat slow and steady under her palm. "I go back mid-January. I can't wait to graduate. One of the counselors at the shelter set up an interview for me a few weeks ago. They said the job is mine if I want it. How long have you been an FBI agent who doesn't use his vacation?"

"Four years." His big palm slowly ran up and down her arm. "This is my first field assignment. I'm hoping they let me have more, but it's not likely. They told me my gift was too unique to risk losing me in the field. I could be hit by a bus on my way to the office one day just as easily, but they don't see it that way."

"If you don't like it, why don't you quit?" She lifted her chin so she could see his face.

He shook his head. "No one else I interviewed with offered a pension. Or the kind of benefits you get working for the government." He shrugged. "It's fine."

"Benefits are important, but what about enjoying your work? I mean, I bet the space program would love to have a weirdo like you. Studying infinite numbers of stars and seeing patterns.

You could find another solar system or something. Or how about starting your own hedge fund? That's gotta be exciting, like gambling, but with you, it'd be much more calculated."

He frowned. "I'm just going to invest for myself until I get the house, then I'll do my time with the agency, retire, and be all set."

She wasn't going to argue with his life plan, but she was curious. "How much have you made toward your house goals by investing so far?"

A shy smile slowly lit his face. "Two and a half million."

"What?" She sat up and faced him. "In four years? That's amazing,"

"I trade commodities. It's almost like cheating for me, it's so easy sometimes."

"And I can see it makes you happy." He had an ear-to-ear grin on his face.

He pulled her back to his side. "What makes me happy is to think I'll have that house on the water in just a few years if all goes well. It'll go even quicker if I can bring Miller and all his pals down. And maybe I'll get a dog. A big one, I think."

"That all sounds perfect. But then you'd still have to go to a boring job every day for thirty or forty years."

"It'll be worth it in the end. So what did you buy me for Christmas?"

Brother. The guy could change the subject faster than a TV remote changed channels. "It's a surprise. Just know that I'm an excellent gift giver. You'll love it. And it's ten times better than a Rubik's cube. Just saying."

"I was kidding about the Rubik's cube." He laid a kiss on top of her head. "I'll buy you something nicer. I noticed you only wear that little heart necklace, no flashy jewelry, which surprises me. And limits my gift choices greatly."

"Jewelry for Christmas is cliché. You can do better than that." She lifted the necklace and opened the heart. "My dad gave me this when I was eleven. He said it was to remind me that when we're apart, I'd always be in his heart. But he tends to bruise mine sometimes."

Brent leaned closer and examined the pictures inside. "That's a cute picture of you." He glanced up and stared into her eyes. "I can't imagine what it'd be like to have someone love me that much. No matter how I treated her."

What was that supposed to mean? "I know my dad isn't perfect. And as far as fathers go, he's been pretty selfish. Using me and Scott for photo ops at his wedding was obnoxious. I get all that. But at the end of the day, he *does* love me."

Brent's hands framed her face, and he lifted it. "Your father used your account to commit fraud. That's why we have to get that data to Zach first thing in the morning. To prove you're innocent and your father is guilty."

Guilty? "Wait. I thought Miller was using my dad. Are you saying my dad might go to jail too? And that by giving you that data, I'll be sending him there?"

Brent's eyes filled with compassion, but his voice was hard when he said, "Yes."

She shook her head and pulled away. She couldn't be responsible for sending her father to jail. What was she going to do?

"Sara." Brent reached for her, but she evaded. "You have to clear your name first and foremost. Your father made his bad choice. Don't let him hurt you any further. The truth will come out eventually with or without your data. Don't make things worse by trying to protect him. It could look as if you knew what he was doing."

His words made sense in her head, but her heart didn't know if she could live with herself if she gave Brent the data.

Could she make a deal for the data to save both her and her dad? Not with Brent. He clearly wouldn't go along with that. But maybe someone higher up. Mario mentioned his family had some incriminating evidence against Miller. Maybe Mario knew of someone else much more notorious involved they could trade for her father?

Brent stood and hugged her. "I know this is hard. But it's the right thing to do. Put yourself first for a change. Please?"

She nodded, but her mind still reeled with other scenarios. Her dad had to have been just a pawn in the bigger picture. She at least had to *try* to save him.

A knock on the door sounded. Thank God for the pizza. Hopefully, it'd put an end to their conversation. She didn't want to have to lie to Brent about what she planned to do.

∞ ∞ ∞

Brent stared at the ceiling as the late morning sunlight slipped between a crack in the heavy curtains. He'd been exhausted by the time he'd crawled into bed around two a.m. Sara had become quiet while they ate pizza earlier. She was up to something. He could practically see the wheels turning in her head.

Then she'd kissed him on the cheek claiming anchovy breath and said good night as she nudged him out the door and back to his bedroom. He'd hoped she'd let him stay.

Maybe he shouldn't have been so harsh, but her dad was a prick with a capital P. It'd be a colossal mistake to jeopardize her freedom for her father's. Even give the FBI a hint that she could've known what he was up to. Because she could have. She needed to separate herself as far from her dad as she could. He needed to talk some sense into her sweet, bleeding heart.

He threw the covers back and stood as a thought struck him so hard, he sat back down on the mattress. He still loved his imperfect mother. Always would. Even though he'd never respect the choices she made while alive. How many excuses had he made for her? How many times had he forgiven her because he loved her with all his heart? Flaws and all.

He might owe Sara an apology, but at the same time point out that her father made terrible choices that he needed to accept responsibility for making. She could visit him in jail. Make sure he had money for commissary in the white-collar prison he'd be sent to and make his stay more comfortable while there, if that'd make her feel better. But she needed to do the right thing and save herself.

After he'd showered and changed into the jeans and dark-green button-down shirt that had miraculously appeared on his bed by the time he got out of the bath, he opened his bedroom door. He lifted his chin in greeting at the new guard who occupied the hallway. Brent was about to knock on Sara's door when the door next to it opened, and Eva stepped out holding Mittens.

Sara's grandmother had been in the room next door? He and Sara hadn't been quiet the night before.

Crap.

"Good morning, Brent. Want to walk an old lady to brunch?" She winked. "That is if you have the strength. It sounds like you showed Sara a good time last night."

What the hell was a guy supposed to say to that? "Well, uh..."

Sara's grandmother laughed. "I haven't made a full-grown man blush like that in a long time. Bet Sara finds that cute about you. Let's go eat."

He pointed toward Sara's door. "I wanted to talk to her about something first."

"I heard Sara leave hours ago, which means we need to hurry. Sara can pack away a hearty breakfast with the best of them. If she ate the Danish Mario always orders in special for me, she's gonna hear about it. That girl has a wicked sweet tooth."

Brent crooked his arm for Eva to take and smiled. He'd never had a grandmother but wouldn't mind one like Sara's. Eva was all right. "Any idea where Sara's love of sweets comes from?"

"You got me there." Eva laughed as they started down the hallway. "But before we get to the dining room, can I ask you a question?"

Oh God. He braced himself. "Sure."

"You have a gift for numbers, but do you believe that people can have other extraordinary gifts? Like the ability to see into the future through dreams or visions?"

Sara must've told them about his gift. "Not really. The FBI has people they use who claim they're sensitive and can help solve crimes, but they're wrong as often as they're right."

Eva nodded. "But when they're right, there's no explaining how they knew, is there?"

"Good guess, I suppose." At Eva's tug on his arm, Brent stopped walking.

"Then tell me this. Why did I see a house in my dreams last night? One with a front door as blue as the Mediterranean Sea, three stories high, perched on a cliff overlooking the ocean? From the rear, it looks to be made of solid glass, and has a shower on the top floor with an amazing view that made me feel like I was on a boat in the middle of the ocean."

How the hell could she know that about his future home? It had never been listed for sale. It'd been in Zach's family since his father had it built. Sara didn't know any of those details. "What game are you playing here, Eva?"

She shook her head. "No games. I see things in my dreams, Brent. I don't always know why I see things, but this particular dream included you."

"Me? In the house?" None of what Eva was saying made any sense.

"No, you were standing at the front door with your hands in your pockets, trying to decide if you wanted to go inside."

She was older. Maybe confused. He'd give her a break. "I think we kept you up last night and so, of course, your dreams might include Sara and me. Sorry about that."

"Sara wasn't in the dream. Just you. You were trying to make a big decision."

Why he felt suddenly sad that Sara wasn't with him in the dream was stupid. The whole conversation was ridiculous. "Let's agree to disagree on this. Okay?" But how she could know about his future home still puzzled.

"You're still skeptical. That's understandable. But it was a similar dream that Annalisa had. It's how she knew to warn Sara about the wedding and Miller's friends. She'd kill me for telling you that. You see, it's not good for her perfect image if her fans think she's a freak. Like you think I am right now." Eva started walking again with increased urgency.

He jogged to keep up. "I don't think you're a freak, Eva. It was just a dream."

Eva stopped and patted the side of his face. "Poor boy. You'll look back on this conversation and see that the dreams make sense of everything soon. But by then, the damage will already be done."

He lifted his hands. "I can't use dreams as evidence in court. I'd rather know the truth."

"I just told you the truth." She let out a long breath. "You're going to have to make a few choices here very soon. I hope you'll keep Sara's best interests in mind, because she loves you, Brent. And love is a fragile gift that, once rejected, may never offer itself up again. Take your phone call."

Eva hurried toward the dining room just as his phone vibrated in his pocket. A chill ran up his spine, leaving him with gooseflesh on his arms.

Coincidence. That was all.

He'd been waiting to hear back from Zach. "Hello?"

"Agent Keiser? Special Agent in Charge John Baker here."

Zach had said Baker would be calling. "Yes, sir?"

"Ms. Chapman sent an email this morning alerting us to her whereabouts. It includes incriminating information we need to talk to her about. Ask her to voluntarily come in for questioning. If she refuses, we still have a warrant for her arrest."

"A warrant issued by Miller that's bogus. Ms. Chapman is innocent. Her father had direction of her account. She never touched it."

"The director wants to know where she got that information. You have your orders, Keiser. We also have a subpoena for a search warrant for Mr. Giovanni's residence and a team downstairs. After you contain Sara and get her clear, let me know."

What the hell?

"Arresting Sara was never part of the deal. We talked about putting her somewhere safe until we can bring Miller in."

"If you can't handle this alone, I'll send someone up to do it for you."

That wasn't what Zach had said to do, but Zach wasn't the agent in charge. "I've got this. But no need for the search warrant. Mario isn't involved." Probably. There wasn't any evidence to support that. Mario had only *offered* to help.

"Are you kidding? We've been trying to get inside the Giovanni circle since I was your age. No way we're giving up this opportunity. Get Ms. Chapman secure, Agent. Now!"

What email did Sara send? And a search warrant? Mario had probably saved their lives. Hopefully, Mario was really as clean as he claimed.

But everything would be fine as soon as Sara wrote down the data from her computer. She'd be questioned and ferried off to a safe house.

"I need twenty minutes."

"What for?" The impatience in his superior officer's voice meant Brent had better come up with a better reason than to convince Sara it was the right thing to do.

"I need Ms. Chapman to give me a vital piece of evidence. It's information that'll save me weeks of reconstruction. My mission was to find the players at the top. Weeks gives them time to ghost."

Baker was silent for a few moments before he said, "You get fifteen minutes. Then we're coming in. Understood?"

"Yes, sir." He disconnected and took off at a run.

Chapter Eighteen

Sara had just finished her third amazing Danish. Who knew how hungry that much sex could make a girl the next morning? Even after late-night pizza. "Mario, these are the best pastries I've ever had."

Dani smiled. "You said that about the eggs and the orange juice too. I guess mind-blowing sex makes *everything* taste better this morning?"

Mario had the good grace to lift his newspaper in front of his face and check out of the conversation. Her mom waited with raised brows for Sara to answer the question.

She refused to be embarrassed about doing what her family insisted she do. "I guess you'd all know if you'd ever had it."

Her mom laid a hand on Mario's arm. "Well, that grapefruit was the best I ever had. How about you, honey? How was your oatmeal?"

Mario mumbled, "Fabulous," from behind the sports section.

He was the only person Sara knew who actually read a paper anymore. Even her mom read the news online. Maybe that was why Mario's hotel had a thirties theme. Maybe he was just an old-fashioned guy at heart.

Grams came in carrying Mittens. "There better be a pastry left for me, Sara."

Whoops. "I'm sorry. I just ate the last one."

Grams leaned down and gave a hard hug. "Any other day, I'd tan your hide. But today, I'll kiss you and tell you I love my Danish thief with all my heart. And I'll watch Mittens until you get back."

Sara's delicious brunch turned to stone in her gut. "Where am I going?"

Mario's newspaper slowly lowered, and the expressions on her mom's and Dani's faces turned pensive. Her mom asked, "You've had a dream?"

Before her grandmother could answer, Brent came flying into the dining room. "Sara. I need to talk to you about something. Now." He glanced around the room. "In private, please."

Grams shook her head. "You can do this in front of all of us, Brent."

Brent's Adam's apple bobbed hard once, and then he nodded and looked her in the eye. "Sara, there's been a change of plans. Please don't freak out, but I have to take you in for questioning. If you refuse, I'll have to arrest you."

Arrest me?

All the air whooshed from her lungs. "I haven't done anything wrong, Brent. You *know* that!"

He nodded. "I do. But we have to do things by the book. You sent an email that my superiors would like to talk to you about. I wish you hadn't done that. But with the data from my computer, we'll have you in and out and to a safe house in no time. Please hurry and write it all down. The team is on the way up."

Mario stood and circled behind her. He laid a hand on her shoulder. "She won't be giving you the data, Brent. She already made her own deal for it. Grab your things, Sara. We have to go now."

Brent shook his head. "I can't let you do that. You're leaving me no choice here." He pulled out his gun. "Sara has to go with me."

In a flash, Mario had his own gun out. She hadn't even seen where it had come from. Mario growled, "You know you can't guarantee her safety. You'll hand her over to strangers and hope they do their job. With me, she'll be safe."

She turned her head back and forth between the two men. "Stop it! Put the guns away. This is *my* decision." What was she going to do? She didn't want to go to jail and then some safe house. She wanted to go with Mario and wished Brent would come along too.

Brent said quietly, "It's *not* your decision, Sara. You have to come with me." He glanced at Mario. "It'd be better if you don't have that gun when my team gets here."

She looked at her mom, then Dani, and then Grams pleading for help with her eyes. Surely they knew what she should do. But they all sat silently observing. "Grams? Am I supposed to go with Brent or Mario?"

Brent barked, "Sara, I'm ordering you to go find some paper and write the information down. Now!" He kept his gun pointed at Mario's chest.

Ordering me?

"Can you guarantee my safety, Brent? A hundred percent? Because Mom and Mario can."

The slightest hint of doubt passed in his eyes and answered her question before he could. She held up a hand. "Never mind. I have my own plan. I'm going to swap my information for a lesser sentence for my father. Tell them I slipped out before you got here."

"Not happening." Brent's face grew hard.

"Yes, it is. I'm going with my family."

"I'll lose my job, Sara."

She stood and threw her napkin on her chair. "Your job is more important than keeping me alive? A job you don't even like? How can you tell me you love me and then do this to me?" Why was Brent even hesitating? It made no sense.

"Please don't make this harder than it has to be. There are rules for a reason. The FBI will keep you safe."

Not the FBI she'd dealt with the past few days.

She took a step closer to him and laid her hands on his arms. "Come away with us. I need for you to be safe too. Please? You'll find another job when this is all over. Who could blame you for going with us to be safe after the way your coworkers have betrayed you? You still can't be sure who you can trust. We *can* trust Mario."

Grams finally spoke. "You have to go with Brent, honey."

She glanced at her mom for confirmation, who closed her eyes and nodded. Dani stood and hugged her. "I love you, kiddo, but I can't watch Brent break your heart. I might have to kill him." She gave one last squeeze and then said as she left the dining room, "I'll get everything ready to go, guys."

Mario's eyes narrowed, and for the first time since Sara had known him, he looked like the former criminal he'd been. He tucked his gun behind his back. "She's coming with us, Brent. You don't have the guts to shoot me, so run back to your little pals.

215

We're leaving now." Mario grabbed her arm and tugged. Brent reached out at the same time and grabbed her other arm.

"Stop it!" Her mom stood up and removed Sara from the men's clutches, hugging her even harder than Dani just had. "Mario, we can't tamper with the future. If my mother says Sara has to go with Brent, then she has to." Her mom whispered, "I love you, sweetheart. And I'll get my lawyers on it right now. You're not to worry."

Feeling abandoned and betrayed once again, she turned and stuck her hands out toward Brent. "Arrest me, then. I'm not going voluntarily." Tears formed in her eyes. How could he do this to her? "No one I know would choose a job over a person. Oh, wait, I guess I do know someone like that. My dad. You're two of a kind."

Brent's head whipped back as if she'd struck him. "I'm nothing... Don't make me arrest you. Just come with me. Please?" Brent put his gun away. "I hate that I have to do this. Can't you see that?"

"I can see just fine." But her heart broke completely apart. She'd thought he was different. That he'd be the one man she could count on and trust. Why had she been so quick to give her love to him? Would she never learn?

But now she had to stand up for herself. For a change.

As he tugged her arm, she said, "Glad I found out what comes first with you now, before we had three kids and a dog. You need to get your priorities straight, or you'll always be alone, Brent."

Brent's stare hardened. "Since when is doing your job a crime? I have to search you for weapons." He ran his hands over her body, nothing sensual like the last time. Then he pulled her along behind him like the stubborn man she knew he could be.

She glanced over her shoulder, and what was left of her heart melted away. Mario had to hold her mom upright because she was sobbing so hard. Grams sat with her head in her hands, crying too. Maybe Gram's dreams had been worse than she'd let on. Maybe Brent was marching her off just to be killed by one of Miller's operatives. Her grandmother's dreams weren't always complete.

How could Brent claim to be falling in love with her and then hand her over to one of Miller's men to die?

∞ ∞ ∞

Brent punched the elevator button to take Sara to the living room a floor below. When the doors parted at their destination, he guided the reluctant Sara into the plush room and sat her on the couch. He was so angry with her, he had to cross his arms before he either shook some sense into her or hugged her.

His instructions were to stay put, so he stood in front of her, blocking any attempts at escape. He hoped she wouldn't try to run off and make him arrest her. "If you'll cooperate, everything will be fine."

She shook her head. "Miller wants you dead too. We'd be safer with Mario."

"We'll be safe with the FBI." He had to trust in the system he worked for.

But he hated how Mario had humiliated him like that in front of Sara's family. Saying he'd not have the guts to shoot. And then Sara making a deal behind his back? Showed how much trust she had in him. None. But worse, she'd compared him to her dad and then said the one thing he'd always feared—that he would always be alone because no one would ever truly love him.

Pissed off beyond reason, he said to a fuming Sara, "Why did you go behind my back and make a deal for the data? Don't you see how bad that makes me look? Besides being a stupid move. It gave away our location."

Sara wouldn't look him in the eyes. "That stupid move got my dad house arrest and a year's probation as long as he pays the money back."

He sat on the coffee table in front of her. "That's what they tell you, but it isn't a done deal until a judge says it is. It's how we get people to do what we want them to do. Why didn't you trust me?" That had hurt the worst of all.

"Trust you? After doing this to me?" She buried her face in her hands. "I can't believe I slept with you."

Another blow to his heart. "Don't do this, Sara. I'm not like your father. Or Scott. I'd never hurt you. All I want is to keep you safe and make you happy."

"So *now* you're concerned with my happiness? I know you don't have family, and I'm sorry for it, but you can't put rules before people. The people you love in life have to come before all else. It's really all any of us has. Money, power, fame are all worthless compared to love."

"Rules keep our society intact. Money puts food on the table. Love is important, but so is the security that rule-following and money bring."

Sara slowly lifted her head. "If Miller gets to me while I'm in a safe house, then I hope you'll still get that promotion you care so much about. Obviously, nothing would make *you* happier."

His patience evaporated. "Really? You think I'm the sellout here? You're going to take a low-paying counseling job to hide from the press and atone for being born into the right family."

"I'm taking that job to help people know there's hope!"

"Good luck with that. They'll take one look at you and think it's nice that Annalisa Botelli's rich kid wants to help, but she hasn't got a clue how life really is."

"You said you misjudged me. But clearly, you lied, based on that dumb comment!"

"I didn't mean that you don't have a clue, I meant it's what others will think. You can't change who you are. The press will always be there, and those people you try to help will think what the press tells them to think."

Sara's jaw clenched. "I've tried to get people like you, who once lived that kind of life, to talk to the kids. People they can relate to. But people like you don't want to look back. Once you break free, you keep right on moving because you're so afraid to stop. Or maybe because it hurts too much to look into those eyes that were so much like yours? I'm all they've got. And if it isn't good enough, then so be it. At least I'm not afraid to try to live the best life I can."

He closed his eyes and counted to ten.

As hard as he tried, he couldn't stop himself. "You're the one who's scared, Sara. You'd rather hide in a little office and *hope* the press leaves you alone. If you really want to help that shelter, which I know you do, then embrace the power you've been handed and own it. Go out and raise money for more shelters just like the one you love in LA. You're an incredible speaker, and people listen because you believe in what you're saying. Instead of running away from the press, you could help thousands more people, raise millions of dollars, simply by embracing the fame you already have."

"And here we go. Right back to money with you." Tears filled her eyes. "Because you know how easy it is to raise that much money, right? And be chased and harassed everywhere you go? You have no idea how long and hard I worked to save that shelter. But maybe you're right. Maybe when you pull your head out of your butt and finally quit a job you hate, one you're willing to risk *my life* to keep, I'll do as you suggest. But until then, I don't need your advice, Agent Keiser."

He drew in a deep breath along with his temper, rather than take any more of his anger out on her. She was upset, angry, and afraid for her life, and so was he. He'd never forgive himself if something happened to her. Especially when Mario might have been able to keep her safe. But taking her to a secure location was still the right thing to do.

"Sara, please listen." He reached out to take her hands, but she pulled them away. "I'll make this right. I promise."

She seethed, "I'm done talking to you. I want to speak to my lawyer."

"Okay. I'll make that happen." A hardness in her eyes he never thought Sara capable of told him he'd lost her. She'd condemn him for doing his damn job.

Then so be it.

Maybe she'd been right. Perhaps their shared experience had heightened emotions that weren't strong enough to survive after Miller was in jail. But if that were true, why did his chest hurt so bad?

He cleared the lump forming in his throat. He needed to make her see the logic. "Sara—"

The elevator dinged, cutting him off, and out poured a team in tactical gear. He stood and held up his badge. "Agent Keiser. This is Sara Chapman. She willingly turned herself into me."

Sara's grunt wasn't loud enough for the others to hear, thankfully.

The leader gave a hand signal, and all the automatic weapons in the room lowered toward the floor. Baker showed his ID, then said, "These men will escort you to the armored vehicle downstairs."

"Yes, sir. The rest of the family is one floor above."

Baker shook his head. "They're not. They spooked on us. Probably the delay you asked for didn't help."

Dammit. That wasn't going to look good in the report.

Baker asked, "Where's the evidence you needed the extra time to obtain, Agent?"

"I wasn't able to get it, sir." Another strike against him.

Baker's eyes narrowed at Sara. "Do you want to add another charge by withholding evidence, ma'am?"

Sara's eyes narrowed right back.

She was mad enough to do something stupid.

Sara opened her mouth to respond, but he cut her off. "Ms. Chapman has made it clear she wants to speak to a lawyer before she comments further." He tugged her arm and hoped she'd keep her mouth shut until they could get her a lawyer. "I'd like to request permission to accompany her to the secure location?" He led her toward the waiting men.

Sara opened her mouth again, so he added, "Just until we're certain there are no more breaches."

"Granted." Baker nodded toward his men. "Johnson and Wentworth, you stay with me. I want to talk to you when I get back, Keiser."

"Yes, sir." Probably to chew him out. Damn Mario for disappearing. If he was innocent, why not stay?

The remaining four men surrounded Sara and him, and as a unit, they walked to the elevator. One of the men handed Brent a lapel recorder, so he clipped it on.

No one spoke until the elevator stopped and the doors parted again. Someone said, "To the right and through the doors."

Armed guards lined up made a path as they entered an empty underground parking garage. One of the men opened the back door to an armored vehicle, and he helped Sara in first. Then Brent slid beside her. As soon as the door closed, they sped off.

Sara whispered so softly, he barely heard her say, "Promise me if you think I'm not safe, you'll let Mario help. Please?"

If the FBI failed her, he would in a heartbeat. But he couldn't say so; he was wired.

Instead, he gently leaned his shoulder against hers, hoping she'd take that as a yes. Then he pointed to his mic on his chest. "I'm sorry, what did you say? I couldn't hear you."

"Nothing." Sara shook her head and closed her eyes. The silent tears that escaped and trailed down her cheeks killed him. Almost as much as the thought of never seeing her again. She was obviously done with him.

He looked out the window as they made their way down backstreets, off the strip, and finally toward the airport. They pulled up to an ugly industrial warehouse and into a large garage where freight might be loaded and unloaded. Once the garage door closed behind them, both of their car doors opened, and they were led into a hallway that had interrogation rooms and holding cells. Not a warehouse at all, but a field office of some sort.

Sara was met by a female guard who led her away. An older agent greeted him. "Agent Keiser? I'm Special Agent Stanger. Can you come with me, please?"

Brent glanced at Sara, who was being led down an opposite hallway. "I need to stay with my witness. At least until she's in the secure location."

"She'll be fine. You can observe the interview, but I'm taking over from here. Ms. Chapman provided some data this morning. We need you to use it to shut Miller's operation down. We're processing the paperwork to drop her arrest warrant as we speak. But I'll still need to question her, and then we'll determine if she's willing to be moved to a secure location."

Alarm skittered up his spine. "She *absolutely needs* to be moved. We can't be sure who else is involved in our organization yet, much less Miller's. I promised to keep Sara safe. I can't do that if I'm not with her."

Stanger raised a brow. "She's safe here. And we can't force her to take our help after the arrest warrant is dropped. It'll be up to her."

He wished he'd arrested her so that they could hold her longer. "Any arrests been made?"

"We've apprehended the agents involved in your office. Now we need you to get busy using that magic brain of yours and tie the new evidence to the key players. I'm told you're the only one who can do it fast enough."

"I can do both. Guard Ms. Chapman and work at the same time."

Stanger slapped a hand on Brent's back. "Not necessary. Don't worry. I got this. You need to do what you do best." He opened the door to a small room that held a table with a laptop. "The director is impressed with your work, Keiser."

Nice, but that wasn't his biggest worry at the moment. "We don't have Miller?"

The agent's jaw ticked. "Not yet. Your buddy Zach lit a fire under the director's ass, so the orders are all coming from the top. We'll get him soon."

"If someone's tipped him, he'd have a plan to disappear. From what I've seen, he's meticulous."

Stanger nodded. "We're on it. Here's the file. Have at it. We've pulled these suspects in for questioning based on what's in there, so move fast. You need to make the charges stick." He held out a folder three inches thick. "Good luck."

Brent accepted the portfolio and sat behind the computer. After Stanger left, Brent opened the file. On the top was Sara's recreation of his computer screen.

What time had she gotten up to get all this done?

Below were pages of evidence from who knows where. Mario must've called in some major favors. He'd risked a lot to save Sara and her father. Because Sara was clearly as important to him as was his biological daughter, Dani. That was what it must be like to have a family who has your back.

Brent dropped his head into his hands. What had he done? Why had he thought they'd let an agent with little to no field experience keep Sara safe when corruption ran all the way to the upper ranks? Stanger wasn't taking the threat to Sara's life seriously.

Dammit. Maybe he *should* have let Sara escape with Mario and her family.

As he beat himself up, he paged through the banking transactions, separating the off-shore accounts and the domestic ones. He studied the names of the people involved Sara had sent. The list was extensive. It had to have taken months to compile.

There were bank managers, law enforcement, real estate agents, title agents, foreign businessmen and women, and celebrities. Probably friends Holden recruited. Like he'd tried to do with Annalisa. They ranged from people with lots of money to those with regular nine-to-five jobs who probably needed Miller's extra-dirty funds to survive.

He scanned the list and the people's occupations. The answer was there; he could feel it. After clearing his mind and closing his eyes, he focused on the pages he'd just read. Combined with what he'd already figured out before the wedding, it was as if a physical line drew itself from the beginning to the end of the money chain in his mind. He stood and uncapped a dry marker, laying the whole operation out on the whiteboard hanging on the wall. The extra financial data Sara had sent had been the missing key.

A half hour later, when he was done, he stepped back and double-checked his work. Large amounts of drug money from offshore accounts traveled entirely through the chain until it became LA real estate. They waited a year or two, sold the real estate, and then the clean money got broken up into smaller amounts and eventually into the players' legitimate accounts. Some got turned over into even bigger mansions worth hundreds of millions. But it all came down to dirty-money-bought real estate, and then when it was sold to a legitimate buyer, the money was clean.

The people buying the properties involved had to look legit. Hence the celebrities holding titles to homes they didn't own in entirety. They owned shares of corporations. The corporations owned the properties. Rich people like Annalisa needed places to park their money. Thank God she'd been too smart to fall into what would look to most outsiders like a legitimate investment property opportunity.

Miller had done a fantastic job of making sure no one knew the real identity of who or what they were dealing with.

Holden's mistake was to involve Annalisa, who involved Mario. According to Sara, no one outside their family knew her mother was dating Mario. Even Holden. Mario's crooked family members probably didn't appreciate Miller's crew playing in their sandbox. But that was how criminals got caught. Secrets always came out eventually, no matter how well shrouded.

He quickly grabbed his burner phone and took a picture of the whiteboard. He sent it to Zach and then to the laptop Mario had given him. Until Miller was caught, Brent was covering his bases.

Smiling, he laid the dry marker on the metal tray and nodded. It all made perfect sense. And that promotion he'd hoped for was looking good once again because all the crooked agents would be gone after he turned the data in to the right people.

But it still didn't explain how Annalisa, who wasn't involved, tipped off Sara. Maybe someone in Mario's family had.

Worse, where the hell was Miller hiding?

Chapter Nineteen

Humiliating.

It was the only word Sara could think of after she'd had another pat down. Ten times more intrusive than those she'd ever had at the airport.

She'd just forwarded these people stacks of evidence Mario's family had already been gathering for their revenge. Although, as Mario pointed out, they'd planned to use the banking information to figure out how to steal the money from Miller, not to hand over to the FBI. But if it meant Miller had to live the rest of his life behind bars, Mario's family could live with that.

And yet the FBI still treated *her* like a criminal. It made no sense.

At least the guard had been kind and given her a bottle of water while she waited for her lawyer. Sara glanced around the small room with a table and four chairs where she'd been dumped. One wall held a big mirror. She'd seen enough cop shows on TV to know that was two-way glass. Was someone behind that mirror? Watching her?

Was it Brent?

The traitor.

He'd had no right to get so angry with her earlier. And say such hurtful things.

She and Mario had to go behind his back to try to help her dad because Brent made it clear he'd never understand why she had to try to help her father. Even if he did make some huge mistakes.

Brent didn't know what it was like to love someone that much. Or what it was like to be truly loved. It made her sad for him, but only for a moment before her anger rushed back and reminded her that Brent would never be the man she'd hoped he was.

He'd had his chance to be loved by her, but not anymore. She was done with him.

Who was he to tell her she'd be ineffective as a counselor? And what was up with the whole thing about how she was going to take a job to atone for being rich?

Technically, she wasn't rich. Her mother was.

Which sounds like something a rich person would say.

There were trusts and property that'd come her way most likely. So maybe she'd be rich one day, but currently, she had eleven hundred bucks to her name and the Porsche her mom had given her. And given the fact that her father was probably going to have to sell their house to help pay back a portion of his debt, she'd have to find somewhere else to live too. And Justin and Zoila would probably be out of a job. That made her heart hurt even worse.

Brent had been right about one thing. They were from different worlds, but he was the one throwing up barriers and then claiming it was her who refused to look past them. His lecture about how she couldn't shake her heritage and that people in the shelters wouldn't take her seriously had been a knife to her soul.

All she'd been striving for the past few years was to be taken seriously for who she truly was.

Thinking about it all left her tired and wounded, and it felt like her heart was physically being ripped out of her chest.

She crossed her arms on the tabletop and laid her head down.

No crying. Time to be tough. Ignore the sick feeling in your gut. Get through this, live long enough until everyone is behind bars, and then prove freakin' Brent wrong.

The door opened, and a dark-haired woman in her mid-thirties wearing a killer black dress and heels stepped inside. After the guard who'd accompanied her left, she laid her briefcase on the table and stuck out her hand. "Hi, Sara. I'm, Juanita Rivera. Your mother sent me to represent you. Please let me do the talking today unless I give you permission."

"Okay. Thanks for coming." Sara returned the shake. Juanita seemed like a tough cookie who came to play. Just what Sara needed.

Juanita slid a piece of legal-sized paper in front of Sara. "Let's go over a few things before the agent gets here to interview you. Are all these things your mother told me true?"

She picked up the paper and read the handwritten note.

--Sara doesn't know anything about the evidence she turned over, except that it was sent to her in an anonymous email. She merely forwarded it to the FBI agent's name it provided.

--Sara knew nothing of her father's activities until Agent Keiser informed her of them. Therefore, she's not a material witness to the case.

--Sara heard Police Commissioner Miller threaten both her and Agent Keiser's lives, making her feel unsafe to go to the authorities. Sara planned to contact the police once she got to the safety of her mother's secure compound.

--Sara is willing to hire her own security team until all parties involved are contained.

Her mother had probably consulted her sizable legal team and compiled the list.

She nodded and handed the paper back. "Yes. This is all true." She didn't *technically* know where the data had come from. Mario had been careful never to say it was from his family.

"Good." Juanita took a seat beside Sara. "Let's talk about the reasons you didn't hand the data over to Agent Keiser."

After they'd gone over what she should say about Brent, along with a few other scenarios, the door opened, and a man wearing a gray suit came in. "Hello. I'm Special Agent Stanger. Everyone understands we're going on record starting now?"

Her lawyer and the agent exchanged some mumbo-jumbo lawyerly things while Sara sat back and let Juanita do her job. Her mother would only send a top-notch person, so Sara would put herself in Juanita's hands and hope for the best.

After an hour of questions, repeated over and over but in slightly different ways, Special Agent Stanger asked one more time about the source of the evidence she'd forwarded again. He wouldn't let it go. But she honestly didn't know where it had come from. Exactly.

Juanita said, "Sara has answered. Let's move on, please."

"Fine. Ms. Chapman, why didn't you share the evidence with Agent Keiser when you got the email?"

She glanced at the mirror. Was Brent behind there?

She turned to Juanita, who nodded her approval to answer the question they'd practiced. "Because when I realized the data Brent asked me to recreate from my memory could hurt my father,

I was understandably reluctant to hand it over. Then the email came, and I saw an opportunity to perhaps help my father. Brent had made it clear that my father didn't deserve my sympathy after what he'd done. That I should put my best interests first." Sara paused and then added her own thoughts. "Brent will never understand protecting family. Because of his background."

"His background?" Stanger's brows lifted. "You're familiar with Agent Keiser's childhood?"

Juanita said, "She's answered the question. Next?"

"Not yet." Stanger leaned closer to Sara. "Is the reason you didn't give the data to Agent Keiser because he knew it was obtained illegally, and you're covering for him? Do you and *Brent* have a personal relationship, Ms. Chapman?"

Personal relationship? Covering for Brent?

It could be tough on Brent's career if she confessed that they'd slept together. But she was the one who'd pushed for that. And sure, someone awful probably sent the data, but wasn't something sent anonymously and then handed over to the FBI fair game? The right thing to do?

But it *could* look like Brent had told her to send it instead of him. She'd been too focused on saving her dad rather than worrying about how going behind Brent's back could affect the case.

Brent told her to tell the truth if asked about their relationship. She turned to Juanita for help.

Brent watched Sara through the glass. Why hadn't she listened to him about her father last night? If Stanger thought the data was obtained illegally, they'd have to release all the suspects they'd detained. If she confessed to sleeping with him, Stanger might cast doubt on the evidence. As would the defense in court. He might as well kiss that promotion goodbye. Maybe his job too. His new house might be a long time coming.

He'd known better than to sleep with Sara. He deserved whatever he got, but Miller's victims didn't. They deserved justice. If his lack of judgment stood in their way, he'd never forgive himself.

He'd told Sara not to lie. It'd be the right thing to do, to tell the truth. But if she did, the whole case could be screwed, along with every aspect of his life.

He held his breath and waited for her response.

Sara frowned as she listened to her lawyer whisper in her ear. Then Sara replied to Stanger, "Wasn't it Brent's job to form a personal relationship with me? To find out if I was involved in whatever was going on with my account?"

Stanger only nodded.

Sara continued, "Well then, he did a good job, because I assumed we were friends when he asked to accompany me to my dad's wedding after Scott dumped me."

Stanger wrote some notes, making Sara sweat, no doubt, before he said, "But you and Brent developed personal feelings for each other after that? Maybe a shared trust while on the road?"

After her lawyer whispered in her ear again, Sara said, "Trust, yes. But it was a mistake on my part to trust Brent. Believe me, there's no personal relationship going forward. Because of his lies, I could be dead right now. If he'd confessed his identity earlier, I might have taken different actions after the wedding that night to ensure my safety."

Brent released the breath he'd been holding. The expression on her face reflected how much she despised him. Sara could sell a line as well as her parents, thankfully. And she'd kept their secret safe.

But Sara would never give him the time of day after the case was over. She said she never wanted to talk to him again. However, maybe now they'd lock a whole lot of people up. Including Miller.

That should make him happy, but what he felt was far from joy. He'd lost the only person who ever made him feel like smiling.

His phone vibrated in his pocket. It was a text from Baker. Probably wanted to give him an ass-chewing for asking for more time when they'd come for Sara. He tapped the screen.

Get Sara out quickly and quietly. Just got word of a possible breach still in place. I'll text you a secure location as soon as I have it.

Brent's heart stopped. Without knowing where the breach was, there was no way he'd trust anyone else with Sara's life. What the hell was he going to do? He could be fired for disregarding a direct order. But he'd made Sara a promise in the car.

He had to protect her. He couldn't let anything happened to her.

He had to decide. No time to waste. Dammit!

What if the breach was Baker? He could be handing her over to her executioner. He'd rather take the hit than risk anything happening to her. He didn't know who he could trust anymore, so he typed back: **Affirmative.**

He had no intention of following orders, though. His career was probably screwed anyway.

He quickly googled the phone number for Mario's casino and then tapped it into his phone. When a male receptionist answered, Brent said, "I need to talk to Mr. Giovanni. It's urgent. Tell him Brent's calling, please."

As he waited, he turned back to the interview. Because Sara refused FBI protection, Stanger agreed to let the lawyer take Sara with her as soon as the proper paperwork came through. He warned Sara to stay available.

Was Stanger the leak?

The man from the casino came back on the line. "I'm sorry, but we can't seem to locate Mr. Giovanni. May I take a message?"

This can't be happening.

"Please tell him to call me as soon as you find him." Brent gave him the number and then hung up. While Brent weighed his options, Stanger left to check on Sara's paperwork.

This is my chance.

He quickly opened the door and met Stanger in the hallway. "Hey. I'd like to ask Ms. Chapman about something for my report before you let her go."

"Fine." Stanger nodded to the guard outside, and he opened the door for Brent. "Bring her up front when you're done, and I'll sign her out."

"Thanks." Brent closed the door behind him. Sara and her lawyer were whispering about something, so he cleared his throat. "Hi. I'm Agent Keiser. I have just one more question for Sara, please. And then we'll get you on your way." He sat in the chair across from Sara.

Her gaze grew hard. "I thought I made myself clear. I don't want to speak to you."

Her lawyer laid a hand on Sara's arm and asked, "What's your question, Agent?"

"It's a request, actually. I need Mario Giovanni's cell number. I'd like to clear up one last issue that's *just* come to my attention." They might still be on the record. He had to be careful what he said. Who knew who was listening?

He slid his phone in front of Sara as he stared into her eyes, hoping she'd understand his meaning.

Sara's narrowed eyes slowly grew wide before she pulled herself back together. She lifted the phone and tapped in a number. "Am I stuck with you until they spring me, Agent Keiser?"

Was that her way of agreeing to let him help her? He hoped so. "'Fraid so. Let me ask Mario this question, and then I'll take you up front so that you can leave." Brent pinned their location in the phone and then texted Mario with the details.

While they waited for a response, he said, "I'd like to ask the guard for a helmet and bulletproof vest if that's okay with you, Ms. Chapman?"

A ding sounded before Sara could answer. Thankfully, it was Mario and not Baker.

Sending my men. Fifteen minutes.

Brent pushed the phone closer to be sure Sara could read the screen too, then he said, "The gear is just for added protection if you agree?"

Sara read the text and then closed her eyes and nodded. Her lawyer said, "Let's get the gear quickly so Sara can go home."

"Will do." Brent jumped up to ask the guard for the equipment and to kill some time to let Mario's men get into place. Sara had to be terrified. But if he could get her out the front door and then safely into Mario's hands, his job would be complete.

He'd argue his case about not knowing who he could trust, but Baker would still reprimand him for disregarding orders and then probably send him back to his cubical in LA until the trial. Or maybe to some remote post in Alaska. What difference did it make where he worked? He had few possessions, let alone anyone to care about. He'd done just fine on his own before, and he'd be fine moving forward.

All that mattered now was getting Sara somewhere safe.

Chapter Twenty

Sara, in full riot gear sans the shield and tear gas, stood beside Brent near the front desk while her lawyer took care of the release paperwork with Stanger. Their backs were to them, and both heads were bent down over the counter. There was no one else around in the little sparsely furnished warehouse-looking lobby. Which was probably a good thing.

She wouldn't be in her current predicament if it weren't for Brent, but at least he'd kept his promise to contact Mario. She hoped she'd not need the heavy gear she wore, but was grateful for it.

She glanced his way. He was texting with someone.

Brent moved way too close. "Just got word Mario's men are in place outside. We have to sneak out quietly. Now!"

The urgency in his voice put some steel back into her spine, and she followed behind him. He was the one good at sneaking around, but luckily, she'd been wearing tennis shoes and not heels when Brent had dragged her to the station, so that helped.

Brent stopped at the door, swiped his card, and then slowly pressed on the bar to let them out. He pushed her behind him. She wore all the riot gear, not him, so she should go first, but he held her in place as he did the scanning thing with his eyes again. Finally, he grabbed her arm and practically carried her at a full run into the parking lot and into a set of massive arms.

"Take care, Sara," Brent said as the big, suit-clad arms tossed her into a waiting car as if she weighed nothing. As she sat up in the backseat, the driver took off. She watched out the window as a huge vehicle drove up. The Baker guy jumped out, talked to Brent, and then pointed to the car she was in.

Baker grabbed Brent and dragged him inside as the tank thing gave chase. "I assume you guys see that big thing?" she said to the men in the front seat. Mario's men she recognized from the plane that'd picked up Brent and her in Show Lo.

The driver nodded and in a perfectly calm voice said, "We're faster and nimbler. Lay down, please."

Sara lay back down on the seat and let the stress of the day overcome her. Tears flowed down her cheeks that she couldn't wipe because of the helmet.

What had Brent told Baker? The truth? Would they try to take her back if they caught her? Brent didn't believe in lying unless it was *necessary*. He'd proven to her that she wasn't *necessary* to him like she'd thought he was to her.

She closed her eyes. It wasn't her problem anymore to worry about Brent. He'd broken her heart. It'd healed before, but maybe the damage was permanent this time.

Everything was out of her control now. Assuming they could ditch the tank, things would progress according to her mother's secret plan. There'd been a system in place to disappear since Sara could remember, and only a chosen few knew what the entire plan was. She wasn't one of the few.

The car picked up speed, and zigzagged through smaller back streets to lose the lumbering vehicle that followed. When the driver pulled the wheel hard, the tires squealed, and her head bumped against the door. The helmet dulled the impact. After fifteen minutes of her being thrown from side to side in the backseat, the driver finally said, "We lost them."

Relief filled her as the car continued to speed to an unknown destination. Now all she had to do was go along with her mom's plan and all would be fine.

Who knew how long she'd have to stay hidden? Until after the trial? A few months? If so, she'd miss her last semester of school. And the classes she needed were only offered in the spring, so it'd be a whole extra year until she could graduate as she'd planned. But for the first time, she was so utterly sad, she didn't care what happened next. Not when the future she'd just begun to visualize with Brent was gone.

Damn her father for ruining her life. She'd always love him, but would she ever be able to forgive him? Probably not this time. She was done being his chump.

As the car sped along, she let her exhaustion overcome her, take her away from her screwed-up life for a few hours, and she closed her eyes to allow fate to do with her what it would.

∞ ∞ ∞

After too many hours to count of traveling, Sara stared at the deep blue water beneath her. Where was she? She'd been given new clothes, driven in cars, jets, boats, and now a tiny prop plane that bobbed at the slightest hint of wind. It made her stomach sick.

She'd tried but hadn't been able to eat more than a few crackers since she'd left Vegas. Probably a good thing.

Her fuzzy brain searched for what day it was, and then it came to her. Usually her favorite day of the entire year. December twenty-fifth.

Merry freakin' Christmas to me.

Or by now, maybe it was the day after? Who knew. But she'd probably spend the holiday alone in some hut on the beach or in the surrounding jungle if the terrain below was any indicator.

What fun.

As the plane made its approach on a grass landing strip, she gathered up the bag someone had given her along her journey. She held it tightly against her chest in case things got rough. But to her surprise, the little plane floated gently to the earth and after only one little bounce, it slowed and taxied right up to a waiting Jeep.

"Thanks," she said to the tall, dark-haired pilot who opened the door for her. None of the people driving her or flying her had spoken a word to her. And she wasn't to speak either according to the escape plan, but please and thank you were engraved in her nature. She couldn't help but be polite even though she wanted to scream in frustration at what might become of her life.

The pilot nodded and held out a hand. He helped her walk down the wing where the arrows pointed. Then she hopped to the grass below.

By the time she'd thrown her bag into the backseat of the Jeep and greeted the driver, the plane had started its engine and taxied away to take off.

So much for changing her mind.

An Asian man, maybe a little older than her, sat in the driver's seat. He pointed to Sara's seat belt, so she clipped in. She couldn't help her smile. Her mother had probably made sure she'd been reminded to wear it. Her mom had made them wear seat belts even in limos. Safety first for Annalisa, but at the moment, Sara had no room to complain. Her mother's diligence had probably saved her life.

But is Brent okay?

Where had that thought come from? Brent was a big boy who'd declined to go with her. He truly believed the FBI would protect him from Miller. Hopefully, that'd be true. She wouldn't wish any harm to come to him. Maybe just a little torture in the form of being buried under piles of paperwork.

Bracing herself for what primitive living conditions were to come as the Jeep bumped along a dirt path through the jungle, Sara said, "This is a beautiful place."

Her driver smiled and nodded.

Great. Was she going to be stuck on some island where she couldn't speak the language? She muttered, "This could be a long few months."

"Maybe."

She whipped her head in his direction. "You speak English?"

"Even managed to graduate from USC. But just by the skin of my teeth." His big smile indicated he was teasing her.

"Sorry. I figured I must be on the other side of the world by now." It'd looked like Thailand from the air. They'd passed over chains of islands that appeared uninhabited. But she could be anywhere.

"No worries." He changed gears and started down a steep path. "I'm John. Head of security here on your mom's island."

Her mother owned an island? Wow. "And where exactly are we?"

John smiled. "Paradise."

Oh. She probably wasn't supposed to know where they were. Got it.

When they got to the bottom of the hill, the jungle parted, and a vast villa appeared. It was three stories high, built into a hill, and every level had decks that looked over the ocean. There was a long T-shaped dock with two speedboats moored beside it, but based on the length and size, it could handle much bigger craft. The sand on the beach was so white, it blinded her. Maybe not such a bad place to work on her tan and get her head straight after all.

"I'll show you to your suite." John pulled the Jeep under a carport and jumped out.

She climbed out too and grabbed her bag from the rear before he could. "Am I the only one here?"

John shook his head. "My family lives next door. I was sent to the US as a kid to live with an uncle right before my family, who are political refugees, went into hiding. Your mom lets us live here in exchange for upkeep. You're safe here."

Sara followed John into the house. They crossed a short landing and then walked down a hallway that had Travertine steps and smooth plaster walls. Far from the grass hut, she'd imagined. But then, it was her mom. She should have known better.

When they got to the top of the stairs, they entered a huge great room with thick glass walls and killer views of the beach and the water. Breathtaking. And most likely bulletproof glass.

John said, "And this is for you. We don't celebrate this holiday, but we knew you did. Merry Christmas, Sara."

Sara turned around, and her heart jumped into her throat. A Christmas tree, all decorated, stood in the corner. It was a fake, but still. She had to be beyond tired, because the sight of the little Charlie Brown five-foot tree with garland and lights, the least beautiful thing in the magnificent room, made her want to cry. "Thank you."

"My pleasure. I stocked the fridge for you. Anything else you need, just let me know." He handed her a walkie-talkie and then led her to a large bedroom with a luxurious bath attached. "Have a rest, and then we have a surprise for you."

"Okay, thanks." She waited until the doors closed behind her and then she threw her bag onto a chair and landed face-first on the soft bed. Too tired to shower or strip, she closed her eyes and passed out.

∞ ∞ ∞

Brent walked into his apartment, totally trashed by the search, and tossed his keys onto the kitchen counter. After getting chewed out for letting Sara go with Mario, Baker had offered a safe house until the trial was over, but sitting around playing checkers with another agent didn't appeal. Miller was still on the run, and that was a personal failure, so Brent had no choice but to find him, but without the help of the FBI, who currently held his gun and badge while he was on paid administrative leave. Code for *when we need your brain, we'll call you. Otherwise, we can handle things without you from here.*

He shook his head and began the cleanup process. Anything to keep his mind off Sara and wondering if she was okay.

He straightened couch cushions and then started cleaning up all the crap in the kitchen his fellow agents had thrown on the floor in the search for his data. Spices, cereal boxes, and cans were scattered everywhere. They'd left the fridge and freezer doors open, so all the food had gone bad too. Not that he had a ton in there in the first place.

As he swept the floor, a knock sounded on the door. Who'd be at his door on Christmas day? Wishing for his gun, Brent laid his broom against the kitchen counter and grabbed a knife from the drawer. Then he crept to the door. When he peered into the peephole, relief filled him.

Zach.

Brent had to clear the lump away from his throat to greet his mentor. He'd been certain he'd spend another holiday alone, which would've been fine, except this time, he'd been missing the hell out of Sara. "Hey. What are you doing here?"

Zach, still built like a fit but gray-haired marine even though he had to be pushing seventy, walked in with a sack. "Everything's closed today. Thought you could use some groceries. This place is a damn mess, Keiser."

"Maid's year off. Come in." Brent accepted the bag and placed it on the countertop. There was a bag of chips, a can of bean dip, and a six pack of beer. Perfect.

Instead of sitting on a barstool at the messy counter, Zach picked up the broom and got busy. Brent grabbed two beers and twisted off the tops. "Cheers."

Zach stopped sweeping and accepted the bottle. "Merry Christmas."

"That too." Brent took a long pull. "Hear anything about Miller?" He laid his bottle down and grabbed a plastic trash bag to throw all the spices, broken bottles, and the spoiled food away.

"Nope. No one seems to know where the guy's holed up. I hear they got most of the thugs who worked for him, though. Some that ran might take a few more days to round up."

Until Miller was behind bars, he wouldn't sleep at night.

They worked in silence for a few minutes until Zach said, "You did the right thing, you know. With Sara. I look back sometimes and wish I'd had the guts to disregard an order."

It was still hard to talk about her. "You have regrets?"

Zach barked out a laugh. "Only about a thousand. Maybe everyone does looking back at a long career. I always told myself I was better off putting my job first above all else. I was a great agent, so I had to be doing the right thing. It wasn't until I got too damn old to be in the field and they made me a teacher at the academy that I realized my mistakes."

"How so?" Brent tied off the first garbage bag then got started on the next.

Zach laid the broom down and took a long drink from his bottle. "After knowing so many agents, I'd look at the kids in my classes and was able to predict with a pretty fair degree of accuracy how they'd turn out. Some were meant to be lone wolves and would make great field agents. Some were going to shine behind the scenes, some were good administrators and leaders, and then there were the few who were simply running from their pasts. The runners never admit it to themselves, just keep running, and end up screwing up their lives because of it. Like me."

Brent stopped cleaning and faced Zach. "You grew up with everything." As Sara had. "An only child, the best private schools, living in the beach house. What could you possibly be running from?"

Zach shook his head and went back to sweeping the spilled pepper from the floor. "Having stuff and happiness aren't the same thing. At least not for me. Except for maybe my boat. She's the love of my life."

So, Zach wasn't going to share what he ran from. "Money is just a necessary evil in life. I'll be happy when I don't ever have to worry about it anymore. Like you."

"But being a slave to it carries a big price."

What the hell was Zach talking about? "I have a solid financial plan I'm going to stick with. You can't be a slave to your own plans. I'm making my own choices."

"Whatever." Zach polished off his beer. "It's late. And you're depressing the hell out of me on this fine holiday. Why don't you come by the house sometime soon so we can talk about finding Miller? That way, you can redeem yourself. Get that precious badge of yours back. Put a smile on that sappy sad mug of yours for a change."

"Okay." Was Zach being facetious? Was he really saying they should try to find Miller on their own, or was his friend trying to tell him something else?

After Zach left, Brent took another long drink of beer, letting the bubbles slide down his throat while letting Zach's words absorb into his brain.

The slave-to-money comment stuck hard. He wasn't a slave to money. He'd just been looking for the best job out of college, one that'd set him up for life. He practically lived like a pauper so that he could save for the future. Zach was wrong about that.

Isn't he?

Chapter Twenty-One

The aroma of something familiar replaced Sara's dream about running away from an oversized chicken. Cinnamon. Sugar. Yeast. And something light and floral, like perfume?

She cracked one eye open.

Still in the bedroom on the island John had escorted her to earlier. Maybe he had a sister so she'd have some female companionship her age. Heck, maybe she'd go find his mom and hang out. She was through with the male species.

Sara opened her other eye and winced at the bright sunlight.

Three cinnamon rolls sat on a plate on her nightstand. Yes! Probably the surprise John had promised her.

She reached out and grabbed one, still warm from the oven, and took a bite. Amazingly as good as her sister's secret recipe. "Maybe it won't be so bad here after all."

"Not even a thank-you?" Dani's voice sounded from somewhere across the room.

That explained the perfume. Sara sat up to be sure she wasn't still dreaming.

Dani joined her on the bed. "You're wearing the same clothes you had on four days ago at Mario's. And John says you've been asleep since yesterday. What's up with that?"

She'd slept for twenty-four hours? "I think it's called depression. But now I'm unbearably happy because you're here." Sara threw her arms around her sister. "And thanks for the rolls. What are you doing here?"

"Currently, I'm being strangled. Good to see you too, kiddo."

Sara loosened her grip, but only slightly. "Seriously. Why are you here? Did something go wrong at home? Are Mom and Mario okay?"

Dani peeled the arms cutting off her airway from her neck. "We're all here to celebrate Christmas with you." Her sister struck an Annalisa Botelli movie star pose. "Botellis are *always* together at Christmas. Even if it's almost New Year's." Her sister's impersonation of their mom was spot-on. "It's rule number fifteen from the *How To Be An Acceptable Daughter* handbook. Did you lose your copy? If so, I'll get you another."

Sara laughed. Her sister could take that act on the road, it was so good. "Did Grams come too?"

"Yes. And a few others you'll be happy to see." Dani took Sara's hands and pulled her off the bed. "But not until you get showered and changed. You're disgusting."

While being dragged to the bath, Sara asked, "But that many people could compromise our location, right? I thought only Mom and Jake were supposed to know where this place is."

Dani nodded. "Mom has another secret place like this somewhere in the world too, apparently. She couldn't bear the thought of you being alone for Christmas. So it was worth the compromise. And you'll probably be moving again soon."

"Great." Sara unbuttoned her shirt and stepped out of her jeans.

Dani turned on the water all the way to hot. "Might need to steam-clean you after four days."

"I'm not interested in being boiled like a lobster, thank you very much." She turned the lever to the middle and then stepped inside. She didn't want to ask, but couldn't help herself. "Do you know if Brent's okay?"

"Brent's fine. Not that you care, of course." Dani slapped the shower door closed. "Hurry up. I'm dying to open presents."

"It might take a while. It's actually been five days since I showered. Brent dragged me to the station before I could get cleaned up," she called out as she leaned her head back and let the warm water sluice over her.

"Thanks for oversharing, Typhoid Mary. Hurry, or all the food will be gone."

"'Kay." How amazing was it that her whole family had come to be with her? It should make her happy to her core, but then, why was she crying, dammit? She opened her eyes and found the body wash.

As she rubbed the floral scent all over, she let her mind go where she hadn't allowed it to for days.

She *might* forgive Brent one day for dragging her to the station and putting her life in danger. But it hadn't happened yet. And she *might even* be able to forgive him for putting his job before her because of his messed-up priorities.

She rinsed off and then reached for the shampoo.

But in the end, they'd never work. She and Brent were just too different. People who'd never see eye to eye on fundamental parts of life. Like her fame. He'd never be able to do another undercover job that he so dearly hoped to do if he was with her. The cameras were everywhere in her life. And Brent made it clear by his actions that his job came first.

She poured conditioner into her hand. It was her usual brand. Her mother thought of everything.

Back to Brent. Money. That was where the crux of the problem lay with them. He was obsessed with it, and she couldn't care less if she lived in a tiny apartment the rest of her life. Fundamental beliefs. People didn't change those unless they made huge efforts to make that happen. And she was finally happy with who she was, so Brent could just go his own way and live in his bubble on the beach.

She rinsed her hair clean and turned off the tap. She grabbed a big fluffy towel that hung on a rack nearby and dried off as she walked to the closet. She'd bet a dollar it was filled with clothes her size.

After wiping the last tears from her eyes, and determined to block any more thoughts of Brent, she slid the mirrored door back, and voila! Designer labels in her size abounded. "Even on a remote tropical island where no one was supposed to see me, Mom? Geez." She chose a dark green top and black silk pants, and then crossed to the dresser. It was filled with expensive lingerie. "Who was this for? John?" Her mother believed that women should always wear nice things underneath no matter what they wore on the outside. Not in case of a car accident like other moms feared. Her mom meant that one should always be prepared in case they run into a handsome man they'd like to sleep with.

After changing into her new clothes and finding a pair of black flats, she grabbed a blow dryer from a hook on the bathroom wall. One nice thing about having short hair was how fast she could get ready. Brent had done such a great job of cutting layers that she could style her new do with only the dryer and her fingers. So okay, that was something she'd probably miss about him. His ability to cut hair. And the way he teased her. And the way he made love—Stop. No more. There was going to be no missing Brent. It was counterproductive to her mood and her sanity.

But being depressed over him helped her catch up on her sleep, apparently. There was always a silver lining in a storm cloud if one looked hard enough. Another of her mother's sayings.

God, help her. She was turning into her mother. She'd be naming coconuts and volleyballs next, left all alone on her mom's island. But safe. She hoped Brent stayed safe too.

See? She could have a civil thought about him. Must already be over the guy. The threatening tears again were happy tears at the prospect of seeing her family. That was all.

Sara switched off the blow dryer and headed toward the great room. The sound of voices quickened her step. Was that Zoila's cute accent she'd heard? And Justin too? Yes! It was going to be a great Christmas after all!

After a fun day of celebrations, Sara cuddled up next to Grams and Mittens on the couch and watched the Christmas lights twinkle on the crooked little tree. "That was the best Christmas ever."

Dani had stayed up after their island holiday celebration too and said, "It was. But I'm ready to go home tomorrow. I miss Michael and the girls."

Grams nodded. "You're going to be the best stepmom ever. They already love you." Then she turned Sara's way. "I hope your Brent will makes things right again so you can go home soon too, honey. But now Mittens and I are pooped. See you both in the morning." She lifted up the cat and headed for bed.

"Night, Grams," they said in unison before Dani turned to Sara. "And how about you? Missing *your* Brent?"

"Nope." She'd tried her best not to think about him all evening. But something he'd said to her wouldn't stop niggling at her brain. "Can you believe he accused me of wanting to take a low-paying job—helping others, I might add—to atone for being born into wealth?"

Her sister shook her head. "You don't have anything to atone for. You do amazing things for the shelter. We're all proud of you for it."

"Thanks. But Brent said because some might recognize me as my parents' daughter, they won't take me seriously." She hated that the most. "And then he said if I really want to help the most people, I should use my fame to raise money rather than be a counselor who no one will listen to."

Dani frowned. "He said no one would listen to you?"

"Well, no. But that's what he meant."

"What he *meant*? You have prophetic powers too all of a sudden?" Dani grinned and got up from the chair she'd been sitting in and moved to the couch too.

"No. He thinks I'm not owning up to a privilege that was handed to me on a silver platter. Like it's so easy to not only be Annalisa's daughter but Holden's too? It's a double whammy in the face. Dodging the press is a huge annoyance. Hardly a privilege."

"Sounds like Brent was simply pointing out the obvious. You have fame whether you like it or not."

"I realize that. But it's annoying, not something I'd want to make worse by calling press conferences like Mom does."

"Mom tried to shield us from it by living in Albuquerque, but you went and moved smack dab into the middle of the spotlight. The press follows you because you're always dressed in

Mom's preapproved astronomically priced outfits, you drive a cool car, and you have fancy friends. You seem to live the life every twenty-six-year-old dreams of. And dreams are what sells a story. Not the good work you do. Move back home and be a counselor there if you don't want all the attention in LA. Or use your fame as Brent suggested."

An arrow to her heart. "I thought you of all people would understand."

Her sister took her hand. "Of course, I understand. But you need to know that your father is part of the biggest scandal to hit Hollywood in years. He recruited a lot of celebrities to invest in Miller's fraudulent corporations. It's all coming out in bits and pieces, and each day, it gets worse. Brace yourself for the press when you get home, because it's nasty. But maybe it could be an opportunity if you make it one. You're so amazing with the paparazzi and more patient with them than I'll ever be. I admire that about you."

Praise from her sister was nice, but she was more worried about her dad. "My father's being painted as the villain?"

Dani shrugged. "His PR team is spinning it as more duped by Miller. But the chances of him getting a commercial or a movie anytime soon aren't so good."

How was her dad going to pay back all the money? "Wait. I just realized that the shelter might have to give back the money I gave them from my account!"

"Then maybe you'll have to get busy raising more money when you get home. I'm going to bed too. Night, Sara."

"Night." Way to ruin her Christmas spirit. "Hey, Dani. Wait a second." She got up and caught up with her sister. "Remember all the things you told me about in your dreams? The Jeep, the three cactuses and stuff?"

253

Dani nodded. "What about them?"

"I found all of them except the pay phone. What was that about?"

Her sister's face lit with a knowing grin. "That's going to be interesting. The decision you make will affect the rest of your life. I hope you'll choose to be happy. Sweet dreams, Sara."

She threw her hands up in exasperation and then headed for bed too. The Botellis and their damn dreams. They all got such perverse pleasure knowing stuff that she'd have to wait to find out. How could a call on a pay phone affect her life in such a big way? Well, it wouldn't take much. The last week or so had pretty much left her life a disaster.

∞ ∞ ∞

Brent stood with his hands in his jean pockets in front of the blue wooden door to the beach house he hoped to own one day, debating with himself. Should he ask Zach the question that'd been bothering him for days or not? Did he want to hear the answer he was afraid he already knew?

When he realized he was mirroring the exact stance in Eva's dream, in the same location, he quickly took his hands out of his pockets and rang the bell. He didn't believe in psychic crap. But it still didn't make any sense how Eva had known about Zach's house. There had to be a logical explanation. He just didn't know what it was.

When the door swung open, Zach appeared with a big smile. "There's the man of the hour. Come have a beer on the back deck and tell me all about it."

Brent stepped inside and closed the door behind him. He followed Zach through the living room and to the rear deck. The waves crashing against the shore and the salty ocean breeze usually brought a sense of calm over him, but not today.

Zach circled the outdoor bar. "Have a seat." He grabbed two beers from the fridge and handed one over. "Did Miller's location come to you in a dream or something?"

Dreams. Again. He was sick of thinking about strange dreams. "No. After you left the other night, I kept thinking about if I were Miller, where would I hide? I had a few hours of mindless cleaning to do, so I ran the possibilities through my head. Miller would have had a hard time leaving the country or maybe even the state with everyone, including the media, looking for him, so why not hide in plain sight until things cooled off?"

"I taught you well. That one is overlooked far too often." Zach tapped his bottle against Brent's. "Good for you. Go on."

"It took me a while, but then I remembered a real estate contract Holden had in his house that I'd found. The contract stated that the home wasn't set to close until next month, but the renters had vacated the property already. And guess who had the keys?"

"Miller."

"Yep." Brent took a drink from his bottle. "I drove out to the house and talked to the neighbors. The couple next door said they'd seen a truck deliver some of those fancy beds. The ones that you can choose the stiffness of the mattress and track sleep."

Zach's grin grew wide. "You went to the mattress store, confirmed the delivery, and then called your boss?"

"Yeah. They got permission to look into the database that records sleep info for people's apps and then confirmed all the beds were slept on the previous night. Later that evening, we waited until all the men were tucked in and snoozing, because the beds can tell when someone is asleep, and then a team went in to extract them. But Miller and his men were heavily armed. They intended to go down with a fight, and they did. They were all killed. Later, when the lab got ahold of their electronics, they showed Miller and his top henchmen were arranging for fake passports to leave the country. It was just dumb luck we got to them before they got their paperwork."

Zach said, "More like smart luck. They give you your badge back after all that?"

"Nope." Brent picked at the label on his beer bottle. "Still being punished for insubordination. But that's okay. I didn't do it to get my badge back. I found him to protect Sara."

A corner of Zach's mouth twitched. "No matter the reason, you did good, son. I'm proud of you."

Brent's heart swelled embarrassingly at the praise. He wasn't used to it. "Thanks. But talking about my case wasn't why I came today. I wanted to ask you which type of student you had me pegged as?"

"Which do you think you were?" Zach grabbed a bag of potato chips from under the bar and ripped it open. He leaned the bag Brent's way.

After taking a handful, he said, "I initially thought the lone wolf."

"But then you went and solved a case for a woman instead of for your badge. So now which do you think you are?"

Dammit. He hated how Zach always saw right through him. "A runner?"

Zach grinned and tapped his nose. "It takes one to know one. That's why I wanted to give you a good deal on this house. To give you roots. And I hoped it'd give you a goal to work toward. And when you reached it, as I've never doubted you will, I hope you'll fill this house with a wife and some kids. And just be happy for a change. Because these beautiful old bones have never housed a happy family."

That was what Zach must've been running from. "What do you think I'm running from?"

"You're the only one who knows for sure, but if I had to guess, you're afraid to be happy. Like if you allow yourself to feel happy, it'll hurt ten times worse when someone or something comes along and steals it from you. So rather than pursuing it, you avoid it. Like people who love dogs, but after losing one, won't get another because of the future heartbreak when the new one will inevitably die. Me? I'd rather enjoy the new dog for as long as I can and be grateful for it."

"And yet, you don't have a dog."

"Right. Like I said, takes one to know one. Don't wait until you're old to figure all this crap out like I did. Go get Sara back."

"I blew it with her."

"Agreed. I made that same mistake once and still regret it. But what hurt worse? Losing your badge or losing Sara?"

"Sara." He'd been in a living hell ever since he'd seen Sara last. But he didn't know how to fix things with her. He'd done the right thing in the end. But she'd made it clear she'd never forgive him for it. And he'd been so hurt by her betrayal that he'd said some hurtful things that hadn't been any of his business.

"So what are you going to do about it?"

Brent threw their empty bottles away then grabbed two more from the fridge. "Don't know. She pretty much hates me right now. Says I love my job more than her. And that I'm afraid to live the best life that I can."

"What does 'afraid to live your best life' even mean?" Zach circled the bar and sat on a barstool too.

"She thinks I'm settling by staying with the FBI for the benefits. That I should find a job that makes me happy to go to work each day. Who's happy to go to work every day? No one I know."

"Yeah. That's a tall order. But after cracking a case no one else could, it's doubtful they'll ever let you out of your cubical again. You're going to be the go to numbers man, my friend. Can you live with that for thirty more years?"

Can I?

Zach held up a finger. "Wait. Before you answer, are you more afraid of dying or being broke?"

"Being broke, hands down. Once you're dead, it's only hard on the ones who loved you. And there aren't very many of those in my case."

"Morbid, but okay, then let's pretend that I gifted my house to you and gave you one of my trust funds worth millions. You'd be set for life. If that were to happen, would you still work for the FBI?"

He laughed. "That's exactly what *you* did."

"We're not talking about me. I don't have a woman I need to win back. And I'm not as dense as you. Answer the question." Zach grabbed another handful of chips and chomped them down.

"How do I know? Is there a point to this? And could you get to it before I'm as old as you, please?"

"My point is that apologizing to Sara obviously won't work. Actions speak louder than words. The only way to get her back and make my house happy too is to change your actions going forward. Show Sara you're not obsessed with money and your job and that you trust in your abilities enough to throw caution to the wind for a change. Live your best life."

"My best life is a financially secure one."

"And one with Sara in it."

"Yeah." She made him happy. That was for sure.

"She's back now, you know. Once they reported Miller was dead, it was safe for her to come home. Saw her on the news getting barraged by the press about her dad."

His heart rate picked up. Maybe this was his chance. He'd find her and apologize. Maybe now that she was home and safe, she'd forgive him. "Gotta go. Thanks for the beer."

"Good luck getting her back."

"Thanks."

But luck wouldn't have anything to do with it. His mission to win Sara back would be his most challenging one to date. But succeeding would have the biggest payoff yet.

He'd never failed at a mission in his four years as an agent and wasn't about to start now.

Chapter Twenty-Two

*B*rent parked his car and walked to the shelter's front door to find Sara. It'd been ten days since he'd seen her, but it felt like months. He'd looked for her at her father's house first. There'd been boxes everywhere. They'd been packing up the house to sell it. Zoila told him Sara had already left for the shelter to log some time before she had to go back to school, so he hoped she'd still be there.

The goodbye hugs from Zoila and Justin had actually hurt. He'd miss them. A lot. Who'd have ever thought a simple assignment could change his outlook so much? Getting to know the people Sara loved, whether they were related by blood or not, made him understand what having a family could do to enrich his life. He hoped Sara would give him another chance. So maybe they could have their own family one day.

He grabbed the handle on the glass door and pulled. The small reception area had two chairs, a metal door with an electronic keypad, and a tall check-in counter. The clock on the wall showed it was just before ten. Too early to ask if she'd like to go to lunch. Maybe coffee.

A man he'd seen with Sara on the platform that day when she donated Scott's ring was on the phone behind the counter. He lifted his finger in an I'll-be-right-with-you gesture and then got back to his conversation about cases of food.

Brent paced off his nerves in the tiny space like a caged animal while practicing what he'd say to Sara. He'd resort to begging if he had to. He would've never seen himself doing that for anyone until her.

The guy hung up the phone. "How can I help you?"

Brent pasted on a smile. "Hi. I'd like to talk to Sara—"

"She's not seeing anyone. I'm sorry."

Just like that? "I just need a few minutes."

He shook his head. "You guys need to leave her alone. She's been through enough."

"I'm not a reporter. I'm..." What was he to her? Nothing, according to Sara. "Could you tell her it's Brent, please?"

"Brent Keiser?" The man whose nametag read Timmy Sanchez laughed. "She left very specific instructions regarding you, which was to send you packing. I'll have to ask you to leave now."

Dammit.

"I only need a few minutes. Please?"

Timmy stood and crossed his arms. "Don't make me call the cops, pal. I'd like to deck you for what you did to her."

Brent held up his hands in concession. "Please tell her I stopped by." He turned and yanked the glass door open and headed for his car. He wasn't going to give up that easily. Maybe he'd catch her later at her dad's house. Or better yet, he'd wait for her.

The visitor's lot was empty except for his car, so there must be employee parking somewhere else. He rounded the side of the large building. A chain link fence revealed a gated driveway with access from the street behind. He could go all the way around the block, but it'd be faster to climb over. The security cameras lining the roof would record his actions, but he didn't care. He didn't have a whole lot to lose at the moment. Except for Sara.

He hopped down on the other side of the fence and walked to the rear of the building. Her car was parked by a door that was marked for employees only. He leaned against her small red car and crossed his arms. The weather was mild for January. He could stay there all day. He didn't have anywhere else he had to be. He hadn't gotten his badge back yet. He was still being punished.

After two hours had passed, the back door opened, and Sara took a step outside, looking madder than hell. With one foot holding the door open and arms crossed, she said, "Are you planning to sit on my car all day?"

The cameras were being monitored after all. He'd begun to worry for her day-to-day safety if they hadn't been. "If that's what it takes to speak to you. How are you?" He stood up and took a step closer.

She held up a hand to stop his approach. "I'm fine. What do you want, Brent?"

He wanted to hug her. Instead, he shoved his hands into his jeans' front pockets. "I'm here to make a donation."

Her brows arched. "Trying to buy my love now? You still haven't learned, have you?"

"I sincerely want to donate to your cause." He dug the check from his back pocket, but she kept her arms crossed.

She said coolly, "Go to the website if you really want to give money to the shelter. Is that all?"

He shoved the check back into his pocket. "I wanted to apologize. Can we go somewhere and talk?"

She shook her head. "I'm busy. And there's really nothing to talk about. Please don't make this harder than it already is."

"I need you to know that I believed I was doing the right thing. The *best* thing for you. That I hurt you by doing it was never my intent."

She nodded. "I know. Thank you for calling Mario. And for finding Miller so I could come home. But I can't be with you, Brent."

Can't be with him? "Why? What can I do to make things right? I'll do anything."

"There's nothing you can do. I just can't deal with another broken heart. But I honestly hope you'll find happiness in your life one day." Sara's eyes filled with tears. When she bit her bottom lip to stop them, it destroyed him.

That sounded way too much like a final goodbye. "*You* make me happy, Sara. And I won't break your heart. Please give me a chance to change."

"I don't want to be in a relationship right now. With you or anyone else, for that matter. I'm focusing on finishing school. So please go now." Tears she couldn't quite hold back slipped down her cheeks.

Didn't her crying mean she still cared? He couldn't lose her. "I don't know if I know how to be happy. Especially without you. I don't even know where to begin."

"Maybe start by getting that big dog you've always wanted. It'll love you back no matter what."

Zach had said actions spoke louder than words. "I don't want to give up on us. After you get your degree, can we talk? I promise you'll see a changed man by then."

Sadness filled her eyes as she whispered, "Okay. But change for you, not for me. Bye, Brent." The door closed with a solid click that reverberated like a gunshot to his heart.

But she'd left the door open for their relationship. It wasn't over between them yet. She still cared. He could see it in her eyes. He'd prove to her that he was able to change.

He slowly walked to the driveway and ducked under the arm that stopped cars from entering without a pass. He could use the time to think as he walked around the block to his car parked in front of the shelter. He needed a solid action plan. But where to start?

Zach had said he was a runner. From happiness. Afraid to allow himself to be happy. So he'd stop running.

What had Annalisa said that day in Mario's penthouse? That he should trust his gift. Use it for the good of others, and he'd find the happiness that'd eluded him. But only after he proved himself by taking a leap of faith. Sara had said her mother was never wrong about her gut feelings.

A leap of faith. That'd mean taking a risk. The biggest one yet.

Sara thought he was too driven to make money. That the security his job gave him was a false one. Quitting his job and giving up his retirement benefits would qualify as the scariest jump he could make.

And doing good for others? How could he do that without a job?

Something Sara had said once gave him an idea. Hopefully he could pull it off before some other lucky guy found Sara and took her off the market. He'd have to get started right away. Five months wasn't all that long to do a complete transformation of his life.

Crossing Double

FIVE MONTHS LATER...

Brent waded through the crowd of graduates wearing royal-blue caps and gowns, searching for Sara on the lush grounds of her college in Malibu. She'd given a fantastic speech about the importance of community service that had resulted in a standing O. Watching her speak with such confidence and grace had made him proud and unbearably sad at the same time. She was so beautiful, it was unimaginable that she wasn't with someone else by now, but he had to see her. To tell her she'd been right about him. And to congratulate her on her success not only for graduating with her masters, but for raising millions that helped open another shelter in San Francisco.

The line for punch and cookies was massive, but the crowd of people and press surrounding Sara and her parents was daunting. He pressed forward into the sea of people. His palms were so sweaty, he had to wipe them on his suit pants, and his heart was beating way too fast with nervous anticipation.

Would she speak to him? Or would she have him removed by one of the many security guards who stood nearby? Had she just told him it'd be okay to contact her to get him to leave that day at the shelter?

A soft hand grabbed his. "There you are, Brent. I've been looking for you everywhere," Sara's grandmother said with a smile. "Hurry, before you miss her. She has to leave soon." Eva pulled him along behind her through the people milling around.

"Hi, Eva. I suppose you're going to tell me you knew I was coming today?"

"Still a skeptic, huh? I even know how this will all turn out, but now I'm not going to tell you. On account of your bad attitude."

Eva tapped people's shoulders. "Excuse me, coming through. Got a love emergency here. Pardon us, please."

Brent smiled and let himself be pulled smoothly through the crowd. Maybe it was Eva's advanced age or her sheer pushiness, but the crowd parted like the Red Sea, leaving a path that led straight to Sara. She wore a cap and gown with sashes draped around her neck for all her extra accomplishments. Her hair was back to its original curly light brown color and had grown just past her shoulders. The way she smiled at the guy she was talking to made his stomach hurt. Was he her new boyfriend? He hadn't seen her with anyone in the press.

Eva grabbed Sara's hand and pulled them both aside. "Grams! What are you doing?"

"I'm sticking my nose where it doesn't belong. So sue me later. But talk now." Eva placed Sara's hand in his then turned around and crossed her arms, daring anyone to disturb them.

Sara pulled her hand away. "Hi, Brent." The coolness in her tone wasn't a good sign.

"Hi." He was so happy to see her that a lump formed in his throat. He cleared it away. "Congratulations. For your masters. With honors. And you look great."

Sara crossed her arms over her gowned chest. "I look like everyone else who graduated today. I see you're still wearing suits."

"Just for today. For you. I mean, for the graduation ceremony. Great speech, by the way." He sounded like a babbling idiot. He needed to pull it together.

Eva said, "Tell her the part about how you work out of that crappy apartment now."

How the hell did Eva know that?

Sara's head cocked. "You quit your job?"

"Yeah." He wanted to hug her so badly. Instead, he took a step closer. "I'd be happy to do some investing for you too. Like we talked about. If you're still speaking to me, that is."

"Oh, my word!" Eva looked up at the sky as if asking for help from above. "Tell her how right she was and how wrong you were before you make an even bigger ass of yourself, please!"

Sara's lips twitched. "I have something I have to do, so..."

"I don't want to hold you up. I just wanted you to know that I... That you were right. I'm much happier working for myself than I ever was at the FBI. Except for the still-missing-you part. So, thanks."

Eva whisper-screamed, "You forgot to tell her about how you give half of all the money you make away. That you learned from her that helping others is good for the soul, or some such."

Eva was starting to annoy him. "Actually, what I wanted to say was that I realize now it takes both money *and* people with big hearts to make a difference."

Sara glanced at her feet. "You were right too. About me and fame—"

A woman with a camera hanging around her neck interrupted. "Sara? We're ready for you now."

Sara smiled weakly. "I have to go take some publicity shots for the college with my mom. Take care."

"You too." He stood rooted to his spot as the only woman he'd ever loved walked away. Again. But then she stopped and glanced over her shoulder. "Did you get the big dog you'd wanted?"

"Yep. A Golden Retriever."

Eva said, "And he named it Ralph."

Did the woman have spies following him? "Do you still have Mittens?"

Sara nodded. "My mom brought her out here just today. Couldn't have her in the dorms. See ya." She smiled and then disappeared into the crowd.

"Well, you mucked that up good." Eva shook her head in disgust. "Let's go get some punch and cookies while we figure out how to fix things."

"Not until you come clean about how you know so much about my life."

"You won't believe me, so why bother? But I would like you to introduce me to your pal Zach. He's a hottie. Maybe you can bring him along with you to Dani's wedding this weekend." She turned and headed for the cookie line.

He caught up. "I don't recall getting an invitation to Dani's wedding."

"For a former FBI agent, you can be a little clueless. Sara needs a date. Get the picture?"

He smiled at the chance to see Sara again. "Did she say yes when I asked her to go to the wedding with me in one of those ridiculous dreams of yours?"

"Don't know. Didn't have that dream. But if she turns you down, you and Zach can come as my guests. I'm old, so they won't get mad at me for messing up the seating chart. But you gotta up your game next time, Brent."

"Will do." He laughed as he threw his arm companionably around her shoulders. "Thanks for the assist with Sara. And I guarantee after I show Zach your picture, he'll want to meet you too." Brent stopped walking and pulled out his phone for a selfie. "Say hottie!" He took their picture.

Eva grabbed the phone. "Let me see if you got my good side." After she nodded her approval, she said, "Send that to me, will you? I like having pictures of me with good-looking young men to make all my girlfriends back home jealous." She gave him her cell number.

After he sent the picture and they joined the cookie line, he said, "I'm surprised Sara doesn't already have a date for the wedding."

"Guys ask her out all the time, but she isn't interested in any of them. Claims she's too busy to date what with finishing school and Dani's wedding. But here's what I think." She poked him in the chest. "I think you broke her heart. And it's about time you showed up to fix it. What took you so long?"

"I had to fix myself first."

∞ ∞ ∞

Sara rubbed the back of her neck as she went over the budget numbers again in her office at the shelter. Thankfully, they'd picked up some new donor corporations in the last few months who'd help keep them afloat. But there never seemed to be enough cash in the account.

After reading the same page five times from lack of focus, she closed out the screen on her computer and decided to finally do what she hadn't allowed herself to do in the two days since she'd seen Brent.

Google him.

She typed in his name, and up popped his webpage. He'd started an investment company with a fancy logo, very sleek and businesslike. His profile stated the college he attended and his time in the FBI. That'd probably make people trust him, so that was smart. His picture showed a smiling and happy-looking guy in a suit standing on a deck overlooking the ocean.

His smile looked so genuine, it made her smile. She'd almost forgotten what a sweet smile he had. And how much that had bothered him at her dad's wedding when she'd pointed it out.

He looked happy. And he missed her. That was the part that kept playing in her head. She'd worked so hard blocking any thoughts of him because they hurt too much, so she wasn't sure how she felt about him anymore.

After she closed his page, she pulled up the budget again. But she couldn't concentrate on the numbers any better than before she'd taken the little side trip to investigate Brent.

Am I happy?

She'd kept herself so busy these last few months with fundraising and school that there wasn't time to be sad. But she *was* a little lonely. She'd turned down invitation after invitation, and she hadn't been sure why, other than she hadn't felt like being social.

Well, she'd have more time now that school was over, and Dani's wedding planning was almost done. She had only a few more things to do for her sister before Saturday. So, she should start accepting invitations again.

As a big first step back into the social world, she'd be sure to accept the next invitation she got, no matter what it was for. Then she'd probably feel like herself again. She hoped.

She dug back into the task at hand because she had to leave soon. She had to pick up the flower girl dresses that had been altered, and the gifts she'd picked out for

Michael's girls. Her new nieces were so sweet, and she looked forward to watching them while Dani and Michael went on their honeymoon. They'd all stay in her mom's suite at the hotel and have popcorn and stay up late watching movies. Maybe she'd take them to Disneyland too.

Feeling immensely better, Sara got busy sorting out the necessary budget items to be paid from the things that could wait until later, determined to make their budgeted funds last through the end of the month.

"Sara?" Timmy Sanchez knocked on her doorframe. "The donor from BDC wants to ask you something."

"Okay." She'd never talked to anyone from there before, but she gladly cashed their large checks. It'd be an excellent opportunity to thank them.

She got up and followed Timmy down the hallway. But he stopped short of the lobby and handed her the pay phone receiver.

A pay phone? No, it couldn't be the last of Dani's clues. It was a donor calling.

She put her hand over the bottom of the receiver. "I thought you meant someone was here to see me. Why would they call on the pay phone?"

"The tech is still working on our line trouble. He forwarded all the calls to this phone."

"Oh. That's why it's been so quiet around here today." She lifted the receiver. "Hello?"

"Hi, Sara. It's Brent."

Brent? Oh, God. It probably was the call her sister warned of. "You own BDC?"

"I do. It stands for Big Dog Corporation. Not very original, but there you go."

Of course, that was what it'd stand for. He'd always wanted a big dog. It made sense. "Why hide behind a corporate name?"

"I wasn't sure you'd take a call from me, but I figured you would from a donor. Is it a bad time?"

"No. Now's fine." He gave a ton of money to the shelter. She should be polite and see what he wanted. But Timmy was sitting at his desk, tapping away on his computer, so she turned her back for some privacy. "What's up?"

"Two things. First, I heard you when you said people like me don't give back. So I'd like to schedule a time I can come and talk to the kids."

"Really? That'd be great. Thank you!" He *had* listened. And he'd made some major changes in his life. So had she. "I didn't get to finish telling you the other day that you were right too. I have more power by using my family's fame than running from it. Especially now that my dad is on everyone's blacklist. Better to talk about the elephant in the room and all."

"I read he had to sell everything. And that Veronica left him?"

"Shocker about Veronica, right?"

He chuckled. "You called that one. How are Zoila and Justin? I didn't get a chance to talk to them at the graduation."

It was sweet he'd ask. "They're good. My mom set them and my dad all up in a new but much smaller house. It was a good opportunity for me to fly from the nest."

"How was dorm life?"

"Different. Loud. Strangely lonely sometimes, even though I had three other roommates in my suite." She hadn't meant to tell him that. Something about Brent always made her spill her guts. "How's the crappy apartment?"

"It gets lonely there too sometimes."

Hearing the sadness in his voice choked her up. She needed to change the subject. "You said you had two things you wanted to discuss?"

"Yeah. I heard you might need a date for your sister's wedding. Just so happens I'm free on Saturday."

Her grandmother had the biggest mouth. "The last time we went to a wedding together, it didn't turn out so well."

He laughed. "True. But the getting-to-know-each-other-afterward part was fantastic."

"It was." She closed her eyes. That part *had* been good. But could she bear to have her heart broken by him again? "I wouldn't be a very good date. I'll be busy at the wedding, doing maid of honor stuff."

"That's okay. I'll wait for you to finish. And I promise not to count how many drinks you have this time."

She smiled. "Good. Because that was annoying. Will you look happy to be my date for the pictures?"

"I've been practicing my smile. All I have to do is think of you, and weirdly, it just happens now."

God, he was killing her. She could picture that sweet smile in her mind. It made her heart ache for him, but in a good way.

He quickly added, "And, we can each have our own five-dollar Mexican food box afterward for old times' sake. You paid last time, so my treat."

"Wow, tacos *and* chalupas? Every girl's dream date. But I have to say no."

"Oh." There was a long silence before he said, "Okay, then. I guess I'll let you go."

"No. Wait. I'm just saying I can't have tacos after. Because I'm watching my new nieces for a few days. I already knew you and Zach were coming because I'm in charge of the seating chart. I was giving you a hard time."

"Nothing new there. Will you at least save a dance for me, then?"

"I don't know. You told Veronica you're not much of a dancer."

"Because I didn't want to dance with *her*. The woman I ran away with would never let a few bruised toes stop her from having fun. What are you afraid of, Sara?"

They weren't talking about dancing anymore. "I have really sensitive toes. And they're still feeling bruised from the last wedding."

"I promise to be careful this time."

"I'm just not sure I want to risk the pain again."

"You're the strongest person I know. Take a leap of faith with me. And I promise that I'll always be there to catch you. Because I love you, Sara. See you on Saturday."

He didn't even give her a chance to respond before he hung up. She'd been wrestling with her feelings for him since she'd seen him at the graduation. And, if she were honest with herself, she'd looked forward to talking to him again at the wedding, but he was right. She *was* scared.

She hung up the phone and made her way back to her desk. Once she sat down, she remembered the promise she'd just made to herself. That she'd accept the next invitation she'd gotten.

He said he loved her. And she'd missed him, no matter how hard she'd tried to ignore it. She hadn't accepted any offers for dates because they weren't Brent asking. And she'd been downright lonely because she'd found and then lost the one person who she could talk to for days and never tire of it.

Dani said the pay phone call would affect the rest of my life. She hoped I'd choose to be happy.

How could she trust that he'd really changed? What if his new job was just a new obsession to replace the old one? But why did he still live in a crappy apartment when he'd given the shelter millions?

She called up his account. The very first donation from BDC was for two and a half million.

All the breath whooshed from her lungs. That was the money he'd saved for his beach house. And he'd given another three million since then. He could've bought his dream house from Zach, and yet he gave it all the shelter?

Maybe he had changed.

Dammit. Should she put her heart on the line again? Give him one last chance?

Her grandmother had sent Brent's new cell number, so she'd send him a text.

Okay, it's a date. I'll meet you on the dance floor after the toasts. Step on my toes again, and I'll send Mario's family after you!

He wrote right back.

I prefer loafers to cement shoes anyway, so you got it. What color tie should I wear? I think we should match and make Justin proud of us.

She smiled.

Bright pink.

Nope. Never mind.

Kidding. Pale yellow.

That works. Looking forward to the dance.

Me too. Bye.

She set her phone down and blew out a long breath. Only time would tell if the choice she'd made was the right one. But she'd never know if she didn't try.

Chapter Twenty-Three

Sara stood next to her sister while the minister talked about the meaning of love. Michael, the groom and a former football player, looked handsome in his dark suit. Her sister, as always, looked like an Italian bombshell in her low-cut ivory dress. And Michael's two girls looked adorable with flowers and curls in their hair.

The afternoon wedding ceremony on a grassy cliff overlooking the ocean was picture perfect. And so far, all the food and decorations inside the private golf club looked amazing. Her sister had wanted to make the wedding as easy on Sara to plan as possible, so they'd decided to have the ceremony in California instead of Albuquerque.

She tuned back in to the minister and his definitions of love.

"Love *isn't* when you hate saying goodbye.

Love *is* when you see 'goodbye' as the possibility of saying 'hello' all over again.

Love *doesn't* cover for your partner's flaws. Love *does* show your partner's flaws for all they are, but you love their imperfections because it makes them who they are.

Love grows.

And encourages growth.

Love isn't perfect.

But it's always close.

And it's nature's way of tricking us into reproducing."

While people in the audience laughed, Sara glanced at the chairs filled with everyone she loved. She saw Maeve, Michael's mother who used to be her mom's assistant and stand-in mother for Annalisa when she'd been away. As had Mrs. Wilson, the world's best chef and drier of tears. Zoila, who watched over her, and Justin, who befriended her through thick and thin. And her mom and grandma, who loved her with all their hearts.

Mario, who treated her like a daughter should be treated, and Jake, her sister's ex-husband, was there with his wife, Gabby, and their twin boys. No two divorcées got along better than Dani and Jake, because they'd always love each other at some level.

Just as she loved those watching in different ways too, Dani and Jake had a deep bond that would always last.

She glanced at Brent, dressed in a dark suit and a yellow tie that matched her dress. He smiled when he caught her staring, and her heart went gooey. Her heart never physically reacted to Scott or to any of her other boyfriends. She'd been happy to see them, but not like Brent.

She wished the minister had said, *Love is knowing you can always trust your partner won't betray you like every other man had who'd come before Brent.* Then maybe she'd have her definitive answer about committing her heart all the way to him again.

But the line about loving people despite flaws was a good one. No one was perfect. Especially her. She'd asked her mom and Dani last night how they knew they were in love and could trust that they wouldn't have their hearts broken, and they'd both said they just knew. Which was no help. She'd felt like she knew that in Vegas, but then things went south, and all she'd known was how much her heart ached. Seeing Brent again brought back all kinds of confusing feelings.

So how did one know for sure they could trust the one they loved?

∞ ∞ ∞

Finally, the last speech was over and the cake had been cut and served, so the music began playing. Brent stood and made his way across the busy reception to the dance floor where Sara said she'd meet him.

Zach and Eva were dancing so close, they'd get kicked out if it were at a high school dance. It made him smile. They were two of his favorite people. How great would it be if they ended up together?

Weaving in and out of the people, he finally spotted a bright yellow ray of sunshine. Sara beamed a big smile at him as he approached.

He held his hand out for hers. "Hi. Great speech, as always."

Sara shrugged. "Roasting my sister was fun. But it might be a while before she speaks to me again."

"Doubt that. You two did some crazy things when Annalisa was away, though." He pulled her to the middle of the dance floor.

"We had fun." She snuggled closer as they moved to the music. "Wait a minute, you *do* know how to dance." She looked up at him and grinned. "You're actually pretty good."

"Better than you. I saw you dance at the last wedding." He spun her out and pulled her back.

"Another new fun Brent fact. I like it. Oh, and my mom said she'd watch the girls tonight if you still want to take me for that taco date."

"Great. I do." When the music slowed, he pulled her closer and kissed her cheek. "I noticed you weren't wearing your locket at graduation, or tonight."

"So observant. I kept it, but it doesn't mean to me what it used to. I don't know if I can handle any more lying men in my life."

He hated the defeat in her voice but was glad she'd taken it off permanently. Her father didn't deserve the honor. "I hope you believe that I'm not lying when I say I love you."

A smile tilted her lips. "Why do you love me?"

"Well, you don't annoy me. And most people do," he teased.

"Seriously?" She leaned back and frowned. "Got anything a little more romantic?"

"More romantic than lack of annoyance? Let me think." He pretended to ponder as he led her off the dance floor and into a quiet corner. "I know. You're the only one I've ever shared my cinnamon twists with and not resented it. Much."

She rolled her eyes. "I'm being serious."

He tucked a loose strand of soft hair behind her ear. "What's the matter? Are you still having doubts about me?"

"No." She scrunched up her nose. "I'm having doubts about *me*. I don't have the best track record with men. I seem to always fall for the wrong guys and end up getting hurt."

"Then let's get serious." He guided her to a nearby bench, and they sat. "I know I love you because thinking about you makes me smile. Just knowing you're in my life made even the most daunting task seem doable. You make me want to be a better version of myself. And you make me believe that it's possible."

She took his hand. "Did you make all those big changes in your life for me? Or for you?"

"At first it was to win you back. To show you I was willing to change. But then once I quit my job and started giving away money I wasn't sure I'd ever be able to earn back, it gave me this strange feeling of freedom. To stop being so focused on having security and just living life. That's when everything I did became for *me*. You gave me the greatest gift. You showed me how to be happy, Sara." He squeezed her hand. "But I knew for certain I loved you when I was shopping for a gift for you the other day."

She blinked away tears. "What happened?"

"I saw a pair of red-bottom shoes like the ones we had to ditch at Scott's house. And I bought them for you."

She laughed. "And you swore you'd never buy me a pair of those. Thank you." Sara lifted his hand to her lips and kissed it. "Don't tell me my shoe size was in my FBI file too?"

"Nope." He leaned in to kiss her but stopped just before his lips met hers. "I guessed. But every time I do this, is another way I know for sure that I love you." He laid his lips on hers.

∞ ∞ ∞

Sara closed her eyes and let Brent draw her under his spell with his kiss. The music and noise from people talking disappeared, and it was only her and Brent in the entire world. She slid a hand behind his neck and drew him even closer. Then he angled his head and made the kiss perfect. Made her feel so light inside, so free, she'd float away if he hadn't been holding her so tight.

How could she have forgotten how amazing it felt to kiss him? The first few times they'd been on the run, in danger, and yet for those brief moments, he'd made her feel safe. And the promise was still there in the way he held her, the way he teased her, and the way he smiled at her like a little kid on Christmas morning, eager to open his presents.

He'd made a mistake. And he'd apologized for it. He'd believed he'd been doing the best thing for her by handing her over to the FBI. But then he'd put his job in jeopardy by calling Mario to be sure she was safe. He'd given up the beach house and taken a risky investment job with no benefits. He'd even gotten a big dog to love.

And he loved her.

She loved him too. Never stopped.

Brent was worth risking her heart. Hopefully for the last time.

He ended the kiss, and all the noise returned around them. He whispered, "And if that didn't convince you, I know what will. Come on. Let's ask the dream ladies how all this is going to turn out." He grabbed her hand and tugged.

She stopped in her tracks, making him stop too. "Wouldn't you rather just be surprised?"

"I want you to be as sure about all this as I am." He led her to the front of the reception where her mom and grandma sat. He said, "Ladies. I have a request, please."

Her mom said, "But you don't believe in our dreams, Brent."

He frowned. "How did you— Never mind. Sara, go ahead. Ask them if we'll live happily ever after."

Sara laid her hands on either side of his face to get his full attention. "I don't need to ask them. I'm good now. And I love you too, Brent. With all my heart."

He smiled. "You're sure? A hundred percent?"

"A hundred percent."

Grams called out, "Then could I interest you in knowing how many kids you'll have?"

"No thank you, Grams." She shook her head. "It's not too late to run if you want, Brent. I'd totally understand." Her family, sometimes...

"Nope. You're stuck with me." He turned to Eva. "You going to make an honest man out of Zach?"

Eva grinned. "Maybe after you make an honest woman out of—"

"Bye, guys." Sara grabbed Brent's hand.

As she dragged him away from the crazies, Brent said, "Can we go back out to the cliffs for a minute? I forgot something."

"Sure." She walked with him outside. The chairs were gone, and the sun was just setting, making the sky a gorgeous hue of pinks and reds. "Looks like they've already cleaned everything up. What did you forget?"

"To introduce you to someone very important to me." He stopped walking and took both of her hands. "Remember when you said you're an excellent gift giver?"

"I do. And I am."

"I think you're about to meet your match."

What is he up to?

Brent turned around and put his fingers in his mouth and blew out a shrill whistle.

She turned to see what or whom he summoned. Zach stood near the clubhouse with a big Golden Retriever on a leash. He let it loose, and the dog ran like the wind toward them, while Zach turned and walked away. "Is this Ralph?"

"Yes."

Ralph skidded to a stop in front of them and sat. He held a box between his teeth, almost too big for his mouth. Brent said, "Ralph, this is Sara. Can you be a gentleman and shake?"

The dog instantly lifted a big paw.

Sara smiled and shook back. "You're such a cute guy. How old is he?" She rubbed his ears and got a doggy sigh.

"He's three. He was a rescue and is a very good judge of character. He wanted to meet you. See if you're good enough for me. He's very protective of his friends. But you might have just won an unfair advantage with the ear rubbing. It's his favorite."

She smiled at how sweetly Brent looked at his big dog. His love for Ralph was evident in his voice. "And how will he tell you what kind of character I have?"

Brent leaned down and said to Ralph, "It's all up to you, buddy. Are you going to let Sara into our friend circle? Or not?"

Ralph moved in front of her, sat down with a thumping tail, and dropped the box at her feet. "Well, thank you." She gave him another rub all over before she picked up the box. "Guess I'm in. Can I open it?"

Brent nodded. "We thought it'd be the perfect gift for you."

Sara eagerly unwrapped the slightly soggy paper. Inside was a Rubik's cube box. It made her laugh. "Thank you. I'll treasure it forever."

"You might want to open the box before you say that. Things aren't always what they appear on the outside. Like how wrong I was about you when we first met." He held out his hand. "Let me help you. It's taped up pretty well."

She handed it back to him. After he took out a little knife from his pocket, she said, "Still armed, I see."

He smiled as he ran the blade around the top. "Old habits die hard." He lifted the lid. Inside the bigger box was a smaller velvety one. Jewelry of some sort. And it was the right size for a ring. Yes!

Her heart pumped with excitement as he grabbed the soft box and then slowly creaked the lid back.

"Oh, Brent." Her hand flew to her mouth. "That is the most beautiful ring I've ever seen." She reached out to take the huge princess-cut diamond surrounded by smaller shimmering ones from the box to try it on.

He snapped the lid closed. "Not so fast." He turned to Ralph. "Can I ask her that question we *speak*-ed about earlier?"

Ralph let out an affirmation bark after he heard the word "speak." "Thank you." Brent swallowed hard. "Little nervous here." He wiped his moist palms on his suit pants then got down on one knee. He cleared his throat and took her hand. "Sara Chapman, will you do me the honor of letting me spend the rest of my life trying to make you as happy as you've made me? Please?"

He was probably so nervous, he forgot to actually ask her the question that went with the ring. Just barely suppressing her desire to jump up and down, she said, "You want me to move in with you and Ralph in your apartment? Is there room for one more?"

He blinked at her. "Yes. I mean no. You don't want to get married?" His face fell like a kid who's just broken his favorite toy.

She placed a hand under his chin and lifted it. "I do want to get married. But since you haven't asked me yet, I'll ask you." She laid a fast kiss on his lips. "Brent Keiser, will you please marry me? But I don't want to live in your crappy apartment. Grams said she saw in her dream that it's a dump. We can live in my slightly less crappy one."

He laughed. "Still so bossy, but yes, I'll gladly marry you." He stood and kissed her again before he slid the gorgeous ring onto her finger. "If you don't like this one, you can pick out another."

"No. I *love* it!" She couldn't help it. She had to jump up and down. Just a little.

When she was done squeeing, she slid the ring off her finger. She was just happy he'd cared enough to pick something so beautiful for her. "Why don't you take this back, though? I bet we could put a big down payment on a small house with the money. I'm fine with a gold band."

"Negative. No matter how many millions I give away, I still seem to be rich. You can keep the ring and also pick out any house you'd like. I'm not picky. And I don't want to hear any arguments about it. I'm sick of living in a dump."

"Me too. But it was all I could afford on forty-five K a year." She hugged him. "Thank you, Brent. I love you. And the ring. And Ralph. I think Mittens will give him a run for his money."

"I think you're going to give me one too." He pumped a thumb over his shoulder. "Should we go tell everyone the good news?"

"They probably already know."

"Right." He rubbed the back of his neck. "That might take some getting used to."

"It's taken me a lifetime. Good thing you're patient."

"It is. Let's go eat."

He surprised her when he scooped her up into his arms and headed for the parking lot with Ralph trotting behind.

"This is nice." She circled her arms around his neck. "But why are you carrying me?"

"I figured I'd better carry you over a threshold now, before you get your hands on those chalupas. You might be too heavy afterward."

She punched his shoulder. "Just for that, I'm not sharing my cinnamon twists with you."

He stared into her eyes and whispered, "But I'll always share mine with you."

And that was it. She was forever his. Because seriously, everyone knows the cinnamon twists are the best part of the five-dollar box.

About the Author

Tamra Baumann is an award-winning author of light-hearted contemporary romance. A reality-show junkie, she justifies her addiction by telling others she's scouting for potential character material. She adamantly denies she's actually living vicariously in their closets. Tamra resides with her real-life characters—her husband, kids, and their allergy-ridden dog in the sunny Southwest. Visit her online at: www.tamrabaumann.com

Other Books by Tamra

It Had to Be Series:
It Had to Be Him
It Had to Be Love
It Had to Be Fate
It Had to Be Them

Heartbreaker Series:
Seeing Double
Dealing Double

Matchmaker Series:
Matching Mr. Right
Perfectly Ms. Matched
Matched for Love
Truly A Match

Tamra Baumann

www.ingramcontent.com/pod-product-compliance
Lightning Source LLC
Chambersburg PA
CBHW031700170626
46808CB00005B/1546